MICK

KINGSTON CORRUPTION, BOOK ONE

JENNIFER VESTER

CONTENTS

Special Thanks	v
Books by Jennifer Vester	ix
Prologue	1
Chapter One	5
Chapter Two	17
Chapter Three	29
Chapter Four	41
Chapter Five	51
Chapter Six	61
Chapter Seven	71
Chapter Eight	81
Chapter Nine	91
Chapter Ten	103
Chapter Eleven	115
Chapter Twelve	125
Chapter Thirteen	135
Chapter Fourteen	145
Chapter Fifteen	155
Chapter Sixteen	167
Chapter Seventeen	177
Chapter Eighteen	189
Chapter Nineteen	199
Chapter Twenty	209
Chapter Twenty-One	221
Chapter Twenty-Two	231
Chapter Twenty-Three	241
Epilogue	251
Coming Soon!	257
Thank you!	263
About the Author	265

Copyright © 2018 by Jennifer Vester
All rights reserved.

No part of this publication may be reproduced, distributed, or transmitted in any form or by any means, including photocopying, recording, or other electronic or mechanical methods, without the prior written permission of the publisher, except in the case of brief quotations embodied in critical reviews and certain other noncommercial uses permitted by copyright law.
This book is a work of fiction. Names, characters, places, and incidents either are products of the author's imagination or are used fictitiously. Any resemblance to actual persons, living or dead, events, or locales is entirely coincidental.

This book is intended for mature audiences only.
Cover design by: Marianne Nowicki @ PremadeEbookCoverShop.com
Edited by: Beyond the Click: Photography & Publishing Services

For more information about the author:
Join my Reader's Group on Facebook! Vester's Vixens
Follow on Facebook and sign up for my Newsletter: AuthorJenniferVester
Author Website: www.JenniferVester.com

ISBN: 9781717950581

SPECIAL THANKS

Jamie Davis – I never quite know when you'll "text hug" me, and I laugh every single time. I'm still not sure why we're pen-pals and yet we both own a phone. So many hashtag moments and thank you for letting me have the cheese. You're my unicorn.

Angela – As always, thank you for the countless hours you spent letting me ramble, question my mental stability, send plots, chapters, message you well after midnight, and just being my friend.

Jane S. Wells – I promise I won't glaze over the next time we start talking about the law. Thank you for the two am chats and needing an HEA. You're beautiful.

Tracey – 24 emails, 482 chat messages, one phone call, and this book is finally born, thanks to you! I'm eternally grateful.

Nadine – Thank you for being tough on me and honest about my writing. Without challenge we never grow.

S. Van Horne, my friend, my brainstorming buddy, thank you. You don't have enough faith in yourself, so I'll have enough faith for both of us. Mick Galloway is yours.

∽

*Muse ~
Pandora's dilemma in a shadow man, a mystery.*

BOOKS BY JENNIFER VESTER

~ Lakefield Series ~

Run

Hide

Break

Chase

Damage

~ Fleming Brothers ~

Smoldering Heart

~ Kingston Corruption Series ~

Mick

PROLOGUE

Mick
Three months ago...

Waking up in a haze, I opened one eye slowly. There was a noise coming from somewhere beside me, that sliced through my head like a sharp knife.

Reaching out, my hand ran across the carpeted floor of my living room. I had no memory of how I got there. Couldn't even remember the bar I'd been at. There was a fuzzy memory of pissing some woman off, and stumbling into a car after multiple rounds of shots. Then the bottle of whiskey that kept me company when I got home.

Rolling over, I groaned when the noise started again. It was too early, I was still drunk from the night before, and all I wanted to do was sleep.

The screeching sound stopped then started again.

"For fuck's sake," I mumbled in a gravely voice. Even to me it sounded like I'd eaten fire and doused it with gasoline the previous night.

Rolling to sit up, my head pounded, and my stomach churned. I eyed my phone, ringing on the floor beside my leg. Wayne Husley's number popped up. My boss at the FBI, he'd been trying to reach me for the last two days.

"Yeah," I croaked as I answered the phone.

"You sound like shit," his deep voice replied. "Did I wake you up?"

I ran a hand over the rough stubble on my jaw. "What time is it?"

"Nearly noon. Look, Mick, get yourself cleaned up. We need you back on the job. Taking two weeks leave, I can understand. I can even understand four, but you've been cleared to come back, and we want you to come in."

"I can't. You got my resignation..."

"I'm not accepting it," Wayne interrupted. "You're grieving, I get it, I've been through it. No one wants to lose a friend like that. No one. None of us knew."

"I'm fine."

"You're not fine, Mick. You were on suspension pending an inquiry that was over weeks ago. I gave you some time to get back in the game, but you're still out of it by the sound of it. We've all lost someone. I'm sorry you had to go through it, it's a shitty situation that no one expected. And like I told you before, we had to open the investigation, it wasn't your fault."

He kept talking as I stood up and stumbled across the living room. Boxes of my belongings lay half open around the edges of my apartment. I weaved around the labyrinth, trying not to trip on them.

Wayne repeated the same things as every other phone call I'd had from him since I left. I listened, just like I was doing right now, but what he didn't seem to understand, was that it didn't make a damn bit of difference.

I stepped in something wet, and glanced down at an uncapped bottle of liquor I'd started drinking yesterday and had apparently finished off last night. Picking up the bottle, I noticed about an inch of brown liquid still left and finished it off. It trailed down my throat, scorching all the way. I set it down on a box, where it teetered for a moment before falling to the floor again. I left it where it landed and walked toward my bedroom.

"What I'm saying is, you're not alone, Mick. What happened was self-defense, pure and simple. It's a sealed case now. Done and over with. Get dressed, get sober and come into the office. We can talk about it and get a counselor assigned to you."

Images of my partner started to roll through my head and my stomach responded. Balancing myself with one hand on the wall, I fumbled my way to the bathroom.

"Wayne, I know you mean well, but I'm not coming back. You have all my credentials and my firearm. I've signed all the non-disclosure agreements. I'm done, that was it. I need to go."

I hung up the phone on his next protest and instantly felt bad about it. Wayne was a good man, decent boss and someone who I'd listened to for advice many times over. He'd been one of my mentors when I'd first joined the Bureau several years ago and didn't deserve my shitty attitude, but he was trying to fix something that was long gone.

My bare feet touched the tile in the bathroom as I entered and made my way to the sink. Grabbing some headache meds, I popped two quickly then looked at myself in the mirror. What I saw was a man I didn't recognize. Not even close.

My once shaven face was now overgrown with a beard that I rarely trimmed. My hair had a couple of months of growth and was currently sticking up all over the place. The only thing that was familiar were the muscles on my bare chest. But even those stared back at me in mockery. I knew beneath them was a man that was half dead.

Guilt and stress had eroded the man I'd been over the past month and hadn't left anything behind. I felt raw, like my emotions had been shredded, and there was only a husk left of who and what I used to be.

My phone buzzed again. Mason calling.

"Yeah," I answered while eyeing the tub. I turned the water on and let it run as I started stripping the slacks off that I'd worn the night before. I had no idea where my shirt, my keys and my wallet were, and didn't care.

"Hey, bro. You still headed this way this weekend?"

"I'll be there. Moving company gets here Friday, packs it, ships it. I'll drive down and they'll deliver a few days later."

"Alright. Dad asked if you wanted to have dinner…"

"No," I cut him off shortly. "I need some space and I don't want to see him."

"Mick," he began, his tone patient. "Look, I know you're going through shit, but maybe coming back here isn't the best idea. I know you quit the Bureau, but don't forget you never liked Kingston. It's different here."

I turned off the water and slid into the bath. My skin protested with the burn from the heat and I flinched.

"It'll be fine. I just need out of here. I'll see you in a few days."

"Yeah, see you soon."

I hung up the phone and threw it on the floor. Laying back in the water, I shut my eyes and immediately regretted it. Images flashed through my head. Things I'd seen and done swam to the surface as I tried to block them out.

I'd been with the FBI for more than five years, and had called it home more days than I could remember. Sleeping in the office on occasion, staying in hotels. Always hunting and searching for the next clue from the dead. That was the normal status of things working in the Behavioral Science Department.

When I'd been transferred to the missing person's department several months back, I'd had hopes that I could do some good, make a difference. It hadn't been my choice to move from behavioral science into that line of work, but I'd tried to make the best of it.

I hadn't realized how much of a toll that would take on me at the time, but I'd learned after the first month. The months following were even worse. And now those cases had me waking up at night, drenched in sweat, and barely able to breathe. Alcohol seemed to kill it some nights, other nights it was women. But nothing ever got rid of it completely and I'd burned out long before I'd gotten here.

Anger burned in my chest. Resentment, rage, and bitterness flowed through me, quickly followed by sorrow. My body hurt, and I felt broken.

Mason was probably right, but Kingston was the only place I could go. The city was calling me home.

CHAPTER ONE

Mick
Present Day...

THE SMELL of decaying flesh this late at night wasn't exactly how I thought my day would end. Whiskey would have been nice. Neat, with nothing else, and whatever the hell was playing on late night T.V.

This? God, no. I felt like I couldn't manage to extract myself from seeing this shit no matter what I did.

The Bureau, at one point, said I had an unhealthy attraction to it. My personal therapist was constantly trying to get me to open up about it. The nightmares and cold sweats just never went away.

It was like a codependent relationship and I was the addict. It happened, I was called in and would get to know the intimacies of the crime. I'd latch on to all the little things, the small details, what they told me and what they didn't. I rarely saw them as humans when I looked at them. Just details, cases, information.

A life was taken by violent means every time I stood over a body. There were very few that weren't riddled with the stink of crime when I was called. Unfortunately, looking at dead bodies and the tales they told was something I was trained for. And like an addict, I digested every violent thing with rabid need and fascination for the particulars.

"Why am I here?" I asked, as my eyes slid over to the barrel-chested man beside me.

He'd been the Chief of Police for many years in Kingston, Texas. An unyielding man with a grizzled complexion and an uglier disposition.

"I wanted you to take a look. That's why you're here."

"I looked. I'm not a body-whisperer. The coroner and M.E. are going to tell you the same thing. Three shots to the upper left part of his chest, close range. And if I'm not mistaken, he was drunk and taking a piss."

My father glanced at me with a serious expression as his crew worked the scene. The back-alley pisser had likely met his fate at the hands of some street punk that spotted his tailored suit and polished shoes. Nothing but a normal homicide, if they were ever normal.

He pointed down at the corpse. "That's George Richardson, son. That's why I called you."

I cringed at the familiarity he used. "Son" wasn't what I wanted to hear from him right now. I wasn't used to it, and it sounded unnatural coming from a man that had been less of a father growing up and more of a tyrant.

I glanced back at the corpse on the ground. The name didn't ring a bell at all. I hadn't lived in Kingston since the day I went to college at Notre Dame on a football scholarship. Something my father knew, but ignored. Except for the occasional holiday visit when my mother was still alive, I hadn't been interested in staying long at all.

After I'd joined the FBI, I hadn't visited much. Occasionally, my brother would visit me, or we'd catch up by phone, but he was really the only reason I'd moved back. Not my father, not the location, and certainly not because I wanted to be standing here in the middle of the night looking at the body of a dead Kingston resident.

Rubbing my forehead, I quietly groaned. "Okay, who is that and why am I up at this hour?"

"Denny King's brother-in-law, and you're here in an unofficial capacity," he replied as he glanced over my shoulder.

I looked back at the random reporters as they snapped photos and yelled questions from across the street. Even at this ungodly hour, they were vultures to their prey.

Glancing over at him again, I let my annoyance show. "I'm not in this line of work anymore."

He shrugged. "The work never leaves you. Might as well come to grips with that."

"I'm going home. I'm going back to bed and I'm not waking up until noon tomorrow."

"Didn't you date one of the King daughters in third grade?" he asked while scratching his chin. "Yeah, Tammy. Anyway, Mr. Richardson here wasn't a faithful man."

"You can't date in third grade and she wasn't a King. It was one kiss behind the bushes and you gave me five swats with the belt for it. Fuck this. You know what? I'm not into your reverse psychology tricks today. I'm not going back and I'm not joining the force. I've had enough."

He smirked, knowing that the game was up. He'd been trying to convince me that my life in law enforcement wasn't quite over for weeks. Ever since I told him that I'd quit the FBI, it'd been one thing after another. He didn't get it and I wasn't about to give up the specifics. It was bad enough for me to think about it on a daily basis, without having to explain what happened. He just knew that I'd left my career as an agent and had no intention of going back.

"Well," he said as he stepped around one of the privacy barricades. "Then maybe you can help me with Denny King when he shows up. You know his son, Alex, is a defense attorney now?"

I shrugged. "No, I didn't know that. Your point?"

"Politics, son. That jackass back there was probably doing one of the local girls. Her pimp rolls him for some cash, kills him. Bad press. But you, being the retired FBI agent that you are, consult on it as a favor, due to your interest in keeping Kingston's founding family in good standing."

"What?" I asked, frowning as he slapped me on the back. "I don't have jurisdiction, much less a badge, and this is way out of protocol."

He tilted his head as he turned us both toward the street and smiled. "It's nice to be a part of the human race again, isn't it? Instead of hiding in that cave you call a bedroom."

"No," I growled. "It's definitely not good and you're way off point. That guy has piss on his shoe and there's a stain on the wall in front of him. The edge of his shirt has a red smear on it that I'm willing to bet doesn't match his blood, but does match the barbeque joint on the corner. That place is standing room only and if you've ever been there, then you know that the men's toilet is nearly always down and there's a long line of dicks in the alley. Mr. Fancy Fuck back there probably couldn't stomach pissing with the rest of them. And from what I saw, he's missing his watch, wallet and cufflinks, if I'm not mistaken. I'm not dealing with Denny King for a simple robbery gone wrong."

He slapped me on the back again. "Thanks for the consult, son. That's all I needed to know."

"What the fuck?" I asked.

Turning, he went back to the scene and began barking orders.

I let out a low growl as I made my way back to my car. It didn't matter how old I'd gotten, my father still knew how to press all the right buttons. He'd dealt with so many agencies and cases at this point that he knew how to get what he wanted. And what he'd just gotten was a sound and truthful theory of possible events, that he could quietly tell Denny King as they worked the case. Politics.

I both hated and admired him right now.

My admiration stemmed from his ability to manipulate and sail through the constant mass of political bullshit. My dislike came from knowing he was better at it than I was.

Picking up my phone, I called Mason.

"Hey, bro," he answered. "It's past midnight. Are you actually awake?"

"Dad pulled me in for a consult on a case. Pisser in an alley with three holes."

He chuckled. "So, did you consult or tell the old man to fuck off like you did last week?"

"Asshole told me he was having chest pains and you weren't

answering your phone. When I got here, his team was like ants to shit. Then he threw out some idiot theory and I gave him my take on it."

Loud music blared over the phone as he let out a thunderous laugh. "I told you he was smarter than both of us. Holy Christ. I wish I would have been there. Out-smarted by the old man."

"Fuck off, Mason, I'm headed home. Just thought you should know because he'll probably pull you in next."

"Nah, I'm done with the force. He hasn't brought it up once. Come up here. I'm at *Erebus Club*. Stop being a fucking hermit and come have a drink."

Sliding into my car, I grimaced. Ever since I'd gotten home I'd stayed out of the way and out of the public. I shared my dad's old house with my brother for now, which worked out for both of us most of the time. He was working on and off. I was trying to forget my life and everything to do with my old job.

My head still wasn't right even after moving back, and I knew it. Too much time on the job and seeing too many things that would have worn a normal man down in a week. Moving back here had been convenient, but it hadn't helped to wipe any of my memories away.

"Yeah, okay," I mumbled. "I'm out of whiskey at the house anyway."

"Noticed that when I got in last night. I'll buy."

"Whatever. Be there in ten."

Looking down at my phone as I hung up, I noticed three new voice messages. I knew who it was. I just wasn't ready to talk to him yet. Wayne had been a great teacher and a close friend, but I couldn't bring myself to return his calls.

It wasn't my life anymore.

Arriving at the club a few minutes later, I noted that the parking lot was packed. The deck on the second floor was full of people milling around, drinking and smoking.

It was a local place that had been in the city for longer than people could remember and although it'd changed ownership many times, the atmosphere never changed.

The sign that hung on the building gave off a red neon glare and blinked from time to time like one of the bulbs needed a replacement.

The stone exterior was deceiving. Painted over by a thousand coats, that had since peeled and faded, it looked like a non-descript place in the middle of Kingston. It wasn't on the main strip, wasn't even close to polite civilization. It was seedy, dark, a place where you could hide in a corner, drink yourself into oblivion and exactly the type of place I'd been avoiding.

Named after the Greek god of darkness and shadows, the neon lettering that said, *Erebus,* blinked and beckoned me to enter. It was so fitting with my mood lately that every time my brother brought it up, I wondered if I hadn't become the same darkness.

Fuck it.

I was dressed in a pair of jeans, running shoes and a grey Henley. Not exactly club attire, but no one gave a shit in this place. They were all there to get drunk, hide in the booths, dance and get laid.

The line to get into the place was twenty deep. I bypassed it, nodded at the bouncer, who happened to be one of Mason's old co-workers, and entered the bar.

Yeah, same place. The air was filled with alcohol, perfume and sweat. The lights were turned so low it was probably a building code violation. The neon lighting on the dance floor, was flashing bright enough to the beat of the music, that I could make my way through the crowd to my destination.

Leaning over the bar top near the entrance, I swept my eyes across the gigantic room. Mason was in the back, sitting at an open booth with a table, and laughing with the guy who sat next to him.

"What can I get you?" the bartender asked, drawing my attention back to the lit bottles of alcohol along the wall, and the man pouring drinks beyond the counter.

"A Four Horseman. Then whiskey, neat, and none of that trashy shit."

"Haven't had anyone request that shot in a long time," the bartender chuckled as he gave me an assessing glance.

"Yeah, I'm old. Just hook me up."

"You got it," he said as he started gathering what he needed. "You new?"

"Nope," I replied, distracted by the dancefloor and the parade of people on it. "Just moved back."

"Where from?"

I glanced at him as he filled my shot, and when he was done I slammed it back. The burn of Jim, Johnny, Jack and Jose slid down my throat like fire from hell.

"Another."

"Thought you might say that," he said as he slid the other one toward me then placed my whiskey beside it.

I slammed the second one, handed him some money and waived off the change. The club was filled with people laughing and joking as I stalked across the room toward Mason. My height alone made me stand out among the crowd. Add my muscled build and I was a beast among lambs in this environment. If they only knew.

The compact mass of bodies made it nearly impossible not to touch people. Tight dresses, cleavage to tease, women giving me interested glances as I passed. I felt a hand or two reach for things they wanted, and I had to smirk at the boldness. If I was in a better mood, I might have enjoyed it for a moment.

Mason greeted me with a smug smile and handshake. "Hey, man, take a seat. I wondered if you were shitting me or not."

"Yeah, wasn't convinced until I got here," I grumbled, looking my brother over. He'd grown a beard and bulked up quite a bit in my absence. He'd always been clean-shaven and even after three months of living with him I still wasn't used to it. He was like a walking arsenal of muscle with a cynical attitude. I'd started working out again in his small home gym, but he'd taken his fitness to another level.

He threw a thumb at his buddy sitting beside him. "This is Jack. He used to work with the vice squad in the department."

I gave him a nod that he returned. Jack had some interesting tattoos that were everywhere. Arms, neck and if I was guessing correctly, underneath the dress shirt he was wearing. Shapes, words and symbols that blended together. It all screamed "trouble" and I wondered if he was. He had a detached, glazed over look on his face, as if his surroundings meant little to him other than to observe. I could almost relate.

I took a drink of my whiskey and scanned the crowd. "How long have you been here?"

Mason glanced at me for a moment before responding. "For a while. There's always some interesting action here. BG's, GG's and GGT's."

"I can guess which ones you've been picking up from the sounds at night."

He shrugged. "It's all good. They know the score."

Jack frowned at us. "BG's? New term for something?"

I chuckled. "Code for bad girls, BG. Good girls, GG. And good girls trying to be bad girls, GGT."

He laughed. "What the fuck?"

Mason shook his head. "It's all Mick, man. When he was up at Notre Dame he had to label them to keep up with all the honeys. Frat parties were more GGT's, though."

"It wasn't like that," I smirked.

Mason slapped his hand on my back. "Fuck that. You know it was. Youngest wide receiver on the team and all that to choose from? I wasn't complaining when I came to visit."

I laughed and relaxed back in my seat, where the darkest spot in the booth was. It enveloped me and kept me out of the light as I stared at the dance floor. "It was an interesting time."

"What made you join the FBI?" Jack asked.

Obviously, Mason had filled him in. I wasn't surprised. Not much was sacred to him.

"Just found my talents in the classroom were being rattled around too much by fuckers built like Mason on the field. Knew it wasn't a life-long thing. Went a different direction."

"No NFL dreams?"

"Not me. Means to an end. The scholarship didn't mean shit if I ended up with a concussion, and I wasn't about to make the draft."

Mason grunted. "Right. You were a god out there. Could be making millions."

I shrugged noncommittally. I wasn't the only wide receiver on the team. Wasn't even the most talented. But my dad and brother thought I walked on water back then. Mason eventually got why I quit the team, but I wondered some days if my dad had ever gotten over it. He'd gone on a tirade the day I told him I'd decided not to play anymore.

Four girls landed at a table in front of us. Mason's eyes went everywhere.

"You should get laid, bro."

"Eh. You've probably done half of them. I'm not sure double dipping into the Galloway family is their thing."

He smiled mischievously. "You never know with chicks. They get their rocks off with some kinky shit sometimes."

A tall brunette walked by and did a double glance at Mason.

"BG," he mumbled. "Hey, Neta."

She smiled in a practiced way and swept her eyes over Jack and me. I was leaning back with my arms over my chest wondering if this was one of the multiple female screamers I'd heard from Mason's part of the house in the middle of the night.

"Mason, it's been a while. You busy?"

"Always, how about I call you later?" he suggested with a smile.

She giggled and looked at me again. My face remained impassive but somewhat amused with my brother's choice of women. Tall, short, brunette, blonde. It didn't matter to him as long as they had a pulse and a killer set of tits.

"This is my brother, Mick. Mick, Neta," Mason gestured to me.

"Hey there," she smiled at me as she leaned in, giving me a healthy view of her chest.

"Not a chance, Neta," I replied.

She gave a slight pout that I doubted Mason even caught. He was too busy hunting something else. It was the tightening of her bottom lip and a small gleam in her eye. I could have taken her home and he wouldn't have given a damn either way. That was Mason. Love 'em and leave 'em. I'd rarely seen a repeat on his arm unless he hadn't gotten in her pants yet. And they all gave it up eventually.

Neta gave Mason a quick glance, smiled and waved as she departed. He looked her over with as much interest as he would a blank wall. Nothing there.

Mason looked back at me and shook his head. "You could have had that."

"Sloppy Galloway seconds. No thanks."

The ladies in front of us were having a good time. Going from my labelling system, since Mason had brought it up, I pegged three of the girls as BGs, and the blonde as a GGT. She looked way too uncomfortable in her own skin to be anything else.

A man wearing a polo shirt and designer jeans stopped by their table, chatting with them. They seemed to know who he was from the expressions on their faces. His eyes landed on the blonde more than the rest and after a few minutes he leaned in and spoke in her ear. His hand circled her wrist as she shook her head. She jerked back suddenly, whether out of surprise or intent, I couldn't guess.

My hands involuntarily fisted for some reason, wanting to punch the guy for whatever caused her reaction. After she twisted her arm away, he moved on and slinked his way through the club. I watched him as he took a seat on the other side of the room, then slid into the shadows much like I'd chosen to do.

One of the women giggled, while throwing a suggestive look at Jack. The redhead eyed Mason with curiosity and he gave her a wolfish grin.

He was a complete man-whore. He should have had it tattooed to his face. But the girls just couldn't resist.

It affected me when women flirted, I couldn't deny that. I was a healthy man with a lot of interest in a wide variety of women. I just wasn't right for any of them and had the tendency of scaring the shit out of most of them. As my therapist liked to say, I'd seen too much cruelty to ever have it leave me. They all sensed it eventually.

The four of them came weaving over to our table. The blonde, reluctantly I noticed, but the other three were more than interested.

Mason turned on the charm and immediately got handsy with two of them. The girls giggled hysterically at whatever he was saying as I sat in my dark corner observing.

It was going to be a loud night if he dragged them home.

Jack was already all over one of the other brunettes, or she was all over him, regardless, there was more than a little touching going on.

My gaze landed on the beautiful blonde standing behind Mason's groupies. Her eyes darted everywhere in nervousness. She wasn't like these three at all. The tight skirt she wore was an obvious attempt to fit in, if the way she kept tugging at it was any indication. It probably wasn't even hers. One of these women must have gotten the bright idea to dress her the way they wanted, and she wasn't used to it at all.

Bad girls were fun for a night, but the blonde trying to find something funny about the situation and panicking, was completely fascinating to me. She was leggy, with just the right amount of curve to her hips and ample chest. Blue eyes landed on my figure nervously several times and I wondered what she thought of my open stare, or if she could even see it.

She wasn't completely innocent if I had to guess, but she was so out of place in the seedy environment. It felt like she'd wandered in here unexpectedly and didn't know what else to do. Something inside me made me want to shove her out the door and tell her not to come back.

I sat up out of the shadows and her eyes went to me with curiosity before she put a smirk on her face. It wasn't a natural smile and was probably something the other three had taught her. She couldn't have been older than twenty-four, while the others were clearly older. I felt like an old man at thirty-two, watching her face and delicate features as she tried not to fidget.

Crooking my finger at her, I motioned her forward. She came hesitantly, weighing the situation. I liked that she'd resisted briefly before surrendering to my non-verbal command. She was trying so hard to be like the others, but the goodness in her made her wary. I wondered what it would be like to have her underneath me following different commands.

"Let's go get a drink."

"Uhm," she replied, as she glanced at her friends. "I don't think..."

"Don't think, just go with it. We're going ten feet over there to get a drink while they get to know each other, okay?"

She swallowed and gave me another fake smirk. "Of course, sure."

I nearly laughed. She was way too beautiful to be here. Especially with me.

CHAPTER TWO

Alisa

I wasn't quite sure what I was doing here with my cousin and her best friends. A night out sounded like a lot of fun initially, but it was clear since the moment we stepped in the club that I was way out of my element.

They called it a welcome home get together for me, but it was more like a bar crawl than anything else. And they were clearly bent on partying a lot more than I wanted to. When I came home from college, my cousin Monica, had been so excited to hear the news, she'd spent nearly every day at my parent's house filling me in on what was happening in Kingston. What places had closed, what had opened, and all the conquests she'd made in the last three years.

She thought I was way too conservative, which I was. She thought I was too naïve, which I was, and wasn't, at the same time. She thought my lack of experience or focus on men was laughable. And so did her friends.

We travelled in separate realms now that we'd grown up from the girls that we used to be. Different lives and experiences that led us to different outcomes. Monica had attended a local college, whereas my parents had sent me to a small, private school in Connecticut. We had plenty of so called "fun" there, with nights of drinking and partying. Despite that, the focus had always been on studies in such an elite women's college with so many competitors vying for grades and then careers beyond school.

I thought I knew what I wanted to do when I went to college. I had the best intentions of becoming a doctor, but had switched my major to social work after the first year. My parents had other ideas though, and wanted me to fall into the family business. Law wasn't exactly my thing no matter how much they pressured me.

I graduated in May and was suddenly thrust back into the family fold with some disapproval to deal with. Hanging with Monica and her friends seemed like one of the only ways to let loose a little bit. But they were *really* loose and not exactly what I was used to.

And now, after two hours of welcoming me back, I was pretty tipsy, unsure if I should drink anymore given that one of us would have to drive. I wasn't getting in the car with any of them behind the wheel. I felt like the odd person out, in my borrowed dress from Monica's extensive closet, that was two sizes too small and way too short for me.

Then he was there, the man in the shadows that stared a hole through me as I tried to play along. When he sat up and into better lighting I thought parts of me were going to melt on the spot. Tall, athletic build, with a broad chest. Short, dark hair and the start of a beard on his face. He looked at me like I was something he owned in a way. The intent in his eyes very clear, despite the friendly smirk on his face. He looked a lot like the man that sat a little further away from him and was currently flirting with Monica and her friend. Both of whom were playfully laughing at whatever he was saying to them.

I tried one of their smiles as the shadow man continued to look at me. It was all in the game, Monica had slurred earlier. Everything about the dating scene, according to her, and at our age, also according to her, was about how well people played the game. From flirting, to initial contact, to dating.

It was like watching some strange movie as I drank with them. It wasn't like the college parties or the nights out that I was used to and that had a lot to do with the friends I'd socialized with at college. This was a whole new territory. I was trying to loosen up and have fun their way, it just didn't quite fit with me for some reason.

When he crooked his finger at me, I was suddenly glad I wore the dress that was two sizes too small, and let them convince me to put on more makeup.

He was, in a very inadequate way of defining him, beautiful. Like the boy next door meets the bad boy. Something about him intrigued me. I wasn't sure exactly what it was that pulled me toward him, but he had a natural charismatic sexual attraction that shamed every man I'd ever met. He exuded self confidence in the stare he gave me, as if my compliance was already a foregone conclusion.

"Of course, sure," I responded, trying to sound more like Monica than myself. It seemed to work for her though, and I really was trying to do this whole flirting like crazy thing.

"What's your name?" he asked.

"What's yours?" I retorted.

"Mick. Your name?"

"Samantha," I lied, not comfortable with giving him my real one if the girls and I were going to move on eventually. I glanced at Monica and saw her tongue halfway down the man's throat beside us.

Mick looked amused for a moment when I turned my focus back to him. "Samantha. So, what's your name tomorrow?"

"What?" I asked, confused.

"Is it a different name every day or just every night you go out drinking?"

I shot him a dirty look and grimaced. The man had good instincts. "That obvious? It could be Breanna the next time I'm drinking. You never know."

He chuckled. A deep throaty sound that I liked hearing.

"Yeah, it's obvious. So, we'll try this again, what's your name?"

"Alisa," I replied.

His eyes swept over my face without a reaction then he motioned toward the bar. "Let's go get a drink, Alisa. Mine's out."

When he stood up, the difference in our height became obvious. He towered over me and his body looked even bigger. He was wearing a shirt that fit over the contours of his muscles. In comparison to his companions it was evident that he wasn't a weight lifter, but was still as intimidating with a body that took diligence to shape.

He turned me around by my hip and pointed me in the direction of the bar. Weaving through the crowd, his hand on the small of my back directed me where to go. He brushed against me several times and I felt cocooned in his overwhelming presence. People moved, or he moved people. Women stared openly, men noted him and frowned.

A man stepped in front of me and smirked as he examined my dress, before he was forcibly shoved to the side by Mick's large hand.

"Fucker," he growled over my shoulder.

The bartender put a shot in front of us as soon as we arrived. Mick cornered me in by placing two hands on the bar on either side of me. He drank the shot immediately then ordered a whiskey on the rocks.

"What are you having, Alisa?" he asked as his mouth brushed over the side of my neck. "Shots? Beer? You look like a mixed drink kind of girl."

I hesitated for a moment. I'd already done more shots than I felt comfortable with, giving me more than a buzz, but I wasn't quite drunk yet.

"I think a water," I murmured.

"That's no fun," he replied against my ear. I could smell the liquor on his breath and feel the warmth of his body against me. "Hanging with those girls I thought you'd like something else. Unless you're done for the night."

It annoyed me that he sounded challenging about it. As if I was someone less for not wanting more.

I squared my shoulders trying to look more confident than I felt. "I...okay, a shot. One. What did you have?"

Mick tapped the bar and the man behind the counter put a shot in front of us. He glanced at me when I took it then slid his gaze to Mick.

Turning my face toward him with his rough hand, I raised the glass to my lips. He gave me a curious look, then tugged on my chin until my mouth opened.

"Hmm," he said as he looked at my open mouth. "Gotta take it all. That's a serious shot of fire you're about to have. A drink your friends might want, but I'm thinking you can't take it."

I narrowed my eyes at him. "You don't know anything about me, Mick."

"Okay," he replied. "Do it then."

I swallowed the shot while glaring at him. It burned a rebellious and fiery path down my throat, making every inch of my chest want to scream.

Sputtering at him, he smiled and dipped his head to brush his lips against mine, before his tongue swept across my bottom lip.

"Another?" he asked, when he leaned back. Amused, no doubt, by my grimace as the alcohol still burned in my throat.

I shook my head. "Water."

He smirked after he licked his bottom lip. "Good girl."

He ordered a water and started maneuvering me back toward the table again. But before reaching it, he guided me to a dark booth in the corner. My cousin and her friends were still within sight, but the darkness of the corner embraced us, making our presence less evident. He sat down, put his drink on the table and lounged back.

I remained standing, torn between joining him and wading through the crowd to join my companions again. They were still enjoying whatever games they were playing with his two friends. Laughing, touching, flirting. In some ways, I envied their ability to play without consequence.

"Alisa, come sit."

I glanced at Mick. He patted his lap as a small smile tugged at the corners of his mouth.

I wasn't sure about this suddenly. A stranger, in a dark corner with friends who hadn't noted my absence. Scanning the crowd, I knew if I screamed, someone would hear me.

"Don't think about it. Just sit," he said while patting his lap again.

Whether it was the alcohol or my own desire to walk on a little wilder side, I couldn't guess as I slid into the dark booth with him and onto his lap.

He adjusted my hips, then leaned back again watching the dance floor like it didn't matter that I was there at all.

Eventually, I loosened up and relaxed in my position. He snaked a hand around my waist and drew me closer to him. I could feel the warmth of his breath against my neck as we sat there for a moment or two.

"What are you doing here?" he asked eventually.

"What?" I shifted nervously on his lap. "You told me to sit here."

"I did. That's not what I'm asking. Why are you here in this bar?"

I gestured toward my cousin. "They wanted to come. It was supposed to be a welcome home thing and I didn't want to celebrate it at home."

"You don't belong here, Alisa," he replied.

I stiffened, and he pulled me back in. "I belong anywhere I want. I have just as much right to be here as they do. You're kind of a jerk."

He rubbed his hand absently down my thigh then back up to the hem of my skirt that had ridden up with my position in his lap.

"I'm not saying you can't be here. Just that you shouldn't be here. And especially not with them."

I glanced at the girls again. "They're fine. They just like to drink way too much."

He chuckled. "Pretty girl, you're the type of woman that's going to end up on a missing person's flyer."

I jerked this time and he still held me in place. The darkness around us seemed dangerous suddenly with his words. I could see that he not only meant what he said, but he had the capability to make it happen. Of all the men in the bar, it felt like he alone was the most dangerous man among them. It was in his eyes, from the calculating look he gave people, to the expression on his face. Feeling uncomfortable, I began to rise from his lap.

"Settle down, Alisa. I'm not the one that's going to put you on it. Look at those girls with my brother. What do you see?"

Following his line of sight, I stared at the other girls. I assumed he meant the big guy that bore a resemblance to him when he mentioned his brother. My cousin was in his lap kissing his neck while her friend ran her hands over the man's chest. It was indecent and yet not anything that the other people around them weren't doing. Grinding, laughing, kissing.

"They're kissing him."

His lips brushed against my neck and my breathing increased. "He's fingering one of them and he'll eventually take one or both of them home. They're different than you. He'll fuck them until he breaks them, and they'll do what he wants. Afterward, they'll leave when he kicks them out. And maybe not tomorrow, but eventually, they'll think back with regret and embarrassment about tonight. They won't be able to look at each other, won't talk about what they did to each other while he watched. They'll get married, have families and sit in church on Sunday convincing themselves that they've repented. But tonight, they won't care."

I clenched my teeth, angry at his words and yet believing every screwed-up thing he said.

"You don't know that. They play games. That's all it is. You seem pretty judgmental of people without actually knowing anything. You were sure I wouldn't do that shot and look what happened."

He laughed against the skin of my neck, sending tingles up my spine as he held me tight.

"What I know is that you're sitting in a dark booth with a man that you shouldn't even be talking to, much less breathing the same air with. You're making me hard every time you move, and I'm having fantasies of you sucking me off under the table. My cum dripping down the back of your throat like that shot you just took. You think one of them would blink if I told them to do it? You don't know me, and you shouldn't be here. But you are."

I shivered again listening to him. Desperate to get away and yet drawn to what he was telling me. His words felt abrasive, but snaked their way into the darkest parts of my desire. He was warning me, telling me with every word that I was making a mistake, and yet I made no move to escape as his hand kept brushing against the hem of my skirt.

I swallowed hard and he chuckled. "Maybe I should leave."

"You should. But you're not going back over there. Do you see why I said you don't belong here?"

My gaze slid from the activity in his brother's booth. He was right about a few things, they probably wouldn't have denied him if he asked. Mick was gorgeous with a blatant sex appeal that he exuded just by breathing. But despite my curiosity and envy of their wildness, I'd never do anything like that.

I wondered what would have happened if the girls had gravitated toward him rather than his brother. Would he have taken them up on the offer? Was he thinking about asking one of them if I left? The thought was strangely deflating in a way and made me want to punch him for being so inhumanly attractive.

I made a move to slide off his lap and he grabbed me by my hips.

"Where are you going?" he growled. "I won't let you go back over there so you might as well get comfortable."

Feeling a little embarrassed about this entire thing, I glanced at him then looked away.

"No, I need to go home, Mick. I feel buzzed and I think I'm just done. You go have fun."

"I have no interest in being anywhere else at the moment."

"Right," I said with some sarcasm. "Hanging out with the last person that you want to, when there's plenty of other women. I'm not buying it."

"For fuck's sake, Alisa. Just sit for a while. I won't bite."

I gave him a small smirk. "You already have."

His eyebrow lifted. "And you like it."

I pursed my lips. "Maybe."

He seemed to be thinking about something as he took a drink and settled me back where he wanted me on his lap.

Slanting his head over my face, I smelled once again the alcohol on his breath, but something more beneath it. His scent or his cologne, I wasn't sure which. It was enough to make me wish that I had more to offer than a conversation tonight.

He leaned in and kissed the top of my nose, then the side of my face. Lingering over my mouth for a moment he waited, breathing me in. My eyelids drifted shut when he closed the distance and his tongue demanded entrance.

He tasted like his drink as he explored my mouth. My body answered with desire for him pooling between my legs. His hand slid up my thigh, his fingers sliding just under the edge of my tight dress.

I felt a rumble in his chest as he groaned. His hips bucked as he shifted me closer and I could feel his hard desire. The music and people around us faded as he explored the contours of my mouth. The firm grip he had on my hip moved to my wrist as he tugged it behind me. It alarmed me until his grasp eased.

We lingered for a moment, then he leaned back, but not before he nipped at my bottom lip. The room came back into focus, his eyes on mine as I stared up at him. He appeared to be searching for something, but for what, I had no idea. The music invaded my ears as he let go of my wrist and tugged my dress down a bit.

His jaw clenched as he looked away and I sat up straighter. Whatever that was, it wasn't just a kiss. He'd shown me what it might be like with him and I found it more than intimidating. I knew nothing about him, but the way he held me, spoke volumes whether he knew it or not. He liked control and I was surprised at the fact that I'd really liked it as well.

"Are you coming here again?" he asked, as he took another drink.

"Probably not," I answered truthfully.

If I ever saw him again, especially in this place with some other woman on his lap, I felt like it might hurt for some reason. He made me yearn for something that I shouldn't want. *Him.*

He swallowed the rest of his drink and set the tumbler back on the table. He frowned for a moment as if thinking about something.

"Come see me again next Saturday night."

I gave him a surprised look. "Here? Where you say I don't belong?"

He nodded slowly. "Yeah, I'll be here. You can dance, drink, and have fun. But you sit right here where you are when you finish."

"Sounds like a contradiction given what you just told me."

He smirked for a second before replying. "If I'm here, at least you know you'll be safe. You can enjoy yourself without having to worry about other men trying to hit on you like earlier. You can feel free to be as uninhibited as you want."

My eyes swept the club for a second trying to see the man he was talking about before turning back to him. "Uninhibited? You mean, meet strange men and sit on their laps? Think I've got that covered now. I don't normally do any of this."

"I think if you were desperate enough to come out with those girls, to get out of the house, then you might want to go out again. If that's the case, come here. But your seat is in my lap. Every single time."

I chewed on my lip for a moment thinking about his offer.

"That is unless you enjoyed whatever that guy was trying to tell you earlier."

I shook my head. "He was at a different bar we were at before this one. He said he followed us, so he could buy me a drink and take me home. It was weird."

Mick's face tightened as I explained, and a palpable menace radiated from him. I felt it for a moment, but it disappeared when he leaned forward and gave me a quick kiss beside my ear.

Moving me off his lap, he said, "Your choice, Alisa. I'll be here."

With that, he turned me toward the entrance and helped me get through the crowd of people near the front door.

"Are you driving?" he asked.

I shook my head. "We drove together."

He pulled out his phone and called for a taxi. Scanning the crowd, I saw the man that had grabbed my wrist earlier. He was weaving his way in our direction, passing us as he stepped outside.

When Mick's hand slid around my hip I realized I'd unconsciously moved closer to him while trying to avoid the stranger's notice. Mick tucked me against his chest as he smirked down at me.

"Phone," he said.

"What? Mine or yours? Was that the cab?"

"Yeah, they'll be here in a couple of minutes. Need your phone, beautiful."

"Oh, I don't have it. Would you like my number?"

He growled and shook his head. "You came out drinking without your phone? Do you know how dangerous...nevermind. Give me your phone number so I can get you home."

I saw the yellow taxi waiting at the curb for me and rattled off my phone number to him.

He punched it in his phone and dialed. "Calling you so you'll have mine. Get in the car."

I crawled in the backseat as he spoke to the driver for a minute. It looked like he was almost threatening the man before he handed him several bills.

When he stepped away from the car he kept staring at me through the window. The driver asked for my address, causing me to turn toward him for a minute as I recited it.

I glanced back to where Mick had been standing on the sidewalk, but he was already gone.

CHAPTER THREE

Mick

Waking up, I stretched and looked around my room. I'd been avoiding unpacking for a while, knowing I was going to eventually get my own place. Living with Mason was convenient, but annoying some days.

He had his routine on the weekends and sometimes the week nights, when he indulged in his pastimes. Last night had been nearly unbearable. When he stumbled in with whomever he'd brought home he'd been loud, even though his bedroom was across the house.

I rolled over and looked at the light peeking through the edge of the blackout curtains on my window. I'd never been able to sleep very well without complete darkness in my room but the problem with that was, I couldn't tell what time of day it was when I first woke up.

Alisa. The woman that had been on my mind when I left the bar and laid down to sleep last night wandered through my head.

I wondered if she'd gotten home okay, even after threatening to murder the cab driver if he didn't deliver her to her house in a reasonable amount of time.

Reaching for my phone, I found her number and texted her.
Mick: *Home okay?*

I rolled out of bed with a slight headache, feeling like I hadn't slept in a week. Which was probably close to the truth these last months. Every night was the same thing. Drink, go to bed, try to forget the past, and pray that the random faces of victims wouldn't plague me. But every night they were there, some familiar and some I was convinced my mind had conjured up to torture me.

I heard a ping on my phone and dug it out of the sheets.

Alisa: *Yeah. Came straight home and went to sleep.*

Mick: *Good girl.*

I tossed the phone back on my bed and wondered if she felt as hungover and rung out as I did today. Probably not, since she wasn't much of a drinker and I suspected that the girl slept better than I did on any given night.

Guilt slid over me for trying to scare the piss out of her at the club. I both wanted her and wanted her to stay the hell away from someone like me. But those eyes of hers had been my undoing. So much beauty there that I could hardly resist needing to keep her close. In the end, I'd surrendered and given myself a small taste.

I could have given her a ride home, but I knew that it would've been a mistake. My interest in her would have had me driving her to the house, into my bed, then pounding into her. She would have regretted it this morning. And although I was a masochistic fuck in a lot of ways, I didn't want to see that reflected back at me from those beautiful eyes.

Showering, I took care of myself while thinking about her underneath me, ruining her while she screamed my name. It'd been such a long time since any woman had piqued my interest, it was short, sweet and explosive. And as I clenched then convulsed into my hand, months of stress seemed to ease out of me as I came.

"Alisa," I mumbled. Fuck, she was better off staying away.

When I stepped out of the shower, I heard another ping on my phone and smelled coffee. Throwing on a pair of sweats, I grabbed my phone and wandered into the kitchen.

Mason was typing on his laptop at the large wooden table in the dining room. He had some sort of home office going on, but the scattered mess of papers and old coffee cups made it look like a disaster zone.

"Made eggs," he called out to me.

I grabbed a plate, some coffee and sank down into one of the chairs across from him.

"What time did you wake up?" I asked.

He continued to type on his laptop as he answered. "Couple of hours ago. Kicked the girls out and got hungry."

Yawning between bites, I stretched again. "Why are you never hungover? I feel like shit this morning."

"That's because you sleep like shit every night. If you had some cardio in your bed to work off the alcohol, then you might sleep better."

"No thanks," I mumbled. "Maybe I should do laps around the block."

He smirked at me. "Not near as much fun, bro. You didn't bring that blonde hottie home?"

I gave him a hard stare. "Off limits. Don't even look at her."

He titled his head and sat back in his chair. "Interesting coming from the demon of doom and gloom. Get anywhere with her?"

I gave him a pointed look. "Just off limits, man."

He chuckled. "Okay. You have my word. If you're digging her, maybe you can get out of the house a little bit. Seems like a good girl compared to those hellions last night. What's she doing hanging out with them?"

I shook my head. "A cousin or something and the cousin's friends. Whatever. I gave her a lecture."

"Wow, you're charming. Hey, girl, come sit in my lap and I'll give you a fucking lecture on how slutty your cousin is."

I rolled my eyes. "Didn't go like that exactly."

"Sure it didn't," he said with a laugh. "Gonna see her again?"

I nodded and opened my messages. "Yeah, maybe."

Alisa: *You feeling okay today?*

Mick: *Not really.*

Alisa: *Too much alcohol? Or just the late night?*

I nearly laughed. Neither the alcohol or the lack of sleep was really plaguing me now. Not after that shower. I wanted to see her. Find out if my inebriated brain painted her in a different light than my sober one would. She might not be half as intoxicating in the light of day.

Mick: *Didn't sleep well. You weren't in bed with me.*

I smirked. She'd run with that response, or should. The asshole inside me wanted her in the worst way. Putting her in a cab last night was one of the nicest things I'd done for someone in a long time. Part of me regretted it, but another part knew it had to happen.

Alisa: *Hmm. I'll buy you a stuffed animal.*

I laughed deeply as I stared at my phone. What the fuck? This girl was strange and too fucking cute.

Mason was eyeing me with interest when I glanced at him.

"Stupid shit," I said to his unvoiced question.

"That's the first time you've laughed in three months."

I threw him a dirty look and stood up. "I laugh. I laughed last night."

"Not like that, you didn't. Tell stupid shit that I like her already."

I rolled my eyes and took my coffee with me to throw on some different clothes.

Mick: *As long as it looks like you in that tight dress.*

Alisa: *I'll have to check "Dirty Teddies". They may be out of stock.*

I stared at my phone and blinked. So fucking strange. Even stranger was the fact that I felt relieved that she was still around.

She was just a girl in a bar that spent some time in my lap. That wasn't unusual, wasn't even unique. She wasn't the first woman that I'd jacked off thinking about, nor was she the only woman that had ever turned me on. It shouldn't have mattered whether she was still talking to me or not, but for some reason this morning I was glad she was.

I'd figure it out later and might text her again. I wondered if she'd go through with showing up Saturday. The possibility both excited and confused me.

Grabbing my keys, I headed to my weekly appointment.

After being back only a couple of weeks and finding myself face-down on the floor, drunk and nearly unrecognizable to myself in the mirror, I'd decided that some counseling might be in order. I was at least trying to move beyond what I felt like was a life sentence of depression and nightmares.

I'd always heard of this happening, witnessed it happen to some of the men and women I'd worked with at the bureau. I didn't ever think I'd need it. When I'd been on cases in my distant past, I compartmentalized my emotions most of the time. Shut down the people that were living and dealt with the dead.

Then there was that one case that broke me at the end. There wasn't a way to avoid finding what I had on that investigation. The darkest place I'd ever gone, had swallowed me whole one day, and the truths I'd discovered about myself had been devastating. To say it was a moment that changed my life would be spinning a fanciful angle on it. It killed me, or at least who I'd been. Nothing would ever be the same in this new reality for me.

The therapist's office was small for the number of doctors they had on staff. Six in all with some therapists, like mine, willing to work over a weekend. Which to me, indicated how many fucked up people lived in Kingston. But since it was only one of three offices in town, there weren't many choices available except for the hospital. And no one ever wanted to go there.

There were only a couple of people waiting. For whom, I didn't know. No one ever made eye contact or talked to each other. It was like people were embarrassed to be there, just like all the other people that sat beside them. It wasn't like we were getting tested for something. We were just all fucked up in some way.

"Mr. Galloway, she's ready to see you," the receptionist said before I could sit down.

I checked my watch as I made my way down the hallway. Five minutes early. She was prompt today.

Opening the door, I found the older woman that had been crazy enough to take me on as a patient, sitting in her usual spot. Incense was burning somewhere in the room and she'd rearranged her antique rugs and furniture again. I wondered if it was for aesthetics, to throw her patients off, or an underlying dislike of sitting in this place for hours on end.

She was a real ballbuster most of the time, which is why I liked her. And if my instincts were good, she was probably a wild one in her youth. She wore some strange tint of pink lipstick and was a believer in a dress suit with panty-hose. Her hair was thinning and looked like she'd either been a red-head or blonde in her younger days. It was always pulled tight in a bun that stretched the skin around her cheeks just enough to hide some effects of aging. Vanity for a shrink was interesting, given that she counselled against it.

I glanced at the wall as I shut the door. She'd finally put her ceremonial accolades for providing law enforcement support on the wall. Something we'd talked about once and I'd dared her to do.

Gesturing toward the frames I sat down on her couch. "So, you're finally admitting you have a dirty side next to all that hippie college crap, huh?"

She raised her eyes from her notepad and peered at me before rolling her eyes. "I thought I told them to call the police the next time you showed up. Obviously, a staffing error. I might have to fire someone."

"You'd miss flirting with me."

She grimaced. "Like a woman misses a pap smear."

I laughed, and she gave me a thoughtful look.

"What happened?" she asked with a quizzical tone.

"What?"

"Did you shoot your brother or torture small animals today? You laughed."

"I laugh," I said with a shrug. "It was funny."

She shook her head. "Are we going to bullshit each other today or are you actually going to talk? Thought we got past the mind games."

"Nothing happened. You and Mason are insane."

Her eyebrows shot up in surprise. "So, you've laughed more than once recently?"

I rolled my eyes.

She put her notepad down and gestured to the door. "Get out."

"What?" I asked, glancing at the door.

"Out. You have two honest relationships. Me and the dead. You want to lie to me, I'm done."

I sighed and sat back on her couch. I told her about my dad pulling me out of a blissfully buzzed sleep for a consult the prior night. Adding that he was still a dick and I still didn't like him, but I wasn't going to leave him hanging if he'd had honest chest pains.

"So, did you get your fix with the corpse?"

I scratched my forehead and shifted in my seat. "It felt good to know I was right."

"I bet," she said a little sarcastically. "Just another case, right?"

I shrugged.

"Then?" she prompted.

"I went out with my brother."

"Oh, Jesus. You left your safety zone? Were you twitching? On drugs? Forced by gunpoint?"

"He asked, and I went, nothing crazy," I replied. "He was doing his regular thing. We had some drinks."

"Interesting. Talk about someone who needs therapy. So, what happened?"

Thoughts of Alisa drifted through my head. She'd happened, and I'd tried to scare her away.

"Met a girl. She didn't belong there. I tried to tell her. Warn her."

"Hmm," she said. "Does she know about you? Or did you scare her away?"

"I tried. I wanted to scare her. She doesn't know a damn thing."

"Were you cruel? You always seem to think you are."

I shook my head. "No, but I wanted to be, I guess. I wanted her to go home, she didn't need to be there. I told her some really messed up things. She should have run, but she didn't."

"Is that scary for you? Wanting to be cruel to help someone? Or was it scary that you actually cared that she was there?"

"I don't know. I just kept thinking of all the bad things that could happen to someone like her. And wondering if I was going to be the bad thing. It's sick, right? I didn't ask to be like this."

"No lies, Mick. You asked the day you joined the FBI. You knew when you joined the Behavioral Sciences Department that you wouldn't come out clean. No one does."

"It was okay being there. It was afterward that..."

She waited on me to finish. That part of my life, we hadn't discussed much. She'd never pressed me to tell her about it and likely never would. She'd been a criminal psychologist before she'd retired and opened her own office in the public sector. She'd heard it all by this point. The honorary awards that hung on her wall, proved that she'd seen more than her fair share of the darker aspects of life.

Changing the subject, she asked, "So, last night, when you were trying to get your friend to leave, did you *enjoy* scaring her, or feel like you *had* to scare her? You and I both know there's a distinct difference."

"No. I mean I enjoyed talking to her. She's beautiful, turned me on. I just think she needed to hear the truth. This man tried to hit on her when I first saw her, and it honestly made me want to punch the guy for no reason at the time. Then she explained what happened later. The guy had followed her to the bar. As soon as she said it, I wanted to take him out to the alley."

"But you didn't."

"Not right then. I mean who follows a girl from one bar to the next? Did I mention he was eyeing her when I put her in the taxi? I followed him to the parking lot and let him know about it. It took a couple of punches to convince him."

Her eyebrow raised. "How bad was it and how drunk were you?"

I shrugged. "I'd had a few. After the first blow he pulled a knife. My anger took over from there and he's probably waking up in the hospital this morning. He wasn't just some lovesick guy following her."

"You don't know that, Mick."

"Doesn't matter now. He won't do it to anyone again."

She sighed and pinched the bridge of her nose. "So, you've laughed more than once today, which is unusual to say the least. You beat up her pursuer without knowing if he was maybe just some random man. Sounds like you might be interested a little more than you're admitting to yourself. Why are you so conflicted?"

Sighing, I sat back on her couch. "Bottom line, it was confusing. She shouldn't have trusted me any more than the guy that hit on her. And yet, there she was, buzzed and sitting in a dark corner on my lap, where I could have drugged her or worse."

"Are you going to see her again?"

"Doc, I'll just corrupt her. She won't ever be the same."

She cleared her throat and sat forward giving me a smirk. "You know what your problem is, Mick? You don't think you're worthy of being liked by a sweet woman. Which is completely wrong."

"Doc..."

She held up her hand. "You're not so lost that you can't find your way back, Mick. Those faces in your dreams won't be going away anytime soon, but it doesn't mean you're completely gone or broken. You could easily be a cruel and corrupting man, you've seen enough of the evil in this world to ensure that. That's always going to be there, like we've discussed. You're going to have to figure out how to handle it. However, for now, don't confuse cruelty, or what you think you did, with just being a plain old horny jackass."

I chuckled.

She gave me a sideways glance. "Ahh, a semi-laugh. I'll take it. See where it goes, you might surprise yourself. When you come back again, tell me about it."

"I thought I was barred from the office," I smirked.

"Well, if the police ever show up, you'll know that someone listened to me. Now get out of here."

"Yes, ma'am," I said as I stood up and shook her hand.

She smiled and walked to her desk as I shut the door.

When I got to my car, I looked at Alisa's last text again, but didn't respond yet.

Instead I dialed my brother, who picked up after two rings.

"Hey, what's up?" he answered.

"I'm out, you want to do lunch?"

"Uhm, yeah. Jack and I were headed to meet someone, but we can eat."

"Where are you at?" I asked, pulling out of the parking lot.

"Mayfair and Haskell. Let's go to Randy's place and get a burger. Meet you there."

"Got it."

I hung up and drove to meet them.

Twenty minutes later, I was sitting in a booth with Mason and Jack who both looked excited about something.

"Okay, what's the deal? Both of you look like you've had nine shots of pure adrenaline and you're itching to run five miles."

Mason's eyes flashed, and he gave me a smirk. "Well, we're working on a case."

I stopped chewing my burger for a minute, then swallowed hard. "Are you back on the force?"

"Fuck, no. You know I've been working some side jobs, right?"

I nodded. "Uh huh."

"So, a few months ago, I went in to see Alexander King. He's a defense lawyer that was helping with my case when the fucking charges against me got dropped. Seemed like a decent man. I think you went to school with him. Anyway, he says something like, all it took was a record lookup from another state to prove I was innocent or something like that."

"That's where I came in," Jack interrupted. "It was easy enough to dig through some old public records down at county for Mason. I was still working at the time and found the guy's record on file."

"Right," I said. "The guy had an obscure prior for falsely accusing a police officer of abuse. I remember."

"So," Mason continued. "Alex asks if I was planning on going back to the force. I told him those guys could go fuck themselves. Then he asks if I want to do a few things for him. For pay."

"Is it legal?" I asked.

Jack and Mason looked at each other for a second then they both answered. "Mostly."

I groaned.

Mason held up his hand. "Before you assume, just listen. It's mostly legal because we took the exam, and we're waiting on our private investigator licenses to come in. Technically legal because we're contracted right now by a defense attorney and we're not doing anything major."

"Okay, so why the excitement?" I asked.

"He says he has the licenses. So, we're good to go. Come with us."

"Eh, I'll pass."

Mason thumped me in the chest with one of his hands. "Come on. I was going to see if you wanted to check it out anyway. You're out of the house, and you're still out of whiskey. You can come take a look and go by the liquor store after. There's one just down the block."

"You make me sound like an alcoholic."

He shrugged. "Nah, just glad to see you out of the house. You can go hide again later."

I nodded. The sad fact was, that I planned to go right back there afterward and do exactly what he said. Work out in his home gym, drink, and try to sleep. Tomorrow, wash, rinse, repeat. But the look in my brother's eyes was hopeful. Like he wanted me to see this. He'd been my steady support for the last few months and I owed him one.

"Yeah, man. I'll go."

CHAPTER FOUR

Alisa

By the time Monday rolled around, I was more than ready to forget about Mick. At least I thought I was, after not receiving any texts back from him all weekend.

Then Tuesday came and went while I settled into my new job helping my brother. No texts from Mick.

Wednesday I had a phone interview with Nelson Hospital for a position as an assistant in their substance abuse department. I was overqualified, but it was a start. They called me back later in the day and told me that, although I had the license, they were looking for experience.

"How am I supposed to get experience if I'm not hired somewhere?" I asked the HR rep.

She answered nicely, "Well, you might want to try something like an out-patient clinic. On paper you have everything, but we're looking for a certain kind of fit in that department. Experience really helps. Or maybe a sponsor."

"I see. Thank you," I replied then hurried to get off the phone.

I slumped in my chair feeling discouraged. It was only my first interview, but I'd felt certain that it was the best position I'd applied for out of the dozen of applications I'd sent.

My thoughts drifted back to Mick as I sat at my desk chewing on a nail. I'd been daydreaming about him for three days. He was just an interesting man I met at a bar, nothing more. Plenty of people met at clubs, drank and talked without getting involved. There was nothing unusual about it. They might run into each other later and just say hello. That was it.

But when I thought of Mick, his square, unshaven jaw, the way he looked distant and yet focused, I wanted to talk with him again. He was complex. There were multiple layers there that I wanted to peel back and examine.

He warned me about the club and the things he saw, yet he made no move to take advantage that night. I was incredibly buzzed on the way home and ready for bed. Although, I wasn't sure I was completely opposed to being in his bed when I got home. When he mentioned it the next day, it sent some seriously dirty thoughts through my head on what that might be like.

I'd never seduced a man. Had I been seduced? Yes. I'd lost my V-card right after I graduated high school. I knew the mechanics of sex, but my experience so far was that it just seemed so awkward and not especially enjoyable. After that, I didn't really have much time, and meeting guys at a private women's college was difficult to say the least.

I wasn't one of those women that was determined to find someone through sex. Like Monica and her friends. I also didn't particularly "hunt" men. Again, like Monica and her friends. Which is why I had no "game" according to Monica, and most likely couldn't keep Mick interested if I tried.

But I found him interesting, nonetheless. After a few internet searches on Tuesday, because I wasn't obsessed at all, I found out his age. He was quite a bit older than I was, but for some reason it didn't bother me at all.

He'd also been a wide receiver, whatever that was, for the Notre Dame football team. Graduated, then disappeared. Not a lot on the internet past that point. Even when I tried various combinations of his name and typed in keywords, dates, places. Nada. However, on a positive note, I also couldn't find a marriage record or social media account with some girlfriend hanging off his arm.

Which really made me wonder who Mick was. Why was there not a wife? Or at least a significant other? He was hot as hell.

I wasn't obsessed. Just curious about the man I'd been dreaming about for the last three days and wondering why my body felt so restless all the time when I thought about him. There were only so many times I could wake up needing to touch myself to the thought of him before I went crazy.

Looking around at the stack of files on the big desk in my brother's office, I wondered what I was doing here.

I'd learned this week that although I'd gone to college, and learned how to alphabetize in elementary school, I was delegated to organizing things. As if it was the only good use of my skills.

I hated everything about this situation and wondered if I should have stayed back in Connecticut to get a job that I wanted. But funds were tight for a college student and I'd only worked part-time, so it was the position I was in.

The door opened, and my brother stuck his head in. "Alisa, I'm headed to the funeral, do you need anything?"

"Nope." I said rather tartly while making sure the documents in one of his files was in the right order.

"Hey," he said, drawing my attention to him. He stepped in the room and shut the door.

"What?"

"Look, I know you're not happy here, but it's something until you find a job somewhere else, right?"

I shrugged.

My brother was a good man, no matter what people thought about lawyers. He'd always been kind to me even when our parents were less than interested in my life. He was tall, with dark hair, just like our father. He had the same large build and stern voice when he got upset. The difference lay in his personality without all the degrees and titles.

He was one thing in public and a different person with me. He was kind and I'd always admired him.

By the time I entered my teens he was already in college. It didn't mean he kept up with me any less. When he was home, he made the effort to spend time with me. Growing up in a house where your gender was seen as a handicap rather than a blessing, it felt good to be doted on by the golden child, who didn't care either way.

I'd learned very early on that my position in the family was looked at more in terms of who I could marry and produce future generations with. It was laughable in this day and age, but there it was. And I was the only woman in my family, that I knew of, that didn't give a shit about wealth, politics or marrying into either. Money didn't mean anything if you couldn't look at yourself in the mirror in the morning. My mother was proof of that.

"Are you saving to move?" he asked as he came around the table.

"I've got enough now, I just don't want to move somewhere that's awful. I think I found a place yesterday. I just need to put a deposit down."

He leaned against the table. "Tell you what, call them and I'll pay the deposit and whatever fees they need. I don't want you to stay with mom and dad any more than you have to. It's not good for you."

Sighing, I looked up at him. "I need to do this on my own."

"You're miserable. There's nothing wrong with letting me help you out. Pay it back at some point when you get your dream job and we'll call it a loan."

Standing up, I hugged him, and he rubbed my back. "It's good to have you home. But I want you to be happy. It's never going to happen in that house."

I nodded against his shoulder, tears threatening to spill. There was so much he understood about me, about my history. Being ashamed of myself for so long, then being sent away due to my parent's disapproval.

He leaned back and looked at me. "Phone number, desk, sticky note with hearts. Pronto. I have to run, but I'll call them when I get back. Or Melanie will, whatever. You know what? Scratch that, just give it to Melanie and she'll take care of it. You know I'm terrible with that shit."

"Thank you, Alex," I whispered. "I'll pay you back, I promise."

He shrugged and gestured at the mess around us. "No big deal. Just help me out for a while and don't disappear. I'm not built for this mess. It just pisses me off."

"How the hell do you even keep up with it if you're on a case?"

Opening the door to leave, he glanced back at me. "One word. Interns. You might even get to meet a few. Okay, have to run. Your uncle's funeral."

I grimaced. "Yeah, no. Never my uncle. He was so weird all the time. Always hanging around the house."

He smirked. "I never claimed him either. Total ass. But I have to make an appearance. I have to go pick up Heather, if I'm late she'll have a conniption."

I shrugged. "Let her?"

He chuckled then his smile dropped. "Yeah. Well, appearances, right? Take off for the day. Go shop or do something fun."

I nodded and smiled at him as he left. Then grimaced as he shut the door, thinking of his girlfriend, Heather. She was a piece of work and I had no idea why Alex dated her.

A happy feeling bubbled up in me at the news that I'd be moving into my own place sooner rather than later.

I wanted to share it with someone, but the friends I'd made at college wouldn't exactly understand. None of them came from the same background it seemed. A small city with a lot of secrets. Where the name of the city started from a decent lineage that had become broken and twisted as the years passed.

I thought about sharing my news with Monica. Even at her worst, she at least understood what it was like growing up as a King. But as my finger hovered over the button to call her, I hesitated. I didn't want her to think it was an open invitation for partying at my house. I was close to her when we were growing up, and still enjoyed our friendship in a lot of ways. But we'd also changed.

Even though she complained about her family, she was yet another King that was confined to living up to the name. Her father was entrenched in land development around the city and it'd been very profitable. She stood to inherit millions one day if the family gossip was true, which it generally was. I knew it was why she acted out. Why she was so wild. She hated the destiny that sat before all of us and strained against the small box they'd built for us.

Before leaving, I finished two more files for Alex and placed them neatly with the other ones I'd completed.

It was well into the afternoon when I left, and I didn't want to go home. There was a window of time that was best for my return to the house. I took advantage of it as much as I could in order to avoid conflict.

Around four-o-clock, my mother would start drinking and popping prescription pills. She'd pass out or be confined to her sitting room, doing whatever it was that she did for the rest of the night at that point, with very few instances where she'd emerge.

My father, who avoided her, and his family in general, apart from occasional meetings with Alex, would come home late, quite often smelling of perfume and liquor. It wasn't hard to catch the tell-tale signs of someone who was cheating. It disgusted me in every way. I felt sorry for my mother at first but from what I'd learned early on, she knew very well what he'd been doing. Sadly, it seemed that she was apathetic about the behavior, or was so in love with her pills that she'd become immune to it. For all I knew, she was probably fucking someone else too.

Since the office was downtown, I took advantage of being near several small Mom and Pop restaurants in the area. I'd visited four so far, but my favorite was owned by the Parkers. Small, deli meat to go, but also had sandwiches and cupcakes. I was addicted to the cupcakes more than anything. The Parker family was just a nice perk to the place.

Generally, David and Geri, worked the place but on occasion their son, Heath, would help. I knew him from high school and he was one of the people that was flirty, but nice to all the girls. He seemed happy, even now, working with his family after all these years, and I envied his situation. I would sometimes imagine what it might be like to have parents that were so normal.

Walking in, Heath called out to me. He was tall, and lanky with brown hair and had a couple of dimples that always peeked out when he laughed. He glanced in my direction as he sliced some sort of meat for a customer ahead of me in line.

"Alisa! You're back again. Same as last time?"

I nodded and smiled. "Yes, please."

He wrapped up what he was doing with the tall businesswoman in front of me and started on my order. The smell of the shop always made my mouth water. A mixture of bakery and roasted something that made me want to eat my weight in whatever they were selling.

"How are things? Getting settled in okay?" he asked as he set my bag on the counter.

"Yeah, I'm good. You?"

"Can't complain," he said with a smile.

"Got some good news today. I'm getting my own place."

He laughed. "Definitely good news. Still working for your brother?"

"He's helping me out with it actually. And yes, I'm still working there for the time being. Had an interview, but it didn't go so well. Just applying where I can."

He rang up my order and I paid.

When I grabbed my bag from the counter, he smiled. "Hey, if you want to go out and celebrate, let me know. Or just go catch a movie or something."

The thought of hanging out with him sometime was tempting. He had a laid-back personality and always seemed affable. I was sure that he'd make an easy friend with no outwardly crazy streak like Monica and her crew. But I wasn't entirely certain that he meant it in a friendly way, and didn't have other designs in mind. Dating him wouldn't be bad, but I didn't feel that way about him.

Unsure of how to answer him, I nodded. "Sure, maybe sometime. A lot of stuff to get settled right now, but I'll let you know."

He shrugged. "Great, you know where I am. Maybe you can have a housewarming party or something. Oh, hey, they're having a grand opening of a gallery near here in the next couple of weeks. You should go, the artist that'll be on exhibit is local supposedly, but no one knows who they are. It's apparently a big secret. Operating under some fake name or something."

Laughing, I wiggled my eyebrows. "Probably has something to hide. The mystery! I'm sure it'll be a swarm of people going just to figure it out."

"I'm going just to see who it is. Fuck the art, this is far more interesting."

"Oh, my God. I forgot how gossipy Kingston was. Probably just someone that knows how to market based on the suspense of it all."

"Maybe," he smirked. "See you there if you're interested."

"Sure," I said as I waved and left.

As I crossed the street, carrying my lunch with me to eat in the park, a car swerved into the far lane and heading in my direction. Behind the wheel was a man in sunglasses, who revved the engine rather than using his brakes. Running, I barely ducked behind a parked vehicle on the street before it passed.

"Learn how to drive!" I yelled after the driver.

I shook off the adrenaline and finally settled on a park bench to eat my messy sandwich as I watched people.

Trying not to think of the idiot behind the wheel of their black BMW, thoughts of Mick drifted through my mind. I wondered if he liked things like movies, art and sitting in a park on a random afternoon. He probably worked somewhere that he didn't have time for those things. I really didn't know much about him at all.

I wiped bread crumbs off my mouth and picked up my phone. Still no messages.

Well, hell. This wasn't getting me any further just leaving it up to him.

Alisa: *I had some good news today.*

I waited and drank my water, listening to the raucous chatter of two birds in a tree above me.

Mick: *What's that?*

Alisa: *I'm getting my own place. My brother is helping me out but still, it'll be mine. I need to be out of that house.*

Mick: *That's good news. What's wrong with your house?*

I hesitated for a few minutes wondering what to tell him. He didn't know my last name right now which was probably best. There was no judgement so far based on my name or what most people thought. He wouldn't automatically assume that as a King, I had a charmed life.

Alisa: *It's just not where I need to be. Or belong. I think that's your favorite word.*

Mick: *If you're using my word then it must be extreme.*

Alisa: *It'll just be a good change. What are you doing this week?*

Some strange desperation in me wanted to see him sooner than the weekend and in my odd need, I hoped that he'd reply back with just as much longing.

I waited for several minutes wondering if I'd been too obvious.

Mick: *This and that. Right now, I'm lying in bed.*

I pursed my lips together at the thought of him anywhere near a bed. The fantasy of seeing him there had rolled through my mind several times no matter how much I tried not to think about him. Shirt off, maybe everything else off, that sexy smirk of his that had me dripping with more than just curiosity.

That thought, also led to another. Had he gone out last night? Maybe to a bar, to get a thrill from someone else? I knew I shouldn't care. I'd just met him. It was silly of me to think that the man might have some interest in me other than a conversation here and there. But he piqued my interest, and something inside me felt like our chance meeting was significant.

Alisa: *Rough night of drinking and partying?*

Mick: *No parties. Not my thing.*

Alisa: *So, being the big bad wolf at the bar wasn't normal?*

Mick: *Only with you. Do you want to go to dinner and celebrate your news?*

I chewed on my lip wondering what he'd meant. I suspected he could be a wolf with any woman, not just me.

Dinner I could probably do, though. If I could manage changing when I got home and leaving without having to answer any questions about where I was going.

Yet another reason why I needed to move out. Nothing remained private there. The expectation to live like a prisoner in that house with occasional parole if your outings involved family, was like a life sentence. If they knew about Monica, that would probably be looked down upon, but since she was family they might not care.

It felt like, even at twenty-four years of age, I was still having to bend to their rules, cater to their whims and live life according to their terms.

I should have never moved back. That was the truth. But I was here now, and surprisingly, a small part of me was glad, simply because I'd met an intriguing, but strangely dark man at a bar.

Alisa: *I'd like that. What time, where? I'll see if I can.*

Mick: *Just do it. Downtown. There's an Italian place called Lucianos. Seven.*

Alisa: *I might meet you there at seven then.*

Mick: *You will.*

I shoved my phone in my purse and wondered what tonight might be like. I could almost imagine the smug smile he had on his face right now, knowing I'd meet him. Which again led to dirty thoughts of him in bed, being bossy while he texted me, and chuckling with that deep masculine voice of his.

Somewhere in the back of mind I pictured it all going well at dinner. But he was probably going to warn me off again, or at least attempt to. Then again, with Mick, he might suggest something lewd. The thought made me smirk with the possibilities.

CHAPTER FIVE

Mick

I WAS ten minutes early to the restaurant, not knowing if she was going to make it or not. I hadn't received a text indicating that she wasn't going to show, but she was probably busy.

She was surprising. I'd tried to back off from her after my appointment three days ago. I'd hoped that she wouldn't show up Saturday night. I thought that maybe if I didn't text back, she'd move on and forget about everything. A girl like Alisa could find another man easily.

The problem was, it cost me. Although it was probably better for her, it ripped me up in a way that I hadn't felt before. It was strange because I didn't know her. Not really. I knew things about her based on a buzzed moment between the two of us, but not the details that most people should know. Details were important and bound people together from my own experience. So, I questioned why she affected me for three days and nights, burrowing into me, making me want to see her again. Something was there but I didn't know what it was.

I had a good day with my brother after the appointment, as short as it was. Met with his new employer, congratulated both of them and talked with Alex for a moment or two. He seemed decent enough. I couldn't find a good reason to dislike him. Although he didn't do it in front of us, he had an addiction to putting pens in his mouth when he was typing, maybe even when he was reading. Whatever the case, I could see the indentations of teeth marks on the ones on his desk. I suspected that he was an ex-smoker or liked to smoke, but hid it at work.

Jack was still a wildcard to me. Last name Hunter according to his certificate. He'd been less jazzed than Mason at lunch, but still excited. It was in his eyes and the smile that occasionally appeared.

While Mason showed his happiness by pounding me on the back and grinning, Jack seemed reserved and extremely professional. For someone who had some very questionable tattoos so visibly on display it was contradictory to what I assumed. He was closed off, observant and struck me as someone who was constantly looking for the "catch" if something good happened. Mason had slapped his license several times, talking eagerly, while Jack had reverently looked at it and kept it in his unmoving palm.

Afterward, I'd done exactly what I'd planned on doing. Bought two bottles of whiskey at the store, drove home, and after a quick workout, drank myself into oblivion. And yet, the nightmares were still there.

I thought about texting her the next day while staring at her last message and feeling like hammered shit. Concluded that I was a fucking mess she didn't need in her life, and drank again. It didn't take away the waking nightmare of someone taking advantage of her, touching her, kissing her soft lips and tasting her.

I wanted that someone to be me. Even with the darkness constantly threatening to spill over every day. Why hadn't she run that night? Why had she stayed? It was a thought that still plagued me.

I was greeted by a hostess that led me to a private booth at the back. *Luciano*s screamed stereotypical Italian, which was why it was considered a nice place to eat in Kingston. Although a little dramatic with the wine country murals, extremely low lighting, candles and semi-private seating in high-back booths. I knew it was the type of place that a woman might enjoy on a date, even if the place was ridiculously contrived.

Loosening my tie, I wondered if I was a bit overdressed for just a small date. It felt like a noose around my neck due to not wearing one these last few months. I'd dug out a nice shirt from one of my boxes earlier, and put on some slacks. I hadn't shaved, but trimmed the stubble on my face. When I'd walked out of my bedroom, Mason's shit eating grin said it all. I'd cleaned up for her somewhat compared to my regular go-to of jeans and shirt.

The waitress handed me a menu and I ordered a whiskey. The candlelight barely gave off enough light to read, but I preferred it over the harsh glare in other restaurants.

Fifteen minutes and another drink later, she walked in and looked around. Her blonde hair was pulled back on the sides, showcasing her long neck. She was dressed casually, black pencil skirt and a cream blouse. Nothing fancy and definitely not the revealing number she'd worn over the weekend. Her makeup was minimal, but she was beautiful enough not to need it on any given day. Her gaze landed on me, and a light pink blush graced her cheeks. She was fucking adorable, a refreshing contradiction to the women I usually associated with.

When she slid stiffly into the seat across from me, she gave me a nervous smile.

I shook my head. "Where is your seat at?"

She blinked at me, confused for a moment then her eyes slid down my chest.

"I can't sit in your lap in the middle of a restaurant, Mick," she replied.

I smirked, pleased that she'd caught my reference. "Well, you could but it would make eating a little difficult. So, we'll have to settle for you sitting beside me."

She let out a small laugh. "Oh, okay. If you want."

I nodded as she stood up and came around the table. Guiding her hip, telling myself that I was only helping and not burning to touch her, I eased her into the booth.

She gave me a slight sideways glance. "Hi. Sorry I'm late."

"That's okay. We all get busy. You look beautiful."

She glanced down at her clothes. "Sorry, if I'd known you were going to dress up I would have put on something different, but I was in a rush."

I leaned over to her ear, which she gently tilted up. I could smell the soap on her skin and the delicate floral scent of her perfume.

"I'm going commando under the slacks, so I didn't dress up completely."

She giggled and pressed the back of her hand against her mouth. "You didn't."

"If you want to confirm, you can slide your hand into my lap."

Her giggling increased and she shook her head. "I think I'll keep my hands above the table and take your word for it."

I chuckled at her embarrassment. It was obvious by her darting eyes, trying to look at anything but me.

"Good girl," I said as I gave her a small kiss on her temple.

"You say that like you don't want me to, but you put it out there anyway."

I breathed against the side of her neck and she shivered. "The choice is always yours, Alisa. Would you like me to give you more choices to choose from while your hand is down there? I can think of half a dozen things that I'd like you to do, if you want."

"Like?" she whispered.

I chuckled. "Like unbuttoning my slacks and having those delicate fingers of yours slide along my cock. Like putting it in your palm and stroking slowly while we pretend we're just having dinner in front of all these people."

"Oh," she responded on a shaky breath. "You'd want that?"

"Of course. You're a good girl because you're making us both behave."

"I guess I'm kind of a bore."

I gently took hold of her chin and tilted until she was looking up at me. "Never."

Leaning down, I gave her a gentle kiss that I wanted to deepen, wanted everyone that might be looking to see. Instead, I tasted just enough of her to have my already hardening dick twitch and regretted it immediately when I resisted the urge to continue.

Letting go of her chin I asked, "Have you been here before?"

She shook her head. "No. I always wanted to see what it was like inside, though. It's been here a while I guess."

"Do you like it?" I asked, wondering if my choice in places to meet had been correct.

She angled her head to stare up at me. "Yes, of course. But we didn't have to do anything fancy. I would have been just as happy with a burger. As long as you were there."

It was my turn to blink at her in confusion as she studied the menu in front of her. As I stared at her, I noted the delicateness of her nose and curve of her cheek. She was too damn good to be here with me. And I was terrified to walk away.

"Do you know what you want?" she asked after a moment.

I wanted her in whatever fucking way I could have her.

"Yeah," I said, as I motioned the waitress over.

We ordered, she sipped her wine and we sat in companionable silence for a few minutes.

Moving her hair off her neck, I asked, "So where is your new place? Have you started moving?"

She chewed on her lip for a moment. "Well, I know where. It'll be over on Rose Street and Hunsley. Do you know the apartments there?"

I nodded, thinking of the area. Decent neighborhood, not too seedy but not too high-end. Middle-class, close to a park and only a ten-minute drive to downtown.

She described the people that lived in the building from a visit she'd had on Monday. According to the apartment manager, mostly young couples and some college age kids. Then she went on to listing the amenities. The words, gym and pool, didn't sit well with me. I didn't want anyone to see her in anything but a fucking coat and three layers of jeans.

"First floor, second floor, how many bedrooms?"

"Well, I haven't seen it yet. I think it's two bedrooms."

I frowned, but my question was interrupted by the delivery of our food. She'd ordered fettucine and I'd ordered lasagna. We both took a moment eating, and oddly, shared some of our meal. It was the first time I'd ever let someone feed me, but I enjoyed watching my fork slip past her kissable lips to taste my food. Her tongue slid across her lip as she watched me and chewed.

If I didn't know any better, I'd think she was trying to tease me with a view like that. It was hard enough not to study the curve of her shirt over her ample breasts, or the tightness of her skirt over her hips. And such a simple involuntary gesture like licking her lip nearly had me dragging her to the car.

I was going to be walking around in a constant state of full erection and ball of nerves if we continued to see each other. Which I was slowly accepting might not even be a choice for me. She had something that I couldn't quite put my finger on, but I needed desperately. The realization of that crept up on me the longer I spent time with her.

Adjusting in my seat, I asked, "So you haven't seen the floor you're on? Is that what you meant?"

"Well," she said as she avoided my eyes. "The deposits are paid as of today. And I did see a layout but not which one. I told Melanie just to pick one…"

Her eyes got round when I scowled down at her. "Who's Melanie?"

"Uhm, my brother's secretary. I couldn't afford to move right now, but he offered to pay for some of it as a loan because I need out of the house. It's a loan, though, I'm going to pay him back. Please don't think badly of me."

I shook my head but felt like I was teetering on the edge of a cliff wondering what was going on at her home. It wasn't the first time she'd said something. What home? Where? With whom? A million different answers flooded through my brain and they were all ones that pissed me off.

I grabbed her arm and turned her so that she was squarely facing me. If she lied to me I wanted to see it in her face, not guess as she looked at anything else but me. "I'm just wondering. Are you living with a boyfriend? Husband? Is that what this is about?"

"No, no," she said quickly. "I'm at my parent's house. I told you I just moved back here. Last weekend Monica took me out for a welcome home thing. I've been back a week."

The tightness in my chest eased somewhat and I realized I was squeezing her arms too tight.

I loosened my grasp but didn't release her. "What's going on, Alisa? No one just fucking pays for an apartment without looking at it. Do you even have furniture?"

"No. I'll figure it out. I'll get a blowup mattress or something. I have some money, I can get a few things when I move in."

"That didn't fully answer the question," I growled.

"Please, Mick. Can we just forget I said anything?"

Her blue eyes pleaded with me as they began to fill with tears. They were truthful, and she hadn't lied, but there was something she was holding back. This wasn't the place to pressure her, though.

"Let's go," I said as I threw some money on the table. "We'll talk somewhere else."

When she turned to slide out of the booth I noticed a red spot on her back.

"Wait," I said as I grabbed her hip. The red spot wasn't from the food we'd eaten earlier. It would have been a smudge that clung to the fabric. This coated the back of her shirt near her shoulder blade.

"What the fuck is this?"

"What?" she asked as she twisted back in her seat.

I gently pressed on it and she gasped. Blood. Pure and simple. A wound. It made sense why she'd stiffly sat down earlier.

"Get up. Walk in front of me. When we get to the door make a right. We're going to my car."

"Mick..." she began, her eyes pleading with me not to ask.

Had she simply said it was from yard work or given me some story, I might have let it go. But that look said everything. Whatever happened, it was from some sort of trouble and that I couldn't tolerate.

"Don't think about it. Just do it."

She did as she was told until we got outside. Then tried to walk away from me.

When I grabbed her arm, she started crying. I hauled her across the parking lot, feeling every bit like an insane bastard, but I needed to know. Needed my questions answered and had to see the fucking wound.

I unlocked the doors on the car and put her in my vehicle as she cried in earnest. I felt locked down, suddenly numb and focused on one thing. What the fuck happened to her?

When I climbed in the car I started unbuttoning her blouse. "I'm sorry, I need to see."

She nodded and didn't make a move to stop me. The freed buttons revealed the undershirt she had on, and at any other time, I would have been pleased to find the lace against her skin.

Maneuvering her, I slid the blouse down her shoulder, the thin strap of her lacy undershirt following. There was a patch of gauze that looked like it'd been hastily taped to her back, the area red with irritation.

Looking at her back in the low light of the street lamp, I inspected the injury closer. This wasn't the first wound she'd received. There were a few older scars that had healed so well that to the normal viewer, they wouldn't have looked out of place.

Peeling back the tape, I stared at a puncture mark that was smaller than a pea. It was deep enough that it bled profusely without the gauze holding it, but not so big that it wouldn't heal quickly. The area around it was red and irritated. It appeared to be a welt of some sort, but what caused it, I couldn't guess.

"Who did this to you?" I growled between my clenched teeth.

Taping up the wound again, I eased her shirt back over her shoulder. She sat crying for a moment before I pulled her back against my chest gently. The blood would be on both of us, but I couldn't stand hearing her pain.

I'd dealt with violence and pain for years. It wasn't something new to me and wasn't the first time I'd heard it from someone. But, not in my life, had I ever heard the wail of a victim or the cries of a family member that affected me like this. I'd learned how to shut it out, control the volume and leave it behind. But hearing this sweet girl cry, wrecked me in ways that I didn't really understand.

"Alisa," I whispered. "It's okay. Baby, please don't cry."

I smoothed her hair back from her neck and planted kisses along her tear stained cheeks. I held her there for the longest time. Whispering to her, that things would be alright, until she calmed, and her breathing became steady again.

Moving the hair off her face, I kissed along her cheek again, determined to fix this with something. Although I couldn't remember the last time I'd showed it, the only thing I had now was my tenderness.

"If you don't want to answer me, it's your choice, but I do need to know a couple of simple things."

I felt her nod slightly.

"Is your car here?"

"Yes," she whispered.

"Okay, do you have anything in there that you need? Is it locked?"

"No, and it's locked."

"Okay, you're not going back home. I'm taking you to my place. We need to get you patched up better, and I need to take a look in better lighting."

"I have to go home," she said on a whimper.

"No, you don't. You don't *have* to do a damn thing you don't want to, and I know for a fucking fact that you don't want to. If you hop out of this car right now and choose to go back, I'm out. No more messages, no meeting up, nothing. I'll call the police and tell them what I just saw. Whoever the hell is at your house is going to have the law shoved so tightly up their asses they won't be able to sneeze without it being reported."

She nodded again without responding.

"You're coming home with me, Alisa. You never have to go back there."

"You don't understand," she whispered.

"What's that?" I asked as I kissed her temple.

"My last name is King."

My hand paused only for a moment while rubbing her arm. This had just become a whole shitstorm of complicated.

CHAPTER SIX

Alisa

Feeling embarrassed, I crossed my arms over my chest as I sat on Mick's worn leather couch. He stormed around the sparsely furnished house for a moment calling his brother, Mason, who wasn't home.

"Just get here before I need bail money," he barked into the phone and hung up.

He tossed a shirt onto the couch in front of me and an open first aid kit on the coffee table. After getting some things out he stared at me for a moment.

"Alright, take your blouse off, Alisa."

Hesitating, I glanced at his front door. "Your brother."

He shook his head and started removing more items from the kit. "He won't be here for a little while. We need to get that patched up better. Blouse. Off."

I slid the now stained blouse off my shoulders as he watched.

"Any way I can get you to remove that camisole?" he asked sweeping his eyes down to my chest.

"I don't think…"

"Don't think, Alisa. Just do it. Take that shirt in front of you and cover up if you don't want me looking."

I tried to maneuver my arms through the straps. He made no movement toward me and waited as his eyes danced across my face.

A small gasp escaped me when I tried to move my arm up and under the shirt. My shoulder was so sore from earlier it was unbelievable. It hadn't been as bad when I left, and if I'd slowed down to patch my back properly I wouldn't be sitting in front of him struggling with something so simple.

I glanced away from him toward the coffee table in shame. One of his hands gently slid up my back as I felt him shift beside me.

"Alisa, look at me."

My eyes met his for a moment before he leaned in and touched his lips to mine. It was soft and patient as he slid his mouth across mine, promising things, but not demanding them.

I felt a tug at my shirt before the material came loose. There was the distinct sound of metal on metal, as he used scissors on the fabric. I clutched the front as it parted down my back and both straps slid off my shoulders.

His mouth moved to the top of my shoulder, slowly leaving a trail of wet kisses in his wake. I whimpered in response as my body grew restless with pain of a different sort. It was a desperate feeling of wanting him, and yet tense from not knowing what this would all mean in the end. He couldn't possibly want to involve himself for long in the King family ugliness.

His tongue glided to the back of my neck as he reached around me. The front of the camisole slid free from my hands.

As he continued to suck at the back of my neck and along my spine, he grabbed his t-shirt and pressed it against my now bare chest. Two of his fingers slid around the fabric to graze the underside of one of my breasts and I started panting.

"I'm trying, Alisa," he whispered against my skin. "I need to patch this, but you taste like honey and smell even better. Fuck, you're beautiful."

A small smile managed to reach my lips. He thought I was beautiful. Even now with blood on us both and in bad circumstances.

Blood trickled down my back a little, but his hand wiped it away. His mouth trailed down to the top on my spine then departed as I felt the tape being removed from the flimsy patch.

"Unfortunately, I've got to do this two-handed," he said gruffly, as I felt his fingers under my breast flex and slide along my skin in retreat.

The tape and covering came off gently and he growled.

"This is going to hurt a moment," he said, as he dabbed the area with something that smelled like alcohol. The sting of it made me hiss for a second.

He trailed a finger down my back and adjusted behind me again.

"Ready to tell me about it?"

I breathed in, knowing what he wanted while he cleaned me up. His long fingers stroked along the angry line in my skin that I knew was there.

"A belt. I think the tongue caught me just right."

He paused for a second in his attentions then continued.

"Okay, and the others?"

He meant the other scars on my back that were so faint, no one had ever said anything about them. Not now, anyway, after years of healing.

"Same," I whispered.

"Okay, you don't need stitches," he said with a tone that sounded detached and clinical. "It just went in deep enough to bleed when you move around."

He kept his hand firmly on the wound for a moment then cleaned it again.

"You have some bruising. Do you want me to call the police?"

"No. It won't help."

"Who's your brother? Did he do this?"

I shook my head. "No. Alex would never do this. He doesn't know."

"Alex?" he asked in surprise. "Alexander King is your brother?"

I nodded.

"Interesting. You don't look alike."

Shrugging I said, "That's what everyone says. Alex looks like...he has the dark hair, looks more like the rest of them."

"You can tell me your dad did this. Or I can tell you. Denny King? Would you like to tell me why?"

Chewing on my lip, I decided it was better to just tell him, he'd already seen the evidence of what my father had done. "He was home early when I got there. I thought I'd timed it right. Should have just stayed away."

"You're done," he informed me. "Let me help you with the shirt."

He leaned against my back as I turned my head to the side and stared up at him. His eyes held mine briefly then glanced down as he slid the shirt out of my hands. They burned at the sight of my bare chest.

"Mick..." I whispered.

"Be a good girl and get dressed for both of us. I can't...I'm not good for you," he whispered.

I opened my mouth for a second, wondering what to say. "I'll be good for you then."

"Fuck," he whispered and closed his eyes. "Please, before I carry you back to my bed and make you regret those words."

"I'd never regret it. Not ever."

He groaned and shifted to stand up, pulling me up with him. Picking me up he carried me to a room with packed boxes and a bed that looked rumpled and slept in.

"Don't move," he said as he laid me down on the sheets then disappeared into the bathroom for a moment to wash his hands.

When he came back, I let the t-shirt he'd given me fall away from my hands and he growled as he gazed down at me. He removed my shoes and slowly tugged my skirt over my hips.

Laying in front of him on display in my black lace panties and nothing else felt overwhelming. I wondered what he thought.

When he didn't move to do anything else or even touch me, I squirmed in nervousness.

"I'm sure you've seen better," I said quietly, as I rolled onto my side and brought my legs up to my chest.

"Don't ever fucking say that to me again," he barked. His measured glare made me blink with regret.

He was so confusing. He wanted the good girl to tell him to behave, but not the words of a woman desperately trying not to feel inadequate compared to what he was used to. Some women would have known what to do, but I just didn't.

I glanced away from him and buried my nose in his pillow. A musky scent invaded me, and I took a deep breath.

I heard movement behind me, then the bed dipped with his weight. His hand came to rest on my back before trailing down my side and over my hip. It lingered there, then slid around to my stomach. Mick's lips found my neck again as he pressed his bare chest against me.

I writhed beside him as he touched and explored my neck with his tongue, sending shooting sensations up my body. I could feel myself getting wet from his attention, a pool of burning lust settled deep in my belly.

He turned me onto my back and latched on one of my nipples with his hot mouth and tongue. He sucked hard causing me to gasp, then bit the underside, roughly.

My panties were invaded by his large hand. I moaned from his attention on my breasts, and he played with my clit, rubbing the sensitive nub in earnest.

He groaned as he found my mouth and my hands found their way around his back.

When he hooked one finger into me I gasped against his mouth. Then he added a second one. I could feel myself coating his fingers as he spread my folds and started a slow rhythm, pumping into my body.

He bit my lip and licked the spot immediately. "So tight. Is this what you wanted, baby? Me inside you?"

"Yes," I whispered as his mouth descended on my neck.

He sat up suddenly, slid to the end of the bed and yanked my panties down my legs.

"Spread your legs for me, Alisa," he said roughly, as he pushed my knees apart and stared down at my center. "Fuck, that's mine."

Before I could question what he said, he lifted me slightly by my hips and his mouth was on me. His tongue licking and sucking as he kept my legs spread around his face.

My mouth opened in a silent scream as I arched off the bed. I couldn't keep up with the sensations that shot through my body. A tear slid down my face at the magnitude of hot yearning that was burning through every part of me as he slid his tongue into me and he flicked my clit with his finger.

The sounds of his groaning response to what he was doing was only making me fly higher. His beard chaffed the most sensitive parts of my legs, the iron grip he had on my hips and his mouth against my clit as he sucked at it harder than before sent me spiraling out of control.

My head thrown back and body arching, I screamed, grasping desperately at sheets, his shoulders, pushing against his headboard to grind into his face. I was spinning and felt so light-headed, I was on the verge of passing out. He continued his onslaught mercilessly until I stopped writhing underneath him and started shivering in the aftermath.

He gave me one last lick that made me twitch and he smirked up at me.

Crawling over me, kissing a trail up my body, he hovered for a second, staring down into my dazed eyes.

"Taste yourself. You're all honey."

Dipping his head, he ran his tongue along the seam of my lips. I opened for him and he plunged inside, making me taste myself and him at the same time. Yet it was his taste, the whiskey and muskiness of his skin that surrounded me.

He licked at my lips then slid away from me. Closing my legs and pulling a sheet over them, he stalked to his bathroom partially clothed in just his slacks that were hanging loose around his muscled hips. He shut the door halfway and I stared after him.

My eyes felt heavy, but my brain was still whirling with what had just happened. I'd never felt so content and somewhat shocked at the same time. He made me feel alive and that was more than anyone had ever made me feel in my life. Whether it was his experience and my lack of it, I didn't know. Much like his personality, the way he touched me felt like he had two sides to him. Rough and yet tender. Surprisingly, I liked both.

I heard the sink turn on and off then sounds of the shower. Steam filtered through the crack in the door as I kept peering at the opening, wondering why he hadn't taken things further.

When he emerged after a few minutes, he had a towel wrapped around his waist. Droplets of water collected and dripped down his chest. He had a smattering of hair that cascaded from his pecks down to the edge of his towel. It looked like he kept it trimmed or it was naturally short. Regardless, it made him look even more like a very virile man.

He gave me a quick glance and a smirk as he grabbed a shirt, and his jeans. He turned around to change, not letting me see him fully nude. I didn't know whether that was out of modesty or privacy, but it felt unfair in a way.

He ambled over to the side of the bed afterward and turned me onto my stomach.

"Still patched. Should heal okay."

"Mick?" I asked, as I gazed up at him.

"Everything's okay, Alisa. Don't think about it too hard. You're stunning."

"Okay, but..."

He trailed his fingers across my mouth. "Just let it be for now. Tell me about what happened earlier."

"Uhm, when?"

He nodded toward my back. "That. I need you to tell me."

"You answer, and I'll answer."

He frowned. "That's not how this works."

"Make it work, Mick. You answer me, and I'll answer you. Truthfully."

"So, it's I'll show you mine if you show me yours?" he asked. "Baby, I've already seen yours, so answer my question."

I blinked up at him, stunned by his tone.

I rolled over and sat up. Inching to the side of the bed and pushing my hair out of my face, I snapped, "Fuck you, Mick."

He sat, stunned at my statement.

I grabbed my skirt off the floor, shimming it up my legs. I didn't even bother trying to find my panties. He could have them.

Covering my chest, I grabbed for his t-shirt on the bed. Mine was still blood soaked and in tatters on his living room floor. It could stay there for all I cared.

When he came around the bed to stand in front of me, I didn't look at him. He sat down on the bed and tried to grab my wrist.

"Where do you sit?"

"Never with you," I bit out miserably. "You can't expect things to be one-sided and tell me that I need to stop thinking about things every time I try to ask you something."

"Well there's that regret I told you about," he said sarcastically.

My eyes flashed at him in anger. "I didn't. The only thing I regretted was not being able to make you feel just as good. What did you say? Get on my knees and suck you off without blinking? Like some club slut I guess. Except it didn't feel slutty ten minutes ago. It felt like the right thing, something I wanted to do with you. I haven't done it before, but maybe it would have been good. At least I would have tried out of wanting to show you that I liked you, instead of being some casual lay."

He grabbed my arm and slid me into his lap.

"No, fuck you. Let me go, Mick," I said as I pushed against his arms that had a vise grip around my waist. I kicked out and he only squeezed tighter.

"Okay, enough!" he yelled at me in a stern voice. "What do you want to know? What do you want me to say? Here's me in a nutshell. I'm a dick for seducing you while you're injured. Even if you'd started bleeding again, I wouldn't have stopped. I'm an asshole because I *want* you to tell me that you can't stand me. Maybe if you did then I'd stop dreaming about you. I'm a jerk because I wanted you to run out of that club, scared out of your mind. Then you'd stay at home like a good girl and find someone that would treat you right. And I'm a fucking selfish man, because regardless of wanting all those things, I want you with me."

"Then answer my questions, Mick," I yelled right back at him. "You're right, you can be a jerk. But I'm still here."

"Fuck, I know. And I hate myself, for the mess I'm going to insert into your life."

"I've got plenty of that all on my own. I'm not asking you to bare your soul. Just...let me understand some things."

He shifted his eyes to the floor in thought or guilt, I couldn't tell which.

Eventually he spoke. "Ask."

"Okay, why are there boxes in here? What's your favorite color? Does going commando in jeans chafe? I'd think it would feel weird."

He looked at me in confusion, his lips tightening then smirking at me.

"You always manage to surprise me. I moved here, but I'm not going to stay with my brother forever. He's got an interesting nighttime routine as you know."

"Do you hear them?" I asked in surprise.

He nodded. "Yeah, sounds carry. It's difficult to deal with when you're not seeing anyone, and you don't sleep."

"Have you ever..." I trailed off and glanced down at his crotch for a minute.

He chuckled then laughed. "Jacked off, Alisa? Jesus. What a question. I don't think you're as good as I thought you were."

I smiled, trying not to laugh at his response and bit my lower lip.

"Interesting," he said, while studying my face. "I wonder if you're secretly a voyeur."

I shook my head. "Not that I know of."

His lips tweaked. "My favorite color today is blue. Going commando does chafe, I guess, depending on the type of pants. Sometimes it feels good, but sometimes it's just for easy access."

"Hmm."

"What else?" he asked.

"Why didn't you let me, do something to you?"

He smirked. "I want that, but can we skip that question for now?"

I nodded. "What did you do before you moved here?"

A dark look slid over his face. It felt like a door slammed somewhere in his demeanor that didn't want to be opened and warned me to keep out.

"I'm not ready to talk about that."

"Okay," I replied. "Do you talk to anyone about it?"

He nodded. "Yeah. Anything else?"

I wondered who he talked to about it if he wasn't ready to answer me. An ex? His brother or family? If the day came that he wanted to tell me I'd listen, but I was certain that wouldn't be anytime soon. Regardless, he'd answered most of my questions. It was just not the most important thing which was why he felt and behaved the way he did.

"No. You've been fair. A jerk about it, but fair."

He sighed, still tense and tilted his head to stare into my eyes. "Your turn."

I chewed on my lip thinking about everything I needed to say. Unlike him, I'd come to terms with things in my life. It seemed like a reality I couldn't escape.

CHAPTER SEVEN

Mick

Staring down into her blue eyes as I hugged her tight against my body, I wondered what kind of creature she was. So damn beautiful and yet so utterly trusting that I wouldn't ruin her.

I knew deep down that I might not meet her expectations. She had to have them. All women did. I warred with the knowledge that I could send her into a tailspin with a word or something I could say one day.

Cold didn't even begin to describe me. I could be clinical, detached, closed off to things that mattered. Her feelings would one day dwindle into bitterness no matter how much she thought she wanted to stay right now.

She'd tasted so sweet in my mouth. So much innocence and purity that it nearly killed me to leave her on the bed. I wanted to sink into her and forget everything, have her wipe away my murky past with her honeyed scent and sweetness.

But it would only be for a moment, before I laid down and the demons tormented me again. Before I was back to drowning in my own mind with the things I'd seen. Her velvety touch would have wiped it away for a little while, though. I craved for that, for her. But I wasn't sure if I could handle what might happen afterward. She deserved a man that wouldn't slip back into the darkness. It would be like taking a small piece of who she was for what I needed, and not something that benefitted her.

I could try, for her. But if I had her, I knew I'd never want to let go.

What I'd told her was the truth. I was a dick sometimes. I wondered what the good old doctor would say about that admission of guilt to this woman. I wasn't sure if it was progress or just another need to warn her that what lay in wait on the fringes had swallowed me whole.

"You know the Kings."

"Everyone does," I replied.

"Well a refresher then, since you haven't known them the way I know them."

I settled back on the bed against the headboard keeping her in my lap.

She let out a huge sigh. "They're one of the most corrupt families I've ever known. Not that I know many people, but they aren't the normal."

"No family is normal," I said.

"Well they're not like my family. I think it really hit me when I was about thirteen or fourteen. Alex was away at college by then. I mean, I knew I wasn't looked at as anything more than someone who would marry well."

"No one should ever be looked at that way, no matter who you are."

She nodded. "I know, but it doesn't mean it's not the reality of growing up as a King. My dad is the District Attorney. It's ironic in some ways how Alex became a defense lawyer given my dad's chosen career. They're on opposite sides of the courtroom, but I wonder sometimes if my dad didn't plan it that way."

"How so? What would be the advantage?" I asked.

"If you think about it, say a criminal case comes up for someone like a family member. Several have over the years. My dad might assign the case to his weakest attorney in the office, then pressure Alex to defend it. There's no law that says he can't defend a family member if they hire him."

Thinking through that, it stood true that there were many instances where a defense attorney represented a family member in court. I'd been witness to it several times when asked to testify on either side.

"Okay, so he defends them. That's legal."

She looked annoyed for a minute. "Glad you agree. I did look it up."

I smirked. "Sorry, continue."

"Okay, so, what if I told you my dad paid for the defense. And it's happened more than once."

"That would be a conflict of interest and illegal."

"That's the thing. Would it be illegal if my father gifted the money to another family member and that money just happened to end up in the hands of the defendant?"

"Yes," I said flatly. "But it's hard to prove collusion in that aspect."

And would warrant an FBI investigation, but I wasn't going to mention it.

"Right. I know. It was a rhetorical question."

I gave her a look. "Please, continue. I'll stop talking."

"No, you won't. Anyway, I overheard a conversation between one of my uncles and my dad one day. I didn't really think about what I heard at the time. Didn't really know what was going on. There were a lot of people that came over, it was an everyday event."

I smoothed the hair away from her face. "Did they see you?"

"I've always been invisible to my dad. Always. There was never any affection there. Not like with Alex. My mother, when she was still semi with it in the world, told me that my place was to marry a nice businessman. Someone of worth in the city. That I should only look for the best and brightest. That's what my reality was."

I nodded and wondered if she knew that she'd found the worst if she decided to stay with me. I was no catch. Not anymore.

"So, you might not remember, there was a case involving one of my cousins. He was twenty-three and accused of raping a woman after a burglary and killing her. Or so I heard."

"Definitely a criminal case. Possibility of death sentence in Texas."

"Right. You're talking again."

I chuckled and kissed the tip of her nose.

"So, one night I overheard a conversation. He never paid any attention to me and didn't know I was there. Or ignoring me, whatever. We have a lot of family in a lot of businesses here. This particular uncle is or was the superintendent for the school district. Obviously, it was bad press for him and his son. But he couldn't, from what I gathered, afford a good defense lawyer."

"Ahh, so he goes to your dad for money to pay one?"

"Yeah, that was the basic conversation. They pleaded it down and he got some ridiculous fine and jail time that was less than half of what it should have been."

"Hmm," I mumbled.

"Of course, I didn't know what the verdict was going to be at the time. I just overheard something about money and a defense case. I didn't know what it was about, specifically. Later, I figured it out."

"So, tell me what happened."

"Well, he caught me listening. And it wasn't like I was really listening on purpose. Anyway, he used a belt on me. I'll never forget it. He dragged me into his office by my hair. Surrounded by fancy furniture and walls lined with references on law, and beat me. It was the first time he struck me in anger and my uncle sat and watched. Six swats across my back with a belt."

My hands clenched as my jaw tightened. Imagining a child being punished in such a way made my stomach churn.

She sighed. "After that I tried not to be around much. At least not when he was there. But there were always run-ins here and there. You've seen my back."

"Yeah," I replied simply, trying to tamp down my anger.

"So, when I say that the King family is corrupt, I mean it. They've got a monopoly in this city that reaches into everything. They're even in the police force. I know that from things I've heard, and when I tell you that I don't want you to call the police about my back, it's because it won't matter. There is no law higher than King law. They're everywhere."

"Politics," I mumbled, thinking of my father and the dead body over the weekend. "What happened tonight?"

She frowned. "I went home, and my father was there. He's usually not home until really late. I think he's having an affair. He's always drunk when he comes in and I make myself scarce enough. But he was on a tirade about something tonight. Screaming into the phone. I tried to just go to my room."

My gut clenched thinking about Alisa facing down the man. I wanted to drive to their house and show him what a real opponent would be like instead of a defenseless woman.

"He was angry, and I wasn't quick enough. He started screaming at me about something that happened before I left for college and then accused me of living off their money. Useless, worthless, whatever. The best way to deal with all his bullshit is not to react at all. When he was just an attorney, he was so good at dressing witnesses down in a courtroom, that it's never good to show him any kind of weakness."

Betting he was a functioning sociopath, I kept my mouth shut, but made a mental note to hurt the man one day.

"I turned to leave when I thought he was done but didn't hear the belt come off. He caught me with the end of it. I ran upstairs, bandaged my back and left."

"You should have called me. I would have come to get you, or met you somewhere. We didn't have to meet at a restaurant."

She shrugged. "To be honest, I just wanted a normal date. I wanted to see you and pretend nothing happened for a while. I thought about calling Alex, but I didn't want to tell him after he'd already helped me today."

"So, he's unaware of what happened tonight."

"He doesn't know. Alex is the only one I trust in the family."

"I saw him over the weekend."

She looked up at me with surprise. "Are you in trouble?"

I chuckled and kissed her cheek. "No. My brother just got his P.I. license and he's basically on retainer to do some work for your brother. Help find things, records, follow people. I'm assuming to help the defendants he represents."

"He's a good man."

My jaw clenched again. I didn't want to tell her my personal opinion now that she'd told me about her home life. If he'd been any brother at all, he wouldn't have allowed her to stay in a house with an abuser.

Anger grew toward Alex and his supposed ethics. He'd talked well enough about them when we'd spoken in his office. He was trying to sell me on something that sounded interesting, but now rankled with the stink of corruption.

Mason bought it well enough. Jack was wary, but then again, Jack was wary about everything it seemed. I should have paid more attention to what the man was saying rather than staying so focused on his damn teeth marks in pens.

"I should call my brother," Alisa whispered.

"It's late, we can call him tomorrow or stop by for a chat."

"I could just crash at his house tonight. It wouldn't be a big deal."

"No," I said flatly. "You're staying here. You're not going to another King household for a while."

She leaned back and gave me a confused stare. "Alex's house is safe."

"Mason will be here soon," I said, changing the subject.

"Mick..."

"You're staying here. Just do this for me. I need you here, otherwise I'm going to worry."

Or kill her fucking family. I wasn't half as pissed off earlier as I was now, and I was ready to beat someone to a pulp earlier. At least if she was here I'd have a reason not to go on a killing spree. She was the incentive. To crawl into bed with her and sleep. She might even keep the nightmares away.

Hearing the front door slam, I rubbed her arms. "Get in bed, baby. Sleep for a little bit. I need to talk to Mason about something."

She slid off my lap and started peeling off her skirt. Seeing her gorgeous mound and hips come into view again made me fantasize about every dirty thing I wanted to do to her. Laying her down to suck at those wet folds of hers again was the highest on the list for the moment.

I pulled the covers over her body all the way to her shoulders as she rolled over. Her blonde hair spread across my gray pillow.

She fit there. In my bed, with me beside her. The thought made my fucking chest hurt. I knew she wouldn't be there forever. I knew it was just a night, perhaps two until we figured things out, but if there was a way to keep her there for a little while, I wanted to make it happen.

I turned off the light and closed the door when I left. Stalking toward the kitchen, I found my brother drinking out of a milk carton in front of the fridge.

"Dude. I like cereal sometimes without your backwash. Do you mind?"

He shrugged and placed it back in the fridge. I made a mental note to mark that one later as the backwash milk.

"What the fuck was so urgent that I left a blonde at the bar?" he asked.

Sitting down at the kitchen table, he joined me.

"What do you know about the King family?"

He leaned back in his chair and whistled under his breath. "Wow. Left a blonde to talk about the fucking King family. Thought you said this was an emergency."

I tapped my fingers on the table. "It is. Alisa showed up for our date."

"Admitting it's a date is the first step in recovery."

"Mason, goddammit. Just fucking listen. Alisa showed up, we're headed out and I see blood on her back. Looked at it, we get back here and she dumps a lot of shit about the Kings in my lap. She's Alisa King. Sister to your part-time employer."

Mason leaned forward, a surprised look on his face. "Holy fuck. The untouchables and you're dating one of them."

I pointed at him. "Don't fuck with me. You had her cousin in your bed over the weekend."

"Yeah, to screw and lose. Not date. That shit doesn't happen. You have to have money or know someone, who knows someone, and that ain't us, bro."

"Fuck that. And it's not like that."

Mason chuckled. "Man, I can smell it on you, don't lie to me. You've been in there playing hide the weasel with one of the King princesses. I have a nose for pussy and that shit's sweet."

I looked up at the ceiling briefly, praying for patience, before meeting his eyes again. "You've become the most vulgar person I know. You don't smell shit. There's a psychological condition called "fucknut" and you're about to meet my boot up your ass."

He laughed. "Alright, alright. Just messing with you. Okay, so what are we talking about. What shit did she lay on you that was such an emergency?"

"Her dad laid a belt on her back and the clasp caught. Not the first time."

"Motherfucker," Mason growled.

My sentiments exactly. I knew Mason would side with me about bringing her home. He might be the biggest prick on the planet when it came to sleeping with women, but he hated abusers. The thing that most people didn't get was that my brother loved women. He was addicted to them. There wasn't a woman alive that he wouldn't do something major for, he just preferred keeping it casual out of simplicity.

"So, what I'm asking is, how far is their reach? She said the police. Didn't want to call them."

"You know how this goes, Mick, you've lived here. It's a corrupt city and the King family is at the burnt and bloodied heart of it. The first and only rule in Kingston is you don't mess with the Kings. Behind every shady event, they're there. Greed, murder, politics. They're a dynasty, an organization that in public seems so legitimate. They have position and power that can sway an entire city. But at the core, they make all the right decisions to help each other."

"Even law enforcement?"

"It's screwed up, I'll tell you that much. Kingston's finest has a lot of cops on the take. I just stayed the hell away. But every once in a while, they'd test your loyalty and do something shitty. You just didn't say anything about it. Like dad always says, it's all political."

Scratching my beard, I considered that news. "So, if I called them about the abuse..."

"You'd probably end up accused of it."

"Fuck. Even with Dad's influence?"

"Mick, Dad's not on the take. But, man, he knows how the wind blows here. And he plays with the political shit every day. They'd fire his ass if he even tried standing up against it. That's *if* they didn't try to do something worse. There are a ton of ways to break a cop and everyone on the force knows that. Shit, you should know."

"Yeah," I replied. I didn't like my dad, but I wasn't vengeful.

"Look, I'd never admit it to Dad, but I think you'll get it. I saw some things going on. There were some guys that strong armed a decent family for some kickbacks once at a restaurant. I was riding with them, didn't like it, said something. One of them was a King cousin. I knew I should have kept my mouth shut, but they were terrorizing those people, and the wife was getting it the worst. The next thing I know I'm facing charges for roughing up a suspect while in custody."

"You never said anything," I replied, shocked at his story. "Why didn't you tell me? I might have been able to pull some strings."

He shook his head. "Nah, and get you fucked up, too? You had great a career, were going places. I never went anywhere. But I worked my ass off, saving what I could, and I've still got some money, even after the lawyer fees. So, I don't have to go back and never will. But since you asked, let me just spell it out. Everything is dirty in Kingston."

"What about Alex? You work for the guy for fuck's sake. Aren't you a little worried?"

Mason started pulling on his beard. "See, I would have said yes before that whole thing happened. But then I met Jack. He knows what goes down in this city. Did some undercover stuff, saw a lot of shit. He doesn't trust anyone. Hell, that guy probably doesn't even trust you or me, but he works for Alex. I may not know Alex very well, but if Jack signed off on him, then he must be better than most Kings. Make sense?"

"Well, I may not kill Alex, then. I just can't justify in my head why her brother would let her stay with her parents if Daddy's been using a belt on his sister for years."

"Look, the guy may be legit, but that doesn't mean he's not a dick. If you want to talk to him, then you know I have your back. Doesn't mean shit to me."

"Yeah, except for your job with him."

Shrugging, he smirked. "Fuck that. Job is a job. Brothers for life."

I nodded and glanced back at the hallway where Alisa was sleeping.

"I can't keep her here forever. We can take her with us tomorrow. If he wants proof, he can take a look. I need to see his face, Mason. He can't hide it from me if he lies."

Mason nodded. "Tomorrow then. What are you going to do if he does?"

"Murder someone."

Mason chuckled. "C'mon, man. That shit's not funny but I get it. I'm headed to bed."

"Me, too," I replied as I got up from the table.

"I bet," he smirked.

"Fuck off."

He laughed as I stalked to the bedroom. I slipped inside the dark room and made my way to the sleeping figure under the sheets. She was a deep sleeper, with little breaths coming out of her mouth as I moved the hair off her neck.

Tomorrow she'd either flip out or decide to have some faith in someone other than her brother. I just hoped that I deserved it if she gave it to me.

CHAPTER EIGHT

Alisa

I woke up in Mick's dark room not understanding what was happening. There was a noise beside me that didn't sound right. A muffled groan, movement, a louder moan.

The room was so dark that only the light from a small digital clock illuminated anything. It threw a red haze over the bed but only within a few feet.

I smelled Mick before I felt him jerk beside me.

Turning over, I saw him on his back, one hand across his chest, flexing. His mouth was partially open and small sounds of pain were coming from him. His whole body jerked, his hand clenched.

He was trapped in some nightmare that wasn't letting him go.

"Mick," I whispered.

He jerked again.

"Mick, wake up," I said a little louder.

He made a whimpering sound.

I touched his arm this time and rubbed while I gently nudged him.

"Mick. Wake up right now. Wake up. I need you."

His body gave one last jerk and he nearly sat completely up. His breathing was coming out in gasps as he fought to escape whatever darkness he'd left behind in his dream.

I rubbed his shoulder slowly trying to comfort him.

"Alisa," he whispered in the dark, then eased back onto the bed and continued to sleep.

Watching him, I kept my hand on his arm for a while, rubbing it gently to let him know that I was there, even in his sleeping state.

There was something to him other than his bravado and dirty mouth. Something that ate at him daily. It was in the way he talked about himself. He could flirt and talk about a lot of different things. He was incredibly smart and tender at times.

It was what he said when he didn't have some flippant remark. It was between the sometimes witty and astute lines. It was somewhere behind his eyes when he was seducing me.

He was a lonely, haunted man. And I knew that man needed me no matter what he said to try and scare me.

His hand covered mine eventually. I wasn't entirely sure how long I'd laid there watching him. When his long fingers slid over mine, I stopped rubbing and eyed him to see if he was still sleeping.

"Alisa?" he asked. "Are you awake?"

I let out a sleepy yawn. "Yeah, woke up and couldn't get back to sleep."

"Hmm," he mumbled as he rolled toward me. "Did I wake you up?"

"Just happens sometimes."

He grimaced. "I have nightmares. I'm sorry."

"What about?"

"Old ghosts. Things that won't ever leave me."

Nodding I whispered, "Me too, sometimes."

"What time is it?" he asked, as his head craned around to look at the clock. "Six? Jesus."

"What's wrong?"

"Nothing. Just haven't been up this early in a while."

"Hmm," I responded, wondering what his normal routine was like. I didn't even know if he had a job he went to every day. "My normal time. Do you have eggs or cereal?"

"Yeah, but I'm smelling coffee which means Mason's up already. He's an egg guy."

"And what are you?"

"Anything that has meat in it. Don't drink the milk in the door. Mason had a swig from it last night."

I giggled. "Gotcha, thanks for the warning."

His hand gently caressed my arm before retreating again. "Your laugh. Are you a morning person?"

"Sometimes, depends on how I sleep."

"Same. Which is pretty shitty most of the time."

I didn't comment about it, knowing he probably wouldn't share why. He was wrapped around something that he kept close to him and he had no reason to trust me with it.

"I'm going to take a shower, but..."

"What?"

I rolled my eyes in the dark, embarrassed about what I was going to say. "I think I probably need a bra. The camisole on your living room floor, was kind of it."

He sat up suddenly. "Fuck. Yeah, you do. Mason doesn't need to see any of that. If he takes one look at you, I'll rip his damn head off."

I smirked at his response. Regardless of the push and pull I felt half the time with him, he was reacting like the pull, the protective part that I'd seen glimpses of, was the thing that affected him most. I wondered if he knew it, but decided that he probably wasn't even aware. Maybe it was in his nature to react to things with a surly stubbornness that forced even the small sliver of good in his life away from him.

That was something to consider about him if he wanted me around. If there was a possibility of things going further, how much was I willing to let him do it and for how long?

"I'll figure something out, we need to go some places today."

He swung off the bed and turned on a lamp. My eyes blinked rapidly with the intrusion of light. When I glanced at him, he was staring down at me with an enigmatic look on his face. His eyes swept over the thin sheets covering half of my body, then to the leg and hip that wasn't.

He was still wearing a pair of sweats that hid absolutely nothing of his physique, not even the bulge that was becoming more pronounced. He was a toned god, lean muscles, broad chest. A beautiful man.

"Fuck, I should have slept on the couch," he growled under his breath.

And there was the push. Too bad for him, I was starting to figure this out.

I yawned and rolled over on my stomach like I hadn't heard him, letting the sheet slip off completely. My nudity from the backside was in full view.

He stared at me then growled again, grabbed his clothing off the dresser, and stormed toward the bathroom. Shutting the door, he used a little too much force to hide what he was feeling.

I giggled into the pillow, then sat up and found my panties on the floor. I wasn't going to fan those flames any more this morning. This afternoon was a whole new ballgame.

By the time he stepped out, he had his usual unreadable mask back on. Dressed in his shirt, that hung to the tops on my thighs, I eyed him as he quickly exited.

Humming a tune, I made my way to the shower. Halfway through it, the door opened to the bathroom. I froze and listened.

"Alisa, I hate to say this, but Mason apparently had a bra in his room. I have no idea whose it was, but until we get to the store, will it do? He *says* he accidentally washed it with his clothes the other day and he hadn't trashed it yet. God knows with him. I'm not even sure what size the damn thing is."

I peeked around the shower curtain, spotting him as he held it up with a grimace on his face. He glanced up at me, the grimace deepening, as he set the bra on the counter, and quickly left.

The smile that crept over my face lasted until I got dressed. The bra was snug, which pushed my breasts up a little more than I was used to. But it worked this morning. Tying the end of his shirt around my waist, and donning the skirt from the night before, I made my way to the kitchen.

The interior of the house looked a little different today. A mash of well used furniture and coloring that screamed either retro or nineteen-sixties, depending on how positive a spin they wanted to put on it. But the early morning light coming through the windows made it look less depressing and more like a space that might house normal humans.

Not that Mason and Mick qualified. They weren't normal by any stretch of the imagination. They were men that seemed on the edge. Of what, I couldn't guess. Societal restrictions maybe. Both gave me the impression that they didn't care what people thought of them.

My nose led me toward the coffee in the kitchen. Passing by the brothers, who were sitting at the table, I ignored them and went straight to my addiction.

"Eggs are on the stove," Mason called out.

"Let me get them," Mick said behind me. "Mason hasn't fed a woman breakfast in his life."

"Thank you," I replied, trying to suppress my amusement.

I turned with my coffee cup and smiled at Mason's reaction. He rolled his eyes and flipped Mick off.

Humming another tune, I made my way to the table.

Mason observed me, then slid his eyes to Mick to give him a questioning glance.

Mick set the plate in front of me, then scowled at Mason and shook his head.

"So how are you this morning, Alisa?" Mason asked while smiling at me.

"Good," I said, around a mouthful of eggs. "A little tired, woke up too early and couldn't get back to sleep."

"Hmm," Mason replied, and gave his brother a smirk. "Must have had something to do with waking up next to that ugly guy in your bed."

"Mason," Mick said, with a definite undertone of warning.

"Nope," I said while taking another bite. "Didn't even notice he was there."

Mason turned back to me, looking innocent. "If that's the case, you can have my room next time you sleep over. You won't even know I'm there."

Mick shoved his chair back so violently it nearly toppled over. The glare he was giving Mason was deadly. "Fuck off, Mason. We have shit to do today."

He all but threw his plate in the sink, still staring daggers at Mason as he stormed out of the room.

"Interesting," Mason said, as his gaze followed Mick.

I chewed my eggs and took a sip of coffee. "I'll say. But at least it's something other than the usual."

Mason looked me over with renewed curiosity and I smiled at him sweetly. A moment hung between us. His detached demeanor toward me suddenly shifted into a smile, then a chuckle.

"Fucking-A. You get it."

I shrugged, finishing my breakfast.

Mason took the plate to the sink for me about the time Mick walked back in, wearing a grey Henley, jeans that sat low on his hips, and carrying a bag.

"Ready?" he asked as he slung it over his shoulder.

A few minutes later, we were all seated in his car as we drove away from his house. Situated in a sparse neighborhood on the edge of the city, I studied the road as we passed by.

The morning light had been deceiving in the house. The sky looked like it was brewing up something nasty on the horizon and the clouds were beginning to darken.

"Where are we going?" I asked as we passed through the neighborhoods and drove into the commercial area of the city.

The buildings and streets looked semi-neglected in this area. Not a place I normally ventured. The neighborhood we'd come from, made more sense now. It was in what was called "old Kingston." It'd been a thriving part of the city a decade ago until new businesses and new corporations spied more prosperous places to build. Along with that, came new houses and new money built on the complete opposite end of Kingston.

It was sad to see old storefronts with faded canopies and barely legible signs in the doors. Most of them were for sale or just so drab that it was hard to imagine that any business had managed to survive.

We passed through familiar territory eventually, and I realized our destination. When we pulled up in front of Alex's office building I nearly wept. The need to see my brother was overwhelming for some reason, even though I felt completely safe with Mick watching over me for the night.

I scrunched up my nose. Maybe not watching the entire night. I felt sure that small detail of a mind-blowing orgasm wouldn't be a topic of conversation.

Hopping out of the car, I waited on Mick. When he stood beside me, he gave me a tight smile. He was as guarded as the first time I met him.

"Thank you," I said. "I'll just…I guess I'll see you soon."

When he put his hand on the small of my back and guided me to the door, I was confused. I thought he'd take off immediately now that I was back in my brother's care.

As he walked past me, Mason handed Mick's bag to him. I gave Melanie a small smile, whose mouth was slightly ajar as Mick's long stride headed to my brother's office and entered without knocking.

My brother stopped typing on his computer and glared at Mick. There was a client in his office that was mid-sentence as we entered.

"Leave," Mick growled at the man as he set his bag on Alex's desk.

"But…" the man stammered out before Mick gave him an icy stare. He stood up and passed us as he left in a hurry. Mason shut the door with an audible click.

"What is this, Mick?" Alex asked before I stepped out from behind his back.

"Alisa," Alex said with surprise.

When he stood up, Mick moved in front of me again, blocking my view.

"How much does it take to buy a defense attorney?"

"Mick?" I asked, as I slid around him again.

He glanced at me then back at Alex. "Alisa, stay where you're at. How much does it take, Alex?"

"What the fuck is going on here? Mason?"

Mason had his arms crossed over his chest in front of the door. His steely gaze was aimed at my brother.

Mick responded by unzipping the bag. "How much does it take, Alex? Or should I just call you Mr. King, like the rest of your family?"

"Mick?" I repeated, an uneasy feeling growing in the pit of my stomach.

Mick brought out a holster and straps that he angled over his shoulders. Two guns came out of the bag next.

I gasped. "What are you doing?"

"Just stay there, baby."

"Baby?!" Alex yelled. "Alisa, come here. She's nobody's fucking baby, especially not yours!"

Mick and Alex were now openly glaring at each other. A mix of deadly intent on Mick's face, anger from my brother.

Mick's hand came out and moved me behind him again, then a strong arm pulled me back. I slapped at Mason's arm as he manhandled me across the small office.

"I'll ask again. How much?"

He reached in the bag and pulled out a stack of money that he threw on the desk. Then another. He kept piling money on my brother's desk until he'd reached the bottom.

"There's no amount of money in the world that'll buy you a good defense if you hurt my sister," Alex growled. "Let her go, right now and get the fuck out of here."

"I'd never intentionally hurt your sister, you ass. But I also won't let her go into another King household that abuses their own. I don't care whether I have to drug her to leave this fucking city, but she's not going home with you."

"What?" he whispered. Emotions played across Alex's face before his eyes met mine with pain evident in his gaze. "What's he talking about?"

"Eyes on me, Alex, I'm the one with the guns," Mick said icily. "How much did your fuckface father pay you to keep it quiet? Was it the price of an apartment? Just enough to shut her up and let it blow over? Or was it college, the job?"

Alex looked horrified. "Get the fuck out of my office. I have no idea what you're talking about, but it'll be a cold day in hell before anyone buys me, including my father. If there's something going on, then you need to tell me right now before I fucking wreck you. You don't stand between Alisa and me."

Mick glanced back at Mason, whose shoulders shrugged.

"Great, then I'll need an attorney. I'm about to shoot your father's hands off," Mick replied as he turned around and started toward the door.

"Whoa, brother," Mason said. "That's not what we came here for. We came to talk to Alex about what's going on, and it looks like he's telling the truth. Don't do this."

Mick shrugged and spoke under his breath. "He's telling the truth. But that jackass put a belt to her back and I'm willing to sit in jail if it means he can't use his hands for the rest of his life."

Mason shook his head. "This isn't the way to do it. I know why you're angry, I get it, but this is insane. You have to calm down."

I wiggled out of Mason's hold and threw myself at Mick, pressing my hands against his chest.

"No, no, no, please, Mick. Please don't do this," I begged.

Alex's voice reached us. "You know very well that I can't defend you in court with prior knowledge. Tell me what the hell is going on before I call the police."

"No," I yelled at Alex. "Don't do that."

Mick's eyes slid to mine. It broke my heart to see the dull gaze of a man I didn't know. This wasn't the Mick I liked, much less the man he'd been this morning. A switch had gone off somewhere and he wasn't there. It was like seeing someone that was catatonic but functional. A repression of himself with only the look of pain and rage fueling him.

On instinct, I leaned into him and pressed my lips against his neck. "Please come back to me, Mick. I need you. My brother didn't know. I never told him. Please."

He shuddered after a moment, then shaky hands slid around my waist.

"Fuck," he whispered. "Fuck, fuck, fuck."

"It's okay," I whispered. "We'll figure something out. Just don't go."

"You stay with me," he said in a tone that didn't invite any argument.

I nodded against his chest.

"Does anyone want to explain what the fuck is happening?" Alex asked. "I'm glad you turned down the job, Mick. You're out of your fucking mind. I didn't realize how much the FBI scrambled your brain. Alisa, get the fuck away from him."

"FBI?" I whispered. When I glanced up at Mick, he was regarding me cautiously. "Okay. Not ready to talk about it. That's fine."

He gave me a nod as Mason tapped him on the shoulder. "You good?"

"Yeah, I think I need to sit down," Mick said as he turned around and gripped the back of one of the chairs in front of Alex's desk.

"You gonna puke, bro?" Mason asked.

Mick shook his head. He had a tight grip on my hand like it was the only thing keeping him grounded.

Some things were adding up in my mind with Mick. The dark moods, nightmares, the pushing, self-loathing. He'd experienced something painful and had it locked away somewhere in his mind. But it was clearly oozing out into his life in the worst ways. Something was eating away at him.

The only thing that seemed to ground him a moment ago was being near me. Whether that was good or bad, I didn't know, but it was obvious he needed a lifeline and I wanted that to be me.

CHAPTER NINE

Mick

BLINKING A FEW TIMES, I tried to straighten myself out. Only the warm sensation of Alisa's hand was helping me calm down.

I didn't expect things to go that far with this. I only knew that my scare tactics hadn't produced what I wanted to happen with Alex. I wanted someone to hurt for the pain they'd caused Alisa.

When she rolled over this morning and the sheets slipped off her beautiful body, I'd taken in everything. The soft round curves of her hips, the small glimpse of her breasts pressed against the bed. Then I'd looked at her back. The bandage was still in place, but the small scars from the past nearly undid me.

I saw red when I imagined her being abused in such a way. The same feelings of anger and need to punish the people responsible had slid over me like an unwelcome guest. It'd been going through my mind all morning. I'd tried to get a hold on it during the drive, but something churned in me to the breaking point when I could tell Alex's shock was genuine.

I'd snapped and seen only one objective in mind. Hurt her father, make him pay.

A surge of emotion had taken over me in that moment. A blur of memories from my past had raced through my mind along with my anger. All the things I'd seen working in the missing persons department at the FBI after my transfer. I'd mainly been called in on cases where we found them dead. Where there were no happy endings and I was the person that catalogued their final moments of pain.

I'd worked very hard to detach the emotion to anyone and anything. Trying to see things without seeing what was around me. Then there was that one last case. The one that turned me upside down and made me doubt my own worth, not only as an agent, but as a functional human. The cruelties I'd witnessed, and the aftermath, had led to a decision I could never undo. I regretted nothing, though, which made me question everything I'd ever valued.

Since meeting Alisa, I was in a different tailspin. One that I didn't know if I could handle. She was so damn beautiful. So utterly genuine. And the only woman that I felt like I connected to in some strange way.

I needed to get my head on straight to deal with this, but it was nearly impossible. Torn between wanting to protect her and trying to keep my distance wasn't working the way I wanted it to. I nearly committed a crime for her.

Something we learned in training, was that there were really no reformed criminals in the system once they turned into repeat offenders. It applied to a lot of serial killers well enough, but even for the petty thieves it was the same mental process. Perhaps not as violent, but the urges to commit crime followed the same patterns. Their minds might have latched onto alternate obsessions, but they were never cured. Her father was the same way. After all these years she'd spent at college, he'd struck her out of his sick need. His malicious urge to do so wouldn't stop. Not unless he was punished.

The irony of this situation was that I too was repeating a pattern. One that I thought I was immune to. Vigilantism had crossed my mind once. Just once and never again since then. Wanting to take someone's life to deliver justice was the same as that first dark time for me. It was why the dead stalked me in my sleep. It was punishment, plain and simple.

I thought I'd never revisit that temptation, but after last night and her tears, I wanted to make someone pay. I thought I was a better man once, thought I had an unshakeable moral compass. My old mentor and the doctor believed I did.

And yet, here I was, sitting in her bother's law firm, willing to attack his integrity in the worst way to find my fucking answers. When my need to satiate my anger with retribution wasn't satisfied I'd seen only one path. It led to jail, but in my mind, it was worth it. There would be some justice for her.

"Fuck," I whispered. I really was insane.

"Alisa, do you mind explaining?" Alex asked.

Her hand squeezed mine. I wasn't sure if it was for me or to give her courage, but I wasn't going to be the kind of man that let her stand by herself.

"Alisa?" I asked as I looked up at her from my chair. "Do you want me..."

She shook her head. The strength of ten people didn't equate to the look she had behind her eyes. I admired her for it. It was yet another thing that drew me to her.

A thought, one of utter possession and yet vulnerability, swam to the surface of my mind.

Mine.

The man that I was, screamed it from some inner place. Something shifted inside me making that one solitary thought the only reason for my miserable existence on earth. Although I couldn't explain it, she'd already become important to me. I wanted her with me, needed to be the one that she had watching over her, and protecting her.

She was also the only reason I stopped and started thinking clearly again. Her gentle pleading had penetrated my rage.

As I listened to her tell her brother everything, I memorized the contours of her face. The pert nose, that needed to be kissed. The soft sweep of her cheek up to her small ears. Two small holes for her earrings, the gorgeous column of her neck.

She started shaking and I pulled her into my lap. I needed to hold her, to reassure her and myself. She settled against my chest with warm tears against my neck and my body relaxed.

"It's okay, beautiful," I whispered into her hair.

She nodded. "I know."

She was stunning. Any other woman might not have done so well. Instead, she told the one person, her brother, whom she clearly idolized and trusted, the whole truth of her ordeal. And why she'd held the truth from him.

Mason cleared the money off the desk and put it back in the bag. It was useful, but stupid to be walking around with that much cash. We had a safe at the house that Mason used for those kinds of funds. I didn't know why he had it there and never questioned it. He knew what I was thinking last night and that I'd probably pull some sort of stunt. He didn't say a word as he repacked it, just did it without judgement.

When he stuck his hand out, I maneuvered Alisa around to remove my guns and handed them over. They were mine. They'd been packed away for so long it was a strange feeling having them on me again.

I eyed Alex over her shoulder as I ran my hands down her arms.

He looked stricken as he slumped in his chair.

He nodded at me and didn't break eye contact for a few minutes. I could see his wheels turning, the madness of revenge beginning to bloom.

"I thought—"

He held up his hand, cutting me off. "I know what you thought. I would have done the same damn thing. I think I might have started with a punch though, and the questions afterward."

"Alex," Alisa said.

"No, if I was in his position, I would have beat your brother to a bloody pulp first. Shit."

"I lost it," I responded. "I know you're not lying, Alex, but I couldn't see straight."

He eyed me for a moment, his gaze darting once to look at Alisa before returning to me. "I just hope you know what you're in for. The Kings are a different breed."

"Wait, before we have this conversation. Have you ever swept for bugs in this office?"

He nodded. "Yes, once a week. Are you kidding me? I'm just about as paranoid as you are. Jack found some a few months ago but we haven't found any since."

"What happened?"

He leaned back in his chair. "I took on a case defending a man that was accused of arson. Small business owner. You have to understand, I try to remain impartial, but the lies some defendants tell you just makes you become—"

"Desensitized."

"Yeah, I'm sure you're familiar," he said as his eyes darted to Alisa again.

I could read the billboard on his face. It read like a warning. He wondered how I'd treat Alisa if I battled with the same sort of issue. I didn't blame him. I wondered the same damn thing.

"Anyway, Jack was working with me on a couple of things. I mentioned to him, that for each thing I filed to get the case dismissed, there was nearly a simultaneous response that blocked it. You've met Jack, not exactly trusting of anyone. So, he swept the office. Three bugs."

"Jesus," Mason mumbled.

"The evidence and all the pressure on this guy seemed overwhelming. I didn't believe the defendant, until Jack found the bugs. Then it made me question whether I'd been manipulated to believe in the evidence in other cases, or whether I'd folded and bargained a little too much under the pressure. Pissed me off."

"I'm sure," I said.

"I hired Melanie after that. Fired the other girl. Replaced the locks, installed cameras that record offsite, and I still have him sweep the office once a week."

"Okay," I responded. I didn't know what Jack's skills were, but Mason's opinion was gold to me no matter what Alex said.

"There are six brothers and one sister, Helena, in the family. You may not remember all of them, but their influence has grown over the last few years. My dad, Denny, you're familiar with. Louis is a land developer."

"Monica's dad," Alisa whispered.

"John King is a retired superintendent of the local school district. He's now working with Warren, who runs several branches of banks here. Bill, is in housing development for the city but also owns a lot of real estate. Malcolm is on the city council. Helena runs a lucrative commercial insurance business and her late husband, George Richardson, was about to announce his plan to run for mayor until he died over the weekend."

"J.D. and Tyson Richardson are cops," Mason said under his breath.

I assumed that they might be the culprits behind some of Mason's troubles last year if he was mentioning it.

"So, from what you're telling me, the King family has control of most of the city. And are you their defense lawyer if they break the rules?"

"I don't take family on as clients. The other people in my firm, can and do, take some of their cases but I've stayed out of it."

I considered Alex for a minute, wondering why he hadn't fallen in line with the perfect setup his family had. It didn't make sense to me. Although he wasn't lying about Alisa's past, it didn't mean he still wasn't shady.

"I don't understand where you fall into place in all of this, Alex. It makes me question your self-proclaimed sterling integrity, no offense. You're a King, which from what you're telling me, means that you have Kingston by the balls."

His eyes wandered to Alisa's shocked face as she opened her mouth to likely yell at me for saying it. I squeezed her tighter and turned her head into my chest.

"Mick!" she grunted while she wiggled in my lap.

I put my lips to her ear and whispered very quietly, "What did I tell you about wiggling in my lap at the club?"

She stopped immediately, staring at me with shock.

Good. She needed a distraction from all of this and if she was thinking about my suggestion of her on her knees, then she'd be far less concerned about my need to grill Alex for some answers.

"You're dirty," she whispered back.

Smirking at her, I didn't disagree. I was dirty, and she seemed to bring out the worst of it in me. It should be a warning, but neither one of us was running yet. I wasn't sure what her reasons were for staying. Mine were purely selfish.

Alex was staring a hole through me when I looked back up at him. I didn't give a shit what he thought either way.

"You can believe whatever the hell you want, Mick. You think they haven't tried to bring me into their fold? I spent years away from this place and their politics. I saw how they treated my own sister after high school ended. It soured me to anything they might have ever offered."

Frowning, I stared at Alex, then shifted my gaze down to Alisa. I wanted to know what happened after high school that was significant enough for Alex to deny his family.

The phone on Alex's desk rang and interrupted before I could ask.

"Yes?" he answered.

He paused for a minute, looking at me.

"She's at my house. She'll be staying with me for a while."

There was another pause as he listened and my arms around Alisa tightened.

"Had a bout of nausea. I picked her up and she's resting there. Sure, I'll let her know you called."

He hung up the phone. "That was my father. Apparently, when Alisa didn't make it back last night he was worried. He's probably just wondering if she went to the police."

I didn't comment, waiting for him to say whatever he was thinking.

Alex stood up and started pacing. "Alright. I'm afraid taking her to my house would just make things worse. He'll likely show up over there."

"She's coming home with me," I replied in a tone that was final. "We'll pick up her car today and move it out there."

He shook his head. "No, take it to my house and park it in the back.

If its spotted at your house, it would cause an uproar if anyone thinks you're with her. No offense."

"We can do that," Mason agreed.

"I have a proposal for both of you," Alex said. "We've been sitting here talking about the things we both detest about my family. I haven't lied about what I've told you."

I nodded, but reserved my continued speculation.

"The firm owns a small building that we use mainly for storage. Old documents, records. It's larger than we actually need, to be honest. The records are locked up there in a back room. We thought about expanding at one point. Possibly putting a few offices over there, but we're not quite in agreement about it so it looks like we'll be storing elsewhere and getting rid of the building."

"I'm not having her camp out in an empty office," I replied.

He shook his head. "Not what I was going to suggest. Mason and Jack just got their PI licenses and for all intents and purposes are on retainer for this firm, but mainly for me. I'll never trust another piece of evidence without some sort of research from them."

"Okay?"

"I'll buy out the building. They can work out of it. We start investigating the family on the side."

Mason interjected. "Alex, that's going to cost a fortune not to mention your reputation if someone found out."

He thought for a moment, biting the inside of his cheek. "Not if you open a legitimate shop and put my last name on it. No one would really question it, and if asked, tell them it's a private business that I branched out with. I'll handle the legalities, make sure it's airtight on paper. You just run your business, take clients if you feel like it, do things for me when I need it."

My eyebrows shot up. "And the side purpose is to bring your family down?"

He shrugged. "They may never end up in a courtroom facing anything legal, but that doesn't mean we can't embarrass them publicly through other methods."

"You're forgetting that we'd need some sort of evidence of deceit to convince the public."

"In the eyes of the media, everything is true."

I shrugged at Mason. "Your call, you're the PI."

Mason stared at me in silence, then shook his head. "You have to be part of this."

"Mason..."

"Look, I know you're dealing with some shit. Doesn't mean you're not still good at what you do. It's surveillance, records, figuring out if something we find means anything interesting. I can't think of a better person that can draw a line between two insignificant things than you. You've done this for years."

Rubbing my chin on Alisa's forehead, I gave it some thought. Right now, I was a liability as far as I could see. I needed to straighten some things out in my life and that didn't leave a lot of room for running after leads for Alex.

Alisa eased out of my grasp and gave me a gentle smile. "I think you'd be perfect for it."

Running my hand down her cheek, I said, "You would."

Mason grabbed the bag as Alisa walked around the desk to hug her brother. The expression on Alex's face was one of relief and protectiveness. I could appreciate that about him, if nothing else, and guessed that was at least a start on the road to trusting him.

When they released each other, Alisa joined Mason at the door and I followed.

"Mick. A minute, if you would," Alex said behind me.

Mason met my eyes, and after receiving my slight nod, steered Alisa through the door and shut it.

"Yeah?"

He narrowed his eyes at me for a fraction of a second, his expression a little annoyed.

"I said I'd think—"

"Alisa. You need to walk very carefully here, Mick. That's my baby sister. She can date who she wants, but I don't want her in the line of fire when you snap again. She's not the kind of girl you guys run with."

I held up my hands. "Whoa. I'm not my brother, Alex. We met her at a bar last weekend with Monica. That chick did what she wanted. I put Alisa in a cab."

"Are you sure that's all you did?" he asked, while giving me a stern glare.

"Nope. But I'll be honest and tell you I've tried to stay away from her. Heads up, your sister is a grown woman. It doesn't matter what you or I tell her. She's going to do exactly what she wants."

"That's what I'm afraid of, Mick," he sighed. "You and I both know she isn't the type of girl that needs a bunch of shit in her life. And frankly, seeing her with you scares the fuck out of me. I don't want to pick up the pieces if you break her."

My jaw clenched at the thought of what he was saying, but I couldn't deny having the same thoughts.

"It's not there yet. She'll figure out I'm not the guy she wants."

"And in the meantime?" he asked.

"In the meantime, I plan on being me. I'm not going to guarantee anything. Right now, I'm not sure if I could give her up either way and that's why I'm exactly the kind of shitty guy you think I am. She's..."

"What?" he asked, when I didn't continue.

"Fuck, I don't know. She has me in knots half the time. I can't figure out what to do with her."

Alex's smirk turned into a smile, then laughter. "Oh, you're fucked. Alright, I'll say this then. You touch her, look at her, think about her in any way other than what she deserves, I'll beat the fuck out of you and bury your body. And, Mick, I've lived here for a lot longer and know of a lot of places where they won't find you."

"That sounds like a pretty serious threat from someone who says he upholds the law, Alex."

He clenched his jaw as he glared at me. "None of us are saints, Mick. The things we do in life may not always align with what we know we should do. It's a tricky, moving line that we draw for ourselves every morning when we wake up. Sometimes, the results of taking actions that we'd normally find abhorrent, garner faster results than normal methods."

"You forget, Alex, I know lawyer language like the back of my hand. That's a bunch of bullshit, wrapped in pretty words to justify criminal intent."

"None of us are completely clean. I know your story, I did my homework. And having the mentality that I do, I can see why you had to leave the FBI."

"That was a closed case, fucker."

He smiled. "Everything can be bought for a price. Don't fuck around with my sister. She's the marrying type, and you don't have it in you."

"Funny you mention price," I said sarcastically. "Weren't we just discussing that?"

"You don't know me when it comes to what I'd do for Alisa. You want the family to pay, we'll make them pay by any means necessary if it comes to that. But you know you're not good for her and she's already burrowing a hole into that fucked up part of you. You're fucked. Either way someone loses in the end. You or her. Make sure it's you."

Message received, I turned on my heel and departed the office with a slam of the door. Pissed off, I stalked through the corridor and down the sidewalk to the car.

Fucker had threatened me which didn't sit well at all. The worst part was that I agreed with him. I was fucked when it came to Alisa.

CHAPTER TEN

Alisa

I FELT a bit out of place in the Galloway house even after two weeks of spending time with the overly stubborn brothers. I wondered if their relationship would fall apart if they ever stopped bickering.

From what I gathered before they immediately stopped talking every time I entered the room, it had a lot to do with privacy. Something to do with me, something with Mick and a lot with Mason's derailed nightly routine.

After our visit to my brother's office, Mick had taken me shopping while Mason dealt with the car and bag full of cash. I'd never seen so much cash in my life, had no idea where it came from and didn't ask. I'd refused Mick's insistence that we spend his money for a few essentials, arguing that I had my own money. The argument got me absolutely nowhere with him. He bought far more clothing than I really needed, and by the time our shopping experience was over, I honestly felt like choking him more than thanking him.

It was sweet, but wasn't necessary by any means. I'd have my own clothes back soon enough according to my brother, who had enlisted Melanie in clearing my things out of the house while my father was away on a business trip. They were being delivered to my apartment by the end of the weekend.

And then, I'd be there too, I assumed. Even unfurnished it was still mine and the freedom that I needed.

For the most part I'd been given some space at the house. I was sleeping in a guest bedroom rather than in Mick's bed. Which was somewhat strange and extremely confusing. Ever since our meeting with Alex, he'd put some distance between us. It wasn't that he didn't talk to me, he just wasn't as overtly flirtatious and that stung somewhat.

After the things we'd shared, I thought that there might be something deeper developing between us. Everything seemed good before we went to visit my brother, but as soon as we left, I'd been moved to the other bedroom. Perhaps in retrospect, he'd decided that involving himself with a King wasn't something he was interested in, even after his show of bravado in my brother's office.

Alex insisted on having me at the office during the day, which I didn't mind since I needed to be working. Mick delivered me to the office very early in the morning every day, making sure to park in the back. He'd walk me to the door, kiss me on the forehead and leave after I locked the door. Again, sweet, but not exactly what I'd expected given our initial interactions.

He was just as moody as he'd ever been, possibly more. His sour mood every morning seemed to be just as bad when he picked me up from work. Whatever was on his mind, it felt like he was biding his time until I left. I wasn't sure how he and Alex were going to get along over time, if Mick decided to work with my brother. But I doubted at this point, I'd be around to witness much of it.

I put the last of my makeup on and gave myself a look in the mirror. Not too bad considering I wore very little of it most of the time. I'd put on quite a bit more than normal for once and felt like I'd possibly overdone it. I adjusted my dress wondering if it was too tight again. It had a skew neckline where one sleeve hung off my shoulder. The front had tiny black beading that sparkled in the light. The hem was a little short, but I liked the ruched design, that seemed to hide some of my curves. It was simple, feminine and considering where I was going, I knew that there would be far more racy dresses than mine.

The art gallery opening was something I'd insisted on going to when I mentioned it to Alex earlier in the week. It wasn't so much that I really wanted to go, but it was better than reading in my room while Mick did whatever he did in Mason's study every night. He'd been very busy doing some research, but had been tight lipped on what it was about every time I asked. He'd sometimes venture out of his self-created cave to watch a movie with me, or ask me questions, but was once again hesitant to answer my inquiries about himself.

When I walked into the living room, I picked up my phone to dial Alex. He'd promised to pick me up, since my car was still parked at his house.

"Wow. Where are you going?" Mason asked from the kitchen table, giving me the once over.

"Oh, well, Alex is picking me up to take me to this art gallery opening near his office. I'm probably underdressed, but it'll do I guess."

Mason's eyebrows shot up. "I think it'll be fine. Has Mick seen that dress?"

I shook my head a little, trying to slip one of my earrings in and juggle my cell at the same time.

"Maybe. I picked it up when he took me shopping."

"Does he know you bought it?"

"What does that matter?" I asked while rolling my eyes. "He gave me a credit card and ordered me to buy clothing. I came out with only a couple of things and he marched me right back in the store. I got this and a few shirts."

"Hmm," he replied. "Does he know you're going out?"

"It didn't come up. He's been busy and honestly, we're all doing our own thing, right? I'm sure both of you will be happy to have me out of your hair on Sunday."

"Wait, what?" Mason's eyebrows shot up another inch, then glared down the hall toward his study. "Motherfucker. Alisa, hold up."

I shrugged as he stalked toward the back of the house. I set my phone on the table and slipped my other earring in.

Hearing Mick bark something and Mason's muffled reply, I wondered what the hell was going on now.

"Oh, fuck no," Mick growled behind me as I reached for my phone. The sound made me jump and the cell clattered to the wood floor.

Bending down to retrieve it, I glanced over my shoulder and found Mick staring down at me. He looked angry about something. He was wearing his usual t-shirt and jeans that I was becoming accustomed to seeing him in every day.

Turning away from him, I tried to ignore the clench in my stomach that happened every time I saw him. He was a very sexy, handsome man, whether he was dressed casually or not, and it always hurt a little to look at him.

"Where are you going?" he demanded.

"To an art gallery, as I explained to your brother," I said as I started scrolling through my phone for Alex's number. "Just need to call Alex and let him know I'm ready. He's taking me."

"The fuck he will," Mick replied.

My head snapped around to look at him. "Excuse me?"

"You're not going out like that," he barked as his eyes swept over me.

I looked down at my clothing and heels, then back at him. "Like what? It's not fancy, but it's just an art gallery so it'll do. I guess I could have worn different shoes."

Mason appeared over Mick's shoulder and gave me a huge smile with a slightly diabolical look. My eyes darted back to Mick who was still grimacing, but was now rubbing a hand down his chest while he took in my attire from head to toe.

He heaved a huge sigh as Mason walked past him to stand by the table.

"I can take her, bro. No big deal. Just need to change really quick."

Mason headed in the direction of his bedroom and Mick growled.

"Fuck off, Mason," he said as he stared at me and blinked. "She's not going."

My chin lifted at his tone. "I'm going, Mick. I'm tired of being cooped up here. I heard about this a couple of weeks ago and it sounds like fun."

"Heard where? At the office?"

"No, at the deli down the street from the office."

He stepped closer to me and crossed his arms over his chest. "So, people go to deli's now and talk about art galleries? Tell me this doesn't have anything to do with Monica and some drinking adventure."

I blanched. "No, I haven't even talked to her, you know that. I went to high school with someone that works there, and he said it was opening tonight. Supposed to be some big…"

"He who?" he asked as his eyes narrowed at me.

I shrugged. "Heath. He works at the deli with his family. I go in there for a sandwich sometimes for lunch."

Mason's laughter carried from the living room and I glanced in that direction.

"Fuck," Mick muttered. He was running a hand down his face and now openly glaring at me.

"What's wrong with you?" I asked, irritated at the conversation. "I don't understand why you're freaking out. Don't you have some computer thing to do like every other night? Or am I missing something? Maybe you wanted to wander out of that cave and watch a movie while ignoring me?"

His jaw clenched, and I felt a wave of anger roll off him. The room in the kitchen suddenly shrunk by half with its presence. It almost felt like the day in Alex's office for a moment when he'd tried to storm out the door to hurt my father. I took a small step back from him, not in fear, but from the sheer force of his emotion.

He turned and stalked back to his bedroom, leaving me scowling after him. Half hoping he'd turn around and at the very least talk to me before I left, but as he retreated to his bedroom and slammed the door, I felt like he was once again shutting me down.

Mason re-entered the kitchen, peering down the hallway after Mick. He turned to me with a smile on his face.

"You look beautiful, Alisa, that's what's wrong. Stubborn bastard needed a kick in the nuts."

"What? I'm not trying to kick anyone or irritate him. It's just a stupid dress."

He grinned at me and grabbed a bottled water from the fridge, motioning one at me.

I shook my head.

"Just hold off on calling Alex for a minute," he said.

"Whatever," I mumbled, as I stalked to my room for my small purse.

By the time I found it, I was ready to call Alex anyway. Stuffing my lipstick and money into the clutch I walked back into the kitchen to the sounds of Mason chuckling.

Mick stood to the side of the table glaring at him, wearing a black suit with a white collared dress shirt. No tie tonight, I noticed, and the top button was undone, giving just a peek at the top of his sculpted chest.

"What are you doing?" I asked him.

He glanced at me and shrugged. "Taking you to an art gallery, apparently."

I rolled my eyes. "I didn't ask you to."

"Too bad," he replied, motioning to the door. "Let's go."

"This is ridiculous," I said as I followed him to the car. He opened the passenger door and I slid into the leather seat.

He stalked around the front wearing a frown on his face like this was the very last thing he wanted to do tonight. I felt a headache coming on and started rubbing my temple as he got in.

The ride downtown was relatively quiet, other than the classical music that Mick turned on as soon as we left. I eyed him several times during the trip. He was usually one to listen to some random station as he drove, but this was different.

He said nothing as we pulled into a parking space along the street. I watched as he stalked around the front, making his way to my side of the vehicle. When he opened my door, he took my hand and helped me stand.

I was turning away from him when his hand landed on the car beside me, blocking me from leaving. Raising my eyes to his, I frowned.

His face was a mixture of frustration and confusion when he spoke. "Alisa, I need you to stick by me tonight."

"Mick, it's just a stupid art gallery."

His eyes shifted toward the street as several couples made their way along the sidewalk.

"You're with me," he said as his eyes bore into mine.

I swatted at his arm to let me leave. "You're just here because I made you mad."

His body suddenly pressed me against the car while his arm snaked around my waist. I could feel the heat of him through his suit and his arousal against my stomach. His head dipped to brush a kiss against my lips.

"You're always with me, beautiful. No matter where you are, you're mine."

My confusion mixed with doubt at his statement. It made my heart clench from wanting to believe him, but his behavior indicated that it wasn't true.

"Why are you doing this?" I whispered against his mouth as he teased my bottom lip with his tongue. "You've been pushing me away for two weeks. You can't say that stuff, and then do the complete opposite."

His mouth slid around my neck, and fire shot through my belly as he kissed me gently.

"I'm trying to be nice to you, Alisa. Every fucking day, I've tried to just let you get to know me the right way. Simple conversations, being around me. I don't want to hurt you."

I let out a small growl of my own. "I like you just the way you are, idiot. You don't have to push me away. And the only hurt you're causing is making me feel like you don't like me back."

He lifted up and rested his forehead against mine as he sighed.

"If you think I don't like you, then you don't know me very well. And I'm trying not to scare you."

"You don't frighten me, Mick."

He leaned back and gave me a pained look before kissing me softly. I opened my mouth to him as he ran his tongue along the seam of my lips.

"I'm trying to be gentle with you," he whispered. "You're so damn beautiful and sweet. I'm not the kind of man that's used to those things and I don't know what to do with you."

"Is that why I got kicked out of your room?" I asked in a small voice.

He leaned back, his eyebrows lifting in shock. "What? No. I didn't kick you out."

"Then why am I in the guest bedroom? And why do you not sound like you anymore when you talk to me?"

He chuckled. "Baby, two things. I have a problem sleeping some nights. I wanted to let you get some rest. Second, if you spend one more night in my bed, I'm going to be between those gorgeous thighs of yours and you'll never be able to leave again. You'll be mine without a choice. I'll never give you up."

"Oh," I replied, then started chewing on my lip.

"Yeah. Oh. So, I'm trying my fucking hardest to give you some space. I feel like a lecherous bastard every time I watch your ass when you walk down the hallway. The way your t-shirts cling to those gorgeous tits of yours makes me hard all the damn time. But I'm a little fucked up right now, and I don't want that to touch you."

I glanced away for a moment. "I don't mind that you're fucked up."

"Alisa," he whispered. "Please don't say that. You don't know."

My hands slid up to his face. "Then tell me. Let me in, Mick."

His eyes were gentle when they landed on mine. The stubble on his chin rubbed against my fingers. Turning his head, he placed a kiss in my palm before he grabbed it and eased me away from the car.

He gave me a small smile as we made our way across the dark parking lot between the parked cars.

I sighed, resigned to the fact that he wasn't going to tell me anything, like usual. But on the positive side, I'd gotten him to at least crack open the closed door he had most of the time, and maybe that was a start. I wondered what it would take to open it wide and whether he would ever do that for me.

He came to a stop on the sidewalk in front of the gallery. The entire front of the building was mostly glass, showing off the vaulted ceilings and circular staircase to the second floor inside. The walls were covered in various paintings that hung at several different heights, in all manner of shapes, colors and subject matter.

A mass of people were milling around, laughing, drinking and looking at the various pieces of work. The volume of the chatter could be heard from where we were standing as we waited for the couple in front of us to enter the building.

My phone pinged in my clutch and Mick looked down at me.

"Probably Alex wondering why I didn't call."

Mick chuckled. "Let him wonder."

I gave him a sideways glance and shook my head. "I'm not sure you two are going to work well together."

Mick suppressed a smile by clenching his jaw and raising one of his eyebrows.

"We'll be fine as soon as he backs the fuck off," he mumbled.

"What does that mean? Did he do something?"

He shook his head once, scanning the room as we entered the gallery. "No, he just seems to think that I can be pushed in one direction or another."

"Well, he's a dominant person. Look at what he does for a living," I said, raising my voice just slightly to be heard.

He chuckled. "That's not what I meant. He threatened to kill me if I wasn't nice to you."

My mouth hung open. "Is that why you've been an asshole to me?"

Mick smirked, letting go of my hand to snag two champagne glasses off the tray of a passing waiter.

"Your definition of an "asshole" and mine are clearly out of sync."

I shrugged and took a sip of the champagne. "You're an asshole when you don't talk to me, not because of what you say."

He narrowed his eyes considering what I'd said. I sniffed, and my chin went up a little as I ignored him.

I pretended to study a painting on the wall beside me, softening a bit when his hand slid around my waist. He lingered over my hip a moment, distracting me from the menagerie of colors in the large landscape painting.

His warm breath hit my ear as he pressed closer.

"So, if I told you I wanted to hike up that skirt of yours and fuck you in the women's restroom, I wouldn't be an asshole?"

"Nope," I replied tartly as my face flushed. I moved to the next painting, his hand still on my hip.

Admiring the portrait of a young woman in repose, his warm breath hit my ear again.

"And I wouldn't be an asshole if I told you I wanted to take you to a table and finger you while we pretend to drink?"

I cleared my throat, as I shivered from his words. "Well, I'm not wearing anything under this, so that might not be too difficult to manage. I thought I might try it your way tonight, so I ditched the panties."

He growled behind me. "Are you fucking kidding me? And you were going to come out without me?"

"I thought I'd try something new and tell you about it later."

"Don't ever fucking do that again, Alisa."

I shrugged. "Why not? You do it all the time. It seems like men get to have all the fun. Go without underwear, play with guns."

I moved to the next painting and his grip on my hip tightened.

"Play with guns?" he hissed. "What the hell?"

I glanced over my shoulder before turning toward him. Smiling sweetly, crowded in by several people trying to get a closer look at the painting I'd moved in front of, I dropped my hand to his belt then slid south in a small gesture. Making my point as my fingers slipped across the hard bulge between his legs, I faced the painting once more.

"Yes, guns," I said and took a sip of my drink.

The woman beside me gave me a curious look that I ignored as I bent to examine the signature at the bottom of the massive framed piece.

Mick brushed against me, harder than he'd been, and slid his hand over my waist as he pulled me slightly into his hips. The small gesture was probably missed by most, likely not even noted, but my body started to burn between my legs.

When I stood straight again, I tried to move on to the next painting, but Mick's hand prevented any movement.

"Not so fast, pretty girl," he growled against my ear. "You're playing dirty."

I shrugged. "I'm just playing the way you would."

"I'm trying to behave as I explained in the parking lot."

Turning in his arms, I peered up at him. "I don't want you to."

The expression in his eyes nearly had my legs going weak. They burned a path down my face, pausing on my lips before they dipped to the hem of my dress.

"I think we should leave," he said in a tone that promised a more interesting destination than the art gallery.

I smirked up at him and shook my head. "No."

His grimace told me I'd better change my mind, but I couldn't help teasing him. He was pulling for once and I was pushing, which seemed to irritate the crap out of him. It was at least something other than the silent treatment he'd been giving me, and I felt like I was winning.

CHAPTER ELEVEN

Mick

THE SMUG SMILE on her face said a lot. She was torturing me like some vixen from another realm. She knew it and felt proud of her ability to get me worked up.

I scanned the room and gestured toward a small set up in the corner with a bartender. I needed a stiff drink, not the champagne we'd been nursing. We'd play it her way for a while, but as soon as we left, she'd pay.

As we made our way through the crowd, Alex approached us with a brunette on his arm. He was in a nice suit and she was in a dress that showed off way too much of her assets. Plastic surgery was the woman's vice by the look of it. Her eyes danced other places rather than on Alex. I wondered if she was even interested in him, as much as it seemed like she was interested in being seen with him.

Standing behind Alisa, I tried to calm my raging hormones. I wiped my thoughts about how much I'd wanted to bend her over only a few minutes before. Sporting an erection, might not be the most appropriate thing when making small talk in public.

"Alex," Alisa said with a huge smile. She embraced her brother in a hug while the brunette on his arm moved out of the way. "I'm sorry I didn't call, Mick wanted to bring me."

Alex's eyes darted to me, his expression unreadable.

"How nice of him," he said with a note of sarcasm. "Heather and I waited for a bit, but I thought maybe you'd changed your mind. I know you said you wanted to come, but I wasn't sure when you didn't text me."

"I told Alex we were going to be more than late if we didn't just leave," Heather said as her eyes slid down Alisa's attire. For some reason it raised my protective instincts and I tightened my grip on her hip.

She turned her gaze to me and gave me a haughty look as her eyes roamed. "Do I know you?"

"I think you'd remember if you did," I said, not giving the woman any other response. She might be Alex's date, but anyone who looked down their reconstructed nose at Alisa, wasn't anyone I wanted to know.

"Sorry," Alex responded. "Heather, this is Mick Galloway. He's just moved back to the area."

She blinked her eyes for a moment then smiled. "Galloway. I know that name."

Alisa coughed as she took a drink of her champagne.

"You okay, baby?" I asked as I rubbed her back.

"Oh, wait, aren't you some NFL player or something?" Heather asked, her face suddenly showing far more interest.

"No, I'm homeless and don't have a job," I responded. Turning to Alex I said, "We were headed to get some water."

Alex nodded with a smirk on his face then steered a reluctant Heather through the crowd.

"What was that about?" I asked as I guided Alisa to the bar and ordered a whiskey.

"She's just a bitch."

I raised my eyebrows in surprise. "Wow. I didn't think it was possible."

"What?"

Scanning the crowd, I said, "For you to be so naughty and harsh in the same night."

"She doesn't like me. She comes up to the office occasionally, and she's been sleazing around Alex for a few months according to Melanie. She knows my dad which doesn't say a lot for her."

"Hmm," I said. My hand went to her hip and drew her back to my side. "Well that explains the attitude, but what about the naughty little play you just made out there, Alisa? You're not being a good girl."

She smiled back at me with a mischievous expression. "If being a good girl means you're going to ignore me again, then I'd rather be someone else."

"Alisa," I whispered in her ear. "You don't have to be anyone but you. Do you know how many times a day I think about you?"

She shook her head.

"It's so distracting that I'm nearly out of my mind by the time I pick you up. You're the first person I think about when I wake up. That first thought involves tasting you, licking you, being inside you. And if that wasn't enough, I just want to be around you. Watching a movie, talking about stupid things. I want to smell your shampoo, see your smile. You're like an addiction to me."

Turning in my arms she gazed up at me, her expression so trusting and innocent.

I moved a stray length of her blonde hair from her face and gave her a small smile. The compulsion to tip her head back and claim her mouth was nearly overwhelming.

My phone buzzed in my pocket and I let out a sigh.

Fishing it out, I looked at the screen. Mason calling.

"Mason," I answered, still looking at Alisa's beautiful face as she turned to the side and scanned the room.

"Hey, man. Have any plans after the gallery?"

Thinking of all the ways I wanted to touch the woman in front of me after I got her out of this place, I groaned. "I might have, but if you need something just ask."

My arms slipped off Alisa's hip as she waved at someone through the crowd and weaved her way around people to a table. She was still within sight as she spoke to a young man. He was polished, in his grey suit, with perfect hair. I caught a flash of white teeth as she approached.

Mason's reply penetrated my growing irritation. "I bought the club."

"Which club?"

"*Erebus.*"

"I'm sorry, what?" I replied with some shock.

"Well, I told you I wanted to use that money to invest in something. When you took it out of the safe and I sat there looking at it, I just... look it's hard to explain, but I figure a lot of those Kings come up here. I know of at least two that are here right now. If we caught one of them doing something it would be on cameras. It's just another way to keep tabs."

Dragging my attention away from Alisa's animated conversation with the guy at the table, I focused on what Mason was telling me.

"So, you bought the club because of this whole thing with Alex?"

"Not just that. It's a good investment. It comes with a lot of headache with staffing, but the woman that's been managing it is staying, and the staff doesn't really have to rotate. They make a lot of money here and with a few modifications it could be a much bigger profit. I want you to go in on it with me."

I blinked a few times wondering how my brother went from frequent patron to owning the club that fed his vice. Whether it helped in catching the occasional transgression or not, it seemed like a drastic move. He wasn't an idiot as much as I liked to call him one. He was extremely intelligent, but owning a business while doing work for Alex, was adding a lot on his plate.

"I'm not sure."

"You're the only person I want doing this with me, Mick. It's the right time. Remember all those talks we had before you left? We were going to rule the city, open all these businesses, fuck all the pretty girls."

"Mason," I said on a sigh. "Those were pipe dreams before we grew up. And I'm not interested in fucking all the pretty girls anymore."

He laughed. "Yeah, you've already got one and you still haven't fucked her."

"Watch it, fucker," I warned.

"It's all good, bro. She's incredible, just wish you could see it. Look, come up here after the party. I need you on this. You're not going back to the Bureau, and the last time I checked, you're not doing anything else. Help me with this."

"I thought we were going to help Alex."

"We are," he said loudly over the music that began blaring in the background. "This is just another way and it's ours. Shit's not black and white anymore, bro. We have to look out for ourselves in this city and you know it. You of all people can see the end game here. If Alex doesn't like something, like you making sweet love to his sister, we're both out. The King family gets wind of this, and we're all fucked. This is the backup plan. In the meantime, we get what we can, when we can, if they step foot in the place."

I rolled my eyes and searched out Alisa. She was still talking to the prick with more hair product in his spikey locks than most of the women in the room. Alex approached them with enough familiarity that made me think they knew each other.

Although Alisa was friendly, she wasn't staring at him the way he was gazing at her. Her body language was closed, arms in front of her, hands crossed, and she was turned sideways as if leaving was imminent if fuckface would stop talking to her.

I wondered briefly if he was the type guy her family wanted her with. Rich, judging by the suit and occasional flash of his watch. If that wasn't enough, it was his bearing that really told the whole story. He was used to impressing people and getting his way. He looked like he could just as easily have been a movie star, rather than just some guy in Kingston, eyeing my woman.

She was mine, though, and I was hers. Wholeheartedly. I may have had some methods she didn't agree with, like keeping her at a distance the last couple of weeks. Mason didn't even understand what I was doing at first and told me about it several times until we talked about it.

She didn't know how many times a day I thought about fucking her into oblivion. Having her around, her scent, her laughter, made it difficult. But the dark man in me knew that she was my light and I felt guilty for thinking it, when I owed her more.

Winning whatever it was she had, that I needed, through sex would have hurt both of us. I wanted her respect, her devotion, her choice, to be with someone like me over the jackass in front of her.

"Mason, you still there?" I asked.

"Yeah, where'd you go?"

Still staring at Alisa, it occurred to me that I'd do anything for her. Beg, borrow, steal. Even kill if it was necessary based on my reaction in her brother's office. I wasn't sure where the darkness in me ended and where she began. The only thing I did know was where it came from.

She was the only person that seemed to combat it without even trying. And yet my tangled emotions twisted around her, grew more ominous when thinking about someone hurting her. It was a double-edged sword that ran its way through my gut, knowing that someone would probably be me.

"Did you buy it yet or is it still in the contract stage?" I asked, eventually.

"I was waiting on you to sign the papers."

"Have you checked out everything?"

He laughed. "Started last week. Everything checks out. I even called in dad for a look, but he couldn't find anything that was out of place."

"Have the owner meet you, I can sign in the morning. I'll transfer the funds to you if you text me the amount."

Hanging up, I waited until I saw his text.

I was surprised by the figure as I stared at it. It seemed a lot cheaper than what I was imagining, and I wondered what the catch was.

Logging into my bank, I transferred the money to his account then called him back.

"Yeah?" he answered.

"Done, should be there tomorrow. Do you want to wait on it?"

"Nope, have the full amount already."

I'd never asked Mason where he'd gotten the funds in his safe. He'd only mentioned it a few times, citing his extraordinary ability to save money. I hoped it wasn't the last of his savings. The amount I'd transferred was so minimal out of my account, I'd barely feel it. I worried that Mason's money was more than he might be able to swing, but didn't say anything.

"If we're doing this, then we're all in. No dicking around with it."

"I know," he replied. "I'll call the owner."

I shut off the phone and made my way toward the most beautiful woman I'd ever met. She glanced at me over her shoulder and gave me that smile I'd become starved to see in the last few minutes without her beside me.

"Hey, gorgeous," I said as I reached her, sliding my hand around her waist.

Alex glanced over at me briefly with the beginning of a smirk that was just as quickly wiped off his face.

Alisa turned toward me, and I kissed her. It wasn't a gentle peck on the mouth that I knew was appropriate for a place like this. It wasn't a small kiss in greeting.

My hands gripped her in possession and ownership, drawing her curvy figure in against my hard one. As my mouth bent to hers and claimed her, she opened and slid her arms around my neck. Lips angling over hers and tongue diving in, I made it known who she belonged to. Fuck the witnesses, she was mine.

When I broke it off, her eyes fluttered open to gaze up at me and she smiled. It pulled at me, and drew me into her sweetness, refusing to let me go, as she had, since the second I laid eyes on her in the club.

Someone cleared their throat beside us, but I didn't give a fuck. I was in her universe, the one that controlled and spurred more of my demons than I could ever hope to harness.

"Sorry, I took so long," I said to her, still locked in her eyes. "Mason needed something."

Her lips pursed as her eyes roamed over my face. "Well, apparently it was a good talk."

"Hmm," I said, not wanting to discuss it in mixed company.

My eyes slid past her to the man who'd been flirting with her. When his eyes met mine, I warned him of every possible way I'd hurt him in one single look. He gave one very small nod that I doubted anyone else noticed and broke eye contact.

Alisa gestured over her shoulder. "Have you met Reid Thomas?"

"Don't need to. Let's go," I replied, and I took her hand and started leading her away.

A hand came down on my shoulder before we made it more than a few feet. When I looked back, Alex was smiling at me in a forced manner.

"Well, if that didn't throw up all kinds of flags and alarms to the family, I don't know what else would have made it clearer. A lot of them are here tonight."

"I don't give a fuck, Alex. Like I said two weeks ago, I can't give her up and won't. Especially to that douchebag. Let me guess, friend of the family?"

A small frown passed across his face before it was gone again. "As much as I'd like to tell you that you're wrong, I can't. He's the least of your worries, though. I warned you. You'd better be sure about this, Mick. If you break her heart..."

I leaned closer to him and smiled like we were sharing a joke. "If you want wedding bells tomorrow to prove something about me, you can have them, I'm there. But don't ever fucking question me again about Alisa. You might know where to bury a body, but I know plenty of ways to make death seem like a better option than an hour spent with me in a dark room."

He leaned back and took me in thoughtfully, continuing to smile as if we were having the most normal conversation. The initial hostility at being threatened, a natural response that anyone would have had, eventually ebbed and a look of wary respect took its place.

His eyes darted to Alisa, as she chatted with an elderly couple beside us.

"You know, I thought you might be the worst person she could have ever chosen to even talk to at one point, Mick. But I think when it comes to making my sister a priority, anyone willing to step toe to toe with my family or me, might be what she needs. Even if I don't particularly like it."

"I'm glad we're in agreement," I replied. "Now either punch me or give me a hard slap on the back like we're best friends. I plan on taking my beautiful date out of here in less than thirty seconds."

He slapped me on the back in a jovial manner. "You're so fucked. Does she know you love her? Do you know it yet?"

I smiled like we were talking about the weather tomorrow. "Fuck off, Alex. I have enough shit on my plate without those kinds of questions."

He leaned in again. "Be ready for anything, Mick. They're cutthroat."

I tapped him on the back in return. "I have no qualms about meeting them with everything I've got. Whatever it takes, just like you said."

He nodded. "I think you're finally getting it."

"What exactly?"

"The line you might have to cross again."

My eyes slid from his face, so he wouldn't see my annoyance and settled on Alisa's back. I gently pulled on her arm and she extracted herself from the conversation she was in.

Steering her through the crowd and out the door, we made our way to the car. After tucking her in to the passenger side, I slid into the driver's seat. When I faced her, I let my hand roam up her leg until I reached the hem of her short dress.

She sucked in a breath and stared up at me with curiosity in her gaze.

"Still want to play the game you started, or are you going to be a good girl and tell me to stop?"

She swallowed hard, then surprised me by leaning in to wrap one hand around my neck as she sucked at my bottom lip. My balls clenched, and my semi-hard dick began to respond again.

"I want you. Is that the game we're playing?" she whispered.

My hand slid up her skirt, her knees parting for me, and I found her soft center. Rubbing her clit, she whimpered into my mouth.

"That's what we're playing. But this is your final warning. Once I'm in here," I said as I slipped a finger into her wet folds. "I'm never letting you go. You'll never be able to leave without me right behind you."

Her gasp on my intrusion told me she was hungry for what I wanted to do to her. It spurred thoughts of so many fantasies I'd had about her over the last couple of weeks. I wondered how far she'd go to make them a reality, hoped that she'd say yes to every single one and knew if she did, I'd make it my life's mission to make sure she enjoyed it repeatedly without fail.

First things first, though. I slid my finger out of the wet heaven that wanted me and let it graze across her mouth. She opened and sucked on it, making me tense with a need to rush something I'd been wanting to do since I met her.

Withdrawing my finger from her mouth I kissed her gently. "Enjoy that?"

She shook her head. "I need more."

I smirked. "Aww, my girl wants me between her legs."

"Mick, don't tease," she said with a small pout.

Leaning away from her, I chuckled and started the car. "We need to eat first."

"Eat? Are you kidding?" she asked, her voice an octave higher out of desperation.

I glanced at her as I drove down the street. The expression on her face was one of confusion and promised violence if I took her out, which amused me to no end as I took an irregular route toward a luxury hotel with a nice restaurant.

The torture was sweet, but so was her face when we pulled in front of the valet. Her eyes swept over the front of the building, then she smiled at me. A thousand angels would have wept at the sight of her in that moment. It was a mixture of excitement, happiness and pure joy. And I was the one she was bestowing it upon.

CHAPTER TWELVE

Alisa

I WAS RELIEVED when we pulled up in front of the hotel. I wasn't sure if he'd changed his mind or if he'd meant eating here the entire time.

Whatever the case, I planned on demanding some things when we got to a room. After the gallery and the car tease, I was getting restlessly angry with him for not following through. My powers of seduction might be nothing compared to his, but I was trying. And the truth was I wanted him in the worst way.

After he'd mentioned it, thinking back on the last couple of weeks, he'd tried to make conversation with me when he'd come out of the study. I was too focused on the shift in attitude from him to see it for what it was at the time, and that felt like time lost with him. That was on me. If he wanted this to work his way, though, he'd have to open up and talk about more than just his favorite movies and what we both liked to eat.

Those small details were important. I wasn't discounting the fact that I loved onions and he didn't, or that his favorite movies were action based rather than my comedy leanings. There were a lot of things that were nice to know. But it wasn't what I truly wanted to learn about him.

I wanted everything. It might have been wishful thinking that he'd open up about his past. The one that I couldn't find on the internet, the one that haunted him. Maybe I'd been moving things forward too soon and he wasn't ready for it.

What I knew now, that I didn't when I met him, was that I couldn't think of anyone else I'd rather spend my time with. That an occasional laugh from him meant the world to me. Catching his dark brown eyes on me, when he didn't think I was looking, and seeing something like reverence in his face pulled at my heart in ways that I'd never felt.

Whether he knew it or not, he made me feel alive when he was being himself. Like I was a woman, desired, cherished, and worth more to him than collateral in a political sphere like my family.

I liked him. Maybe even loved him, but for reasons I couldn't explain or pinpoint. He was both gentle and rough. Sweet and naughty. Aggressive and giving. So many polar opposites wrapped into one person.

I'd thought he was complex, but it really didn't encompass everything. There was some intricate design to the man in the way he thought and expressed himself. I couldn't begin to unravel it and wasn't sure if I ever would. It settled in my chest that it was okay if I couldn't figure everything out about him, but I needed to know at least a small amount of the complex parts if he wanted something more than just a casual relationship. And I wouldn't settle for anything less with him. I wanted something more. If in my probing, he refused, I wasn't sure if I could take the man without knowing at least a little bit of his soul.

The valet opened my door, but it was Mick's hand that slid into mine to help me out of the seat. Once standing, his hand slid around my waist as he guided me inside. The white marble floors gleamed in the light thrown from the large chandelier above us. Footsteps and chatter from guests echoed across the enormous room, as an elevator chimed, the doors opening to a couple that was dressed for a night on the town.

My heels clicked as we made our way across the lobby to the entrance of the restaurant. It was the type of place that my father probably had brunch in with some associate or client. Neat champagne colored linen, candles, cutlery precisely placed, tables for the casual diner and private booths on a second floor overlooking the tables below. The low lighting made it cozy, but elegant for dinner guests or the single drinker around the lighted glass bar.

The hostess greeted us, but only had eyes for Mick. Something I'd gotten used to whenever we were out together.

Even at the art gallery, there were looks, some innocent, some full of debauchery and I couldn't really blame them. His appearance rivalled anyone I'd met in my life. The suit, the shirt, his height and broad shoulders, his dark hair and eyes, the look of dominance on his trimmed but unshaven face.

Even in heels, he was still much taller than me. But it was his presence that said more than what appearances did. He filled a room with a darker and possibly dangerous demeanor, his eyes roaming as if directly searching for a threat.

It'd been the same at the club, I realized, but I'd been too nervous to really see it until tonight.

As we followed the waitress to the stairs and began to climb, I leaned into him.

"You know, I think that the other guests might start evacuating soon if you keep scowling at everyone."

He smirked at me. "I'm not scowling. Just checking the room. Old habits."

We were shown to a booth high enough above the diners below that we had an aerial view. I glanced around the room before sliding into my seat set back from the glass rail. Mick slid in beside me and waived off the menu when offered.

"Whiskey, neat. Margarita. Top shelf," he said and glanced at me. "Steaks and oysters I think."

He stood to unbutton his jacket and discuss something with the pretty hostess that still had eyes on him. I scanned the rest of the second floor wondering why there weren't many people seated on this particular level given the view.

He sat again and ran a hand down my back. "Was the food okay with you?"

I nodded as the hostess drifted away. "I've never eaten oysters."

"They're an acquired taste. I thought you might like to try something new."

I grinned at him. "All of this is new. I've never been here."

"I've been here once. Mason dragged me out of the house. He said the best view in the place was here."

"Mason came here?" I asked, a little shocked.

"He brought a date or something once. It was probably some woman he needed to impress in order to take her home."

I laughed. "Your brother is a complete womanizer, but I still love him. I don't think anyone could possibly hate him."

He tilted his head to the side and considered me. "I'm sure there's a list of women that would disagree. What is it about you and thinking the best of complete jackasses?"

Our drinks arrived, and I took a sip of mine. "What do you mean?"

"You look past things that would normally piss most women off. Mason for instance. You accept him for what he is and don't care. The same is true for me and my nature."

I chewed on my lip, debating my response. "I think there's more than a little bit of goodness in everyone if their intentions are earnest. That may not always manifest in the way we want, but it's still there. Then there's the other half of our nature that sometimes draws closer to corrupted things. That may be by design or accident, but it doesn't make someone completely depraved."

He sat back and smirked at my answer. "So according to you, if I wanted to get you in bed, but had the best of intentions, it wouldn't be completely evil if I used every method at my disposal to get you there?"

I laughed. "Well if you drugged me then that's different. But something like that, I suppose. You and your brother are, I wouldn't say perfect people, maybe a bit tarnished. But neither of you are evil. I think Alex is the same way. There's good somewhere in everyone."

A small frown shot across his face before his eyes scanned the room.

"You don't believe me?" I asked.

He gave me a stiff smile. "I've known a lot of evil in the world. I can verify that there are some people that are too far gone to have any goodness in them."

I hesitated while he sipped his whiskey. "Is that something you saw at your old job?"

He didn't immediately answer, staring down at the amber liquid swirling in his glass. After a minute, he took a large drink and set the tumbler on the table.

"Yes. That was something I learned at my old job. There's not a shred of good intent in some people."

"Did you ever come across people that were maybe a bit of both?"

He laughed. "Yeah, coworkers. Not so much criminals. At least not the ones I went after. They could eat a man's soul just looking at their deeds."

"Did you have your soul eaten, Mick? Is that why you seem so sad sometimes?"

He straightened, finished his drink and waived at the waitress for another. "If you'll excuse me, I need to use the restroom."

My hand slid to his lap. "Mick?"

He gazed down at me with an almost panicked expression. I moved closer to him, running my hands up his chest as I placed a kiss on his neck.

"I'm sorry," I whispered.

He took a deep breath as his arm held me tightly against him. "Don't be. There's just some things I don't know if I can tell you. I may never be able to. It terrifies me that you might forgive me for things I don't deserve to be forgiven for."

"Why?" I whispered against his neck.

"To accept those things and move past them, you'd also have to accept the burden of knowing those deeds."

I rubbed my lips over his neck, wondering what he could possibly tell me that would be that bad. Not knowing a lot about what he did, it made my imagination flare with the possibility of bribery or false reporting. And sadly, he was right, I could forgive both.

"You'll never scare me away, Mick. You might make me angry enough to leave you, but you'll never scare me. I'm not sure what you were like before you came here…"

"A better man, a long time ago," he replied flatly.

"Well, I don't know that man, but I know this one. And I know that you're still a good man, no matter what you've had to do to get here."

"Alisa, you can't understand."

I leaned back and scowled at him. "You're right, I don't. What I do understand is the way you look at me. Like you'd never get tired of it. And the way you talk to me. It may be dirty or sometimes a little angry, but it's honest. I want you to tell me what's wrong, Mick, not because I wouldn't see some evil offense for what it is. I'd see it. But I want you to trust me with some of what tears you up because I care about you."

He sighed and tugged me into his lap. I sat with my face on his shoulder as our food was delivered silently.

"I can't tell you some things, Alisa. It's not that you wouldn't listen, it's that some of the things I've worked on were parts of cases that I can't tell you about. Do you understand?"

I nodded.

He shifted before taking another drink. "Good. So, the other half of that is…well, I need you to understand that there are things that I've done that…I'm not…fuck."

Emotions played across his face as he struggled to voice what was eating at him. It was clear to me that he was trying to let go of something in his past that wasn't ready to loosen its grip on him.

Finally, he said, "I've never felt so out of control in my life. Everything was always planned. Football, college, the academy. Even with work, I had a set routine. That system was really clear to me, helped my team put away a lot of bad men. I worked the facts over and over until I could see the little anomalies in things. If they existed, then they didn't belong in the pattern and sometimes that led to clues."

"Seems like a good talent to have."

"It was. I guess still is, since I'm scowling at people downstairs. The part that I need you to understand, is that sometimes to see into the darkness it requires you to view things darkly. It changes you. I'm not the good man that I was, but I'm not the bad guy that I could be. I'm a cold bastard sometimes, and that rubs off on people."

"You've never let it rub off on me. You can tell me things and it won't hurt me."

"You're not understanding," he sighed. "You make me feel things that I don't handle well, and that make me a little insane sometimes. My obsessions take over my life, and in the past, have been the only things I can focus on. It was always about closing the case, finishing the job. No matter what I had to do to get there, no matter who got hurt or suffered, it happened. And for me, since I'm a cold man, it was easy to walk away once the day was done."

"Okay?" I whispered.

He glanced down at me with a tight smile. "I can't do it with you."

Frowning, I pursed my lips for a moment trying to interpret what he'd said.

Sliding off his lap and onto the seat beside him, I hesitated, trying to swim through my confused thoughts. I wasn't sure what sort of game this was, but I'd possibly misunderstood some things.

He couldn't do this with me? Could he with someone else? Was that the reason he pushed? I wondered if I'd heard that right. If he wanted to be with other people, then I wasn't going to keep embarrassing myself by trying to get to know him.

"I think I should go," I said. "If you want to date other people, feel free. I have no idea what I was thinking. I'm so sorry for pushing you."

His hand reached out and grasped my wrist as I tried to move away.

"What the fuck?" he growled. "Sit down."

I shook my head. "I don't know what I wanted with all of this, Mick, but it was something more than just a temporary situation. I hate to be such a naïve person, but I guess I thought we could maybe be together for a while."

He pulled on my arm and dragged me closer to him. "Whatever the fuck you're thinking, get it out of your head. Don't think."

I wiggled back from him and tried to free my hand.

A tear slid down my cheek. "So, we're back to don't think, just do it? Was that what fingering me earlier was about? Look, I was—"

His hand reached my jaw and titled my head back. "Stop, Alisa. Stop fighting me for a second."

I jerked my head back from his hand and averted my eyes.

"For fuck's sake," he barked at me. He dragged me across the booth and up against him as he stood up.

I refused to look at him, but tried my best to act somewhat dignified as he hauled me across the second floor, past only two other seated tables and a private bar.

Stepping into an elevator he punched a button and the doors slid closed.

"Where are we going?" I asked.

"Somewhere we can have a private minute."

"Upstairs?"

His jaw clenched as he watched the numbers ascend. "Reserved a room."

"When?" I asked as I glanced at his moody face.

"The hostess arranged it, told her...forget it. Just give me a minute."

We rode in silence the rest of the way until the doors opened, then I walked beside him down one of the long hotel hallways. He stopped at a door and put in a code.

I looked back down the hallway toward the elevator briefly before I was hauled into the dark room by a set of incredibly strong arms.

My eyes didn't adjust to the darkness, but I could feel Mick pressing me against the wall. His breath landed on the side of my face before he kissed me gently.

"You are such a pain in the ass."

"At least I'm not a jerk."

He chuckled. "Now listen to me. What you think you heard and what I said just blew up in that pretty head of yours. Do you remember what I said?"

His scent wrapped around me so completely I could barely think. Being this close to him, his hips pinning me to the wall, hands against my ribcage and jaw, was sending shockwaves through my body.

I swallowed forcibly, trying to think. "You can't do it with me."

"That's right," he whispered against my ear before he kissed it. "And why can't I?"

My lip trembled a little bit. "I don't belong with you?"

He bit my earlobe. "Try again."

"You can't tell me about what hurts you."

His mouth moved to my neck and sucked before nipping at me. "Try again."

I let out a shaky breath as my body started to melt from the slow attention of his tongue and mouth nuzzling right below my ear. His hand slid up to cup my jaw and tilt my head to the side before he kissed a wet, hot trail to my shoulder.

"I don't know," I said weakly.

"Alisa, you missed some things. I'm obsessed with you. And I'm afraid that with the way I am, you'll never be happy with the answers I can give you. I'll never be able to walk away from you, though."

"Mick? I don't understand," I whimpered.

"Baby, I'll never get enough. It doesn't matter what I have to do to be with you, I'll never leave you alone. You're going to get hurt and you're going to see and hear some dark things from me. But the things you make me feel, I can't let go. I can't walk away from you at the end of the day, even knowing that I'll hurt you. It tears me up, knowing you deserve so much more than I can give you."

My heart ached hearing his voice crack as he finished speaking. He was broken, yet beautiful to me, no matter what he thought of himself. There was so much he'd said that called to the things I needed to hear. I didn't want to be hurt, but I couldn't walk away from him either. Whatever bound us together, we were both going to have to come to terms with it.

It was clear to me now that this man was as much a part of my soul as I was his. The sentiment settled in my chest and I welcomed it without hesitation. It started the night I met him and had been building to this. The how and why wasn't even important. The lack of time between now and then didn't matter. Mick was the man I wanted to be with no matter what happened from here.

My mouth opened to him when he stopped whispering against my lips and I leaned in. My hands snaked up his sides and wrapped around his shoulders as I kissed him softly.

When he broke off and started to say something, I bit his lip.

"Mick, make me yours. All I need is you."

CHAPTER THIRTEEN

Mick

Those five little words, spoken so sweetly, rocked me to my core.

All I need is you.

No one in my life had ever just needed me. They'd taken what they wanted, seen what I'd shown them, but at the end of the day, they needed things I could do for them. Not Alisa. My salvation. The only light in my life.

A rumble in my chest was the only warning she received before I picked her up and made my way to the king-sized bed.

She didn't know what she was asking for, or what she'd get, but I was tired of fighting my own demons when it came to her. The need to posses her far outweighed my reservations for holding back.

I tossed her on the bed, pinning her body down with mine, and began kissing her as I removed my jacket. My knee nudged her thighs open as she helped unbutton my shirt then I grabbed her wrists and held them to the bed above her.

"Keep your hands there, Alisa, don't move."

She grabbed at me when I tried to shift away from her. I growled and held her wrists to the bed again, my other hand going to her throat.

Her movements settled after a moment of holding her in place.

I needed this dominance. Needed her complete and utter surrender. My life was already a hurricane of things I couldn't control, and this was always going to be my domain from the moment I met her.

Unbuttoning my pants as I stood up, I reached for the light and turned it on. She lay on her back, blinking at the light, arms resting on the blanket above her. The darkness might have worked any other time, but this was the last woman I knew I'd be taking to my bed, and I needed to see her.

She stared up at me with so many questions in the blue depths of her eyes that I knew I couldn't answer. A better man, the man I might have been a year ago, before all the cases and cruelty had taken hold of me, would have left. Even if it meant breaking her heart right now. That man might have seen early on how foolish it was to fall in love with a sweet girl, knowing the shadows that lurked within me.

But I wasn't that man and I needed her more than she'd ever know.

Removing my clothing hastily, I kept my eyes on her face. If she had any reservations she didn't show them as my hands glided up her legs to the bottom of her dress. I both loved and hated the damn thing as it slid from her body. A body that was only mine to admire, and the dress didn't leave much to the imagination.

I leaned over her when the last of it was off and slid my hand around her back to unhook her bra. When she was finally naked in front of me I listened to her unsteady breathing, gazed at her chest as it rose and fell with anticipation.

She hadn't worn panties. Such a small thing to be turned on by in a public place but seeing her bare now I clenched my jaw thinking of the possibility that I would have missed it.

"Alisa," I breathed as I settled on the bed between her thighs and kissed her. "Don't ever go without panties again unless you're with me."

Her whimpers as I sucked along her neck, only increased the discomfort of my hardened cock. It made me want to take her hard and fast without preamble, but I knew if I did I'd regret it.

She was intoxicating, her tongue tangling with mine as I tried to control myself. I needed to bury myself in her so badly I could barely breathe. The flesh of her soft thighs rubbed against me as my hips angled against her.

Sucking on her bottom lip, I leaned back and marveled at her flushed, lust-filled face.

"Fucking beautiful."

Her arms trembled when I slid my fingers across the velvety skin of her nipples. She was struggling to do what I'd asked, and it pleased me that she was willing.

My hand slid down between us, over the soft skin of her hip until it reached her center. Slipping a finger inside her wet opening, I leaned in and kissed her as she moaned quietly.

"Alisa, I need to know if you're on anything."

I rubbed my thumb across her clit and she arched her back.

"Wha..."

I smirked. Fuck, she was so responsive, I could play with her all night.

"Hmm," I chewed on my lip, as her mouth opened and closed with the small flick of my thumb. I added another finger and gently began a slow rhythm.

Her hands gripped my shoulders, fingernails biting at my skin.

I sucked in a breath. "Alisa."

She moaned as her hands flew to the blankets and clutched at them.

I withdrew from her slowly, teasing her clit as I pulled back.

"No, no," she gasped. "More."

The head of my dick rubbed against her wet opening and her hips tilted to meet me.

Clenching my jaw, trying to stay in control, I debated asking about birth control again. Her body against mine, her wet entrance that begged me to take her bare was just too much.

I grabbed her hip and pushed slowly into her tight body. She let out a long moan of pleasure that matched mine.

The warmth that wrapped around my cock was so incredibly tight and wet that I paused, worried that I was about to hurt her.

"Fuck, baby, are you a virgin?" I hissed.

"No," she responded on a gasp.

Disappointment swept over me for less than a second before I slid further into her. Whether she was or wasn't didn't matter to me, her body was mine now. She was so tight around my thickness that I had to move slowly as her muscles clenched around me, welcoming my invasion. I pulled out a bit then slid even further in.

"Mick, oh my God," she whimpered.

My hand reached up to knead her swollen breast then my mouth found her nipple. I slid my tongue around the peak, and she moaned as I gently nipped at her. Raising above her, sliding my tongue into her mouth I pulled back and slammed home.

Her scream echoed through the room, slipping past my lips on her mouth. It eroded the last thread of my control, slipped into the very fiber of my soul and begged me to make her do it again.

My mouth found her neck and started to suck as my hips pumped into her. I rubbed at her nipple and she screamed again.

A smile slipped across my face, when I saw my mark I'd left on her neck. A small dark spot that everyone could see. A mark that no one could possibly miss.

I leaned back on my knees, grabbed her hips and watched as my cock slid in and out of her. Gently rubbing her clit, she arched off the bed in pleasure as I felt her hot release engulf me.

Her eyes fluttered open as I bent over her to kiss a tear that ran down her cheek.

Her hands slid around my neck and forced me down to her mouth. Her dominance in the kiss was sweet, but only lasted a moment before mine overpowered her.

Grabbing her hair, I tilted her mouth where I wanted her, and I teased her with my tongue, until tortured, small cries of desperation erupted from her.

"You're mine," I said against her ear, as my jaw clenched, and I surged into her again. This time I didn't hold back. Digging my knees into the bed I stretched her until she cried out against my neck.

I needed to pull out soon but her moans as the head of my dick reached the end of her, made my head spin. My need to fill her was primal, instinctual, nearly impossible to resist.

This woman was mine to conquer, to stretch, to bend and to fuck. She would come to know what it felt like to be worshipped in my bed, would discover what it meant to be possessed by a man whose only ambition was to take care of her in any way possible. I wanted to ruin her right now if it meant that she'd never forget who she belonged to.

"Mick," she moaned as her muscles once again clamped around my throbbing dick.

Her legs tightened around me as she tilted her hips into me. She was gasping for breath, so far gone in the bliss of pleasure that she was barely coherent as she said my name over and over again.

A tingling slid down my spine making me swell and throb. "Oh fuck, Alisa. Fuck, I have to pull out."

I leaned back but her arms wrapped around me causing her to lift with me and sink further onto my shaft. My hands slid around the soft flesh of her ass and held her in place as I pumped into her harder.

Her lips found my neck, and I couldn't let her go. My hunger for her taking over my better judgement. Grinding inside her, hips still thrusting, we fell to the mattress where I pummeled into her until she screamed.

Balls tightening, head spinning, grunting as I invaded her sweet world, I forgot everything but her. Nothing existed but the scent of her skin, the softness of her body against mine, the throaty sound of her voice as she called to me.

Her walls clenched me, and she cried out again. I groaned as I unexpectedly came, a thick rope of cum pouring into her before I pulled out. Grabbing my cock as I slid out of her, still high on my own orgasm, I pulled at my shaft and came against her opening.

My moans were muffled against the soft mounds of her breasts as I licked at them one last time.

I didn't move for a moment then shifted my body weight, rolling to the side and dragging her on top of me.

My eyes closed for a moment before I felt her shift, then saw her bright eyes gazing at me.

Her fingers skipped across my jaw, rubbing against the stubble on my face. Her eyes followed the same path until she got to my mouth. Nipping at her fingers gently, she smiled.

"Did I hurt you?" I whispered.

She shook her head. "No."

"Tell me."

"Just a little sore."

My arm wrapped around her tighter, feeling possessive and guilty. "How long has it been?"

She groaned as her head hit my chest.

Frowning, I rolled us over again until I was on top of her. Sliding my leg between her thighs, I brushed a hand over her face and saw an embarrassed blush steal across her cheeks.

"After high school and right before they shipped me to college."

My eyebrows arched. "Seriously? No boyfriends?"

Her lips pursed. "I dated a couple of guys, but I just never went that far again."

"Why?" I asked as I kissed along her cheek.

"Uhm..."

"You keep mentioning something. So, what the fuck happened after high school?"

She opened her mouth to answer then shook her head. "My dad caught me dating someone that he didn't approve of. We'd had sex, but it wasn't like that. Not like you. I got angry and told him while we were yelling at each other."

"And?"

"The belt. Then a doctor to check if I was pregnant. He said if I was, he'd get rid of it."

I stiffened in anger, trying not to feed my impulse to kill him.

She gave me a sad look. "It wasn't anything, you know? I knew I wasn't or didn't think I was. He was just a nice friend from choir and things..."

"I don't need to know, Alisa. And don't want to."

She frowned.

I tipped her jaw up with my finger until she looked at me again.

"Baby, I'm not trying to be mean, but you're with me now. No one from your past exists anymore."

She shrugged. "A few days later, he came up with a perfect plan to keep me more in line with the family focus. He thought I couldn't see it, like I was too stupid to figure it out. One of his friends had a son who was a lot older than me. I was eighteen, I think he was about thirty. He brought him over a few times a week for dinner. He always talked and talked about me like I wasn't even there."

My jaw clenched in anger as her eyes slid away from my face.

"He encouraged me to date him. I know he was thinking that maybe I'd marry him or something. That would have been advantageous, I suppose, for my father's connections in the city. The man does some sort of business overseas. I really didn't pay much attention at the time. So, I refused, and I know he called Alex about it. I think it was Alex's idea to have them ship me off to college."

I sighed and sat up, bringing her with me. I flipped the top blanket off the bed and onto the floor as I nudged her toward the bathroom.

She gave me a questioning look.

I chuckled. "It was a mess."

The hot spray of the shower as I turned it on, filled the room with steam. I gently guided her in after me, rubbing her arms as I pressed her up against my chest.

As we stood in the warmth of the water, I tilted her head to look at me.

"Don't ever feel like you have to keep things from me."

"But…"

"No. You're mine now, Alisa. Do you understand? No one will ever hurt you again. And if they try it, I'll do everything in my power to end them."

She regarded me, then nodded. "That works both ways."

I chuckled. "Really? Would you kill someone if they hurt me?"

She frowned while biting her lip.

My grip tightened on her. "That's the difference. I know what you're thinking, that I shouldn't hold back with you. I know you care, but there are some things I need to work out about my past. Just know this.

For you, I'll work on it. For you, I'd do anything. But there will always be some things that won't heal, and I won't tell you. I can't change those things."

"Okay," she whispered and laid her cheek on my chest.

I kissed the top of her head and wondered whether she truly understood the path that we'd laid. If her father ever touched her again, I'd make him pay in the worst imaginable way.

Grabbing the soap, I lathered it and began washing her shoulders, gently rubbing the thoughts in her head away.

She was a fighter, whether she knew it or not. Everything that'd happened in her life would have broken a weaker woman. They would have complied, would have stuck with what her father wanted. Given the information that I had on their family, most of them already had.

I'd never have guessed she had such resilience in her, as I hadn't seen it the first night we'd met. But now, I realized she had more inner strength than most. It was subtle, not overwhelming in any way. It helped me, drove me, and motivated me to do, maybe not the best things, but better things than I'd been doing. No more drunken nights on the floor, no more wallowing in self-hatred. She was my world now and I'd be damned if she ever lived another moment being unhappy in her life.

My hands reached the fullness of her breasts and massaged. Her head tilted back, eyes closed, and my dick hardened at the sight of it.

Smirking, I rubbed over her nipple. She let out a tiny gasp.

"Those sounds you make are getting me hard again and you're sore. Let's get you dried off and back in bed. I'll order some food."

Her mouth formed a little pout. The things I wanted to do with that mouth were endless, but tonight wasn't the night.

She gazed up at me, my eyes locked on her breasts as soap slid down the mounds to pool at her feet.

My hand grazed over her cheek. "Be a good girl for once."

She smirked, then frowned.

"What?"

She shook her head and tried to move past me.

My mouth met her ear when I stopped her. "I love you. Is that what you wanted to hear?"

She smiled up at me and my heart clenched.

"I love you too, Mick. No matter what."

I felt gut-punched hearing those words from her. I knew how I felt, but our definition of love was probably so dissimilar she wouldn't recognize what it was in me. Love was defined rather inadequately as a feeling of deep affection. To me, it was everything that was Alisa. Not just affection, but need, as if her departure from my life would rip me to shreds and burn down whatever remained of my grip on the world. I'd never leave her, to do so would be like jumping off a cliff into a bottomless, dark pit.

When she left the shower, I took a deep breath and buried my head in the water. As the hot spray landed on my face and shoulders, I wondered if she'd love me if she knew how dark my soul was, and still could be.

My thoughts wandered inevitably to what happened at the Bureau. I closed my eyes and saw my partner's face. The demon in his eyes that he'd hidden from me.

All the facts ran through my head. The database filled with young, missing women. A string of small clues on several cases for months. Days where nothing added up and the missing continued to be found sporadically. There'd been so many other cases, that I hadn't seen three of them for what they were. Even with my background, the training, the ego of my own abilities.

Then that day, that one fucking day. The body on the ground. Cold, lifeless eyes staring up at me. I was already numb from past cases when we walked into the field together and looked over the body privately. I'd seen so many by that point that I'd already shut down.

She was young, angelic even in death, gazing vacantly up at the blue sky on a cloudless day. Sweat trickled down my back from the heat of the field she'd been found in. The clothing beside her, folded in a neat pile just like the other three victims. The knowledge that this was a serial case made my stomach clench.

My partner's hand twitched in my peripheral vision as if he wanted to touch her. His fingers ran across the fabric of his pants in a strange caress. Blood under her fingernails. Something that had never been found on the other three. The scratch on the back of his neck that I'd given him hell for. Something he'd said last week. The woman he described fucking over that weekend had been an angelic blonde, but "feisty" according to him.

Movement behind me as someone approached. My hand on my pistol before the person reached me. My head whipped around to find his friend. My friend too. Whom I'd shared a drink with, laughed with after a long day at the office. Gun in hand he aimed at me, but I was quicker. His body dropped with my bullet in his face. When I turned to my partner, he was smirking, crouching over her body, touching her leg. His other hand twitched near his gun, then I put a bullet in his head.

My hand shook as I lowered my weapon. The acrid odor of spent gunpowder reaching my nose. He hadn't drawn his weapon. Thinking about it? Maybe. That fucking smirk, though. The same one that I'd seen on his face nearly every day. So human, and yet so utterly evil. He'd been playing a sick game for months at the cost of my sanity. I hated everything about him.

We'd held everyone back at a roadblock a mile in the distance, but the sound of my weapon alerted them. Distinct voices of people yelling and coming closer penetrated my haze.

I'd killed him at close range and his blood coated my shirt. His weapon lay in the holster on his hip. Taking a pen from my back pocket, I yanked it out with some effort and placed it on the ground near his hand, right before the first officer arrived over the hill.

Glaring at him, I walked past him on shaky legs, knowing my life had just gone to hell. I didn't care. He was just another dead body.

CHAPTER FOURTEEN

Alisa

WATCHING Mick put on his clothes the next morning, felt like a natural thing couples do. It wasn't like I hadn't seen him dress at least once, but it felt different this time. Somehow normal and right. He was mine. Every single inch of skin that he covered in pants, socks and shirt was voluntarily given only to me.

After our shower, he'd come to bed distracted and I'd wondered why. It was either something that he wasn't ready to talk about, or couldn't for now. I wondered very briefly if it had to do with me, but as the long night wore on and he told me a hundred times that he loved me, I knew it was something more to do with him. He was letting me in slowly and it was enough for now.

The night had gone so differently than what I'd expected. But like anything with Mick, nothing was ever predictable. I'd gone from thinking he'd dismissed me, to hearing him say that he loved me. A crucial turning point for both of us.

He looked at my dress for the hundredth time and frowned as he gathered his things. Last night had been one of the best of my life. He loved me. Something I might have guessed at, given enough time, but he'd freely given me the words I'd needed to hear and that to me was significant.

He wasn't basing it on a familial connection or what I could do for him. It was just love, formed over the past few weeks. I didn't have to be anyone I didn't want to be. Didn't have to prove myself to him. I wasn't living my dream life, with a job that was fulfilling. I had very little money and couldn't provide him with any financial gain. It was just me with my faults and past.

"I know you still hate the dress, Mick, stop scowling," I said with a smile.

He rolled his eyes. "It's the lack of clothing under it."

I slid the hem up a little as I leaned back on the bed. "Would you like to take it off again?"

He ran a hand down his face in frustration. "You're sore. You tried that all night and it's still not going to happen."

I threw him a haughty pout.

"Pouting won't get you anywhere either. Give it a day."

"Bossy."

He glanced at me and held out his hand. "Get used to it."

Taking his hand, I followed him through the door and down the long hallway to the elevator. When the doors closed he pulled me up against him and ran his fingers through my hair.

"We'll go by the house to change, then head to *Erebus*."

Mick's decision to buy the club with Mason confused me when he'd mentioned it the night before. I knew exactly why it bothered me. Mason's addiction to anything with a pair of boobs was one thing, but it also meant that Mick would be around the same temptations. I was hoping last night that he'd tell me he was going to be a silent partner. But the more he talked about it, the more I realized that Mason wouldn't be able to run the business on a daily basis without him, and I worried.

I would have never thought I'd be a jealous person. At least not with a man. I envied other people's families, relationships that seemed normal, their happiness. It was never really something I'd thought about too much until last night.

There was a line in my life that was distinct now. Life before Mick, and life after meeting him. The reality was, despite being surrounded by friends in college, excelling at the things I wanted, I wasn't happy. Not truly. I was only waiting for the next bad thing to happen. Especially with men.

Apart from Alex, I didn't have any influential person that I idolized. No one I admired for their resilience or even their ability to make me feel safe. Not my mother and certainly not my father. But that was the King family way.

Then there was Mick. My eyes slid across his face as he stared at the elevator door. Mick, my complicated and troubled man. He was mine and I was determined to keep him.

Mick's phone rang when we stopped at the third floor. He answered as a couple, who appeared to be lost, peered inside the cab, then started arguing about which floor they were supposed to be on.

The doors closed without the additional company and I turned toward him. The expression on his face was alarming.

"What did you say?" he barked in an angry tone.

He paused, listening, his eyes sliding over my face.

"No. We weren't home," he said with another pause. "Alex, I don't owe you a goddamn explanation. What the fuck do you mean her car was broken into at your house?"

My eyebrows furrowed with concern as I listened.

"Your house? What the hell would they be looking for? Forget it, we're headed home right now."

The elevator dinged and I realized we still weren't on the lobby level. The doors slid open and a man with a grizzled complexion stared back at me. His scruffy face looked like it hadn't had a shave in a while. His clothing, t-shirt over a pair of slacks, seemed somewhat rumpled.

My eyes clashed with his, and I knew instantly there was something wrong. As he stepped in he noted Mick, then barreled into both of us.

I felt a sharp pain in my side and cried out.

Mick's large hands grasped my hips and shoved me to the side. My body hit the wall and slid down as I stared back at Mick. The man that had joined us was now locked in a wrestling match with Mick against the opposite wall. His teeth gleamed as he let out a howl when one of Mick's fists hit him in the side. The man elbowed Mick in the face, punching his ribs. Mick's palm came up and started squeezing the man's throat as he kneed him in the leg.

The doors were shutting when Mick was punched in the jaw. Off balance, he managed to throw a punch of his own squarely in the man's chest, but the attacker was already stumbling out of the cab. He took off down the hallway with speed and Mick was nearly after him before he glanced at me to make sure I was alright.

His face froze as his eyes swept over my body, then he was on top of me.

I reached for him but the pain in my side increased.

"Oh, fuck, Alisa," Mick yelled as he wrapped a hand around my back. "Fuck, baby. Stay still."

His other hand pressed into my side and I cried out again. The fury on his face was unmistakable.

Looking down at his hand, that was causing so much pain, I let out a small scream. Blood covered his hand as he pulled away from my torn dress.

He picked me up in his arms, still furious and punched the lobby button several times. Red smears covered the panel as he slammed the button repeatedly until the doors closed.

"What..."

"Baby, just breathe and try to relax. I have to get you to the lobby."

When the door slid open he strode out among other guests who gasped. One screamed as Mick's long legs carried me to a couch.

Someone was shouting for security as others stared in horror.

Mick was on the phone speaking with someone then dropped the phone and placed both his hands over my side.

"Baby, just hold on and breathe. Ambulance is on the way."

Two men in security uniforms came rushing over. Mick barked out information to them while I tried to remain calm.

Just like the belt. It was nothing. Everything healed. It wasn't as bad as it looked.

The same mantra kept rolling through my head as I tuned out

everything around me and stared at the large vase on the table in the lobby. Mick's voice carried through the room and he yelled something.

When his face hovered in front of me again he was speaking.

I blinked, wondering why I heard him, but couldn't focus on what he was telling me. He looked so angry and confused at the same time. His face changed to one of concern then he leaned in, kissing my temple, my forehead, my cheek.

His hands slipped from my side and another face replaced his. Unfamiliar, but kind, a woman, who pointed a light in my eyes. She was pretty, tight-lipped and focused as she gave me the once over. Her eyes darted down my body then back at me and she gave me a gentle smile. When I closed my lids, feeling sleepy, the sounds of the room rushed back to me. Sirens, people talking.

And Mick yelling ferociously.

"What do you mean, you didn't catch that crazy fuck? He had to have exited through the side entrance. There are only three ways out of here."

"Sir, there's an exit through the restaurant. We'll pull the cameras, once the police get here."

"Motherfucker," Mick growled. "He's probably already halfway across the city."

"Mick," I whispered.

A woman's voice answered. "It's okay, we're taking you to the hospital. We need to get you patched up."

"Mick," I said again.

"Hey, man," the woman said. "Are you Mick? She's asking for you."

"Fuck," he barked as he stormed across the lobby. "Alisa, it's okay, baby. They're going to take you. Mason will be there."

His hair was ruffled, a red smear on his cheek while his wild eyes regarded me. I'd never seen him so out of control. Of all the times he'd tried to scare me away from him, nothing compared to the look in his eyes as he scanned the room, fists clenching, snarl on his face.

"You?" I asked as I was moved to the side, my eyes closing.

"I have to stay here. I'll be up there as soon as I can."

My body was lifted, then we moved as I heard someone talking in codes.

"Baby," I felt a hand against my face. "I'll be there, just hold on."

~

When I woke up, it wasn't Mick who was leaning over me, it was Mason.

"Hey there," he said with a smile. "Just relax."

My arms felt sluggish as I tried to sit up.

"What..."

There were men's voices in the hallway arguing. Mason's head tilted to the side as if trying to listen to the conversation. A man I didn't know walked into the room, nodded at Mason, sat in one of the chairs and pulled out a magazine.

"So," Mason said, turning back to me. "While you were getting a nice set of drugs in surgery and stitches, Mick showed up with your brother and my dad. Alex stepped out, but he'll be back in a minute."

"Surgery?" I whispered.

"Yeah, the guy that was in the elevator knifed you. Not sure where he was aiming but it was a lucky miss. Nearly clipped your lung. You're alright, though."

"Where's Mick?"

He raised his eyebrows and nodded at the hallway. "Having a talk with the old man. They don't get along. Has he told you anything?"

I shook my head.

He pursed his lips for a moment. "Not a pretty bedtime story, but the long and the short of it is that my dad was a dick when we were kids. He's still a dick, but not like that."

He gave me thoughtful look.

"You get it when it comes to my brother. You see him now, and I think you can see how bad he could be. He wasn't always like this, but he was always strong. I looked up to him, wanted to be him some days. My dad was a piece of shit a long time ago. Mick took most of it until he got into sports, then dad found a new way to be a dick, constantly on his ass. But when my mom died he changed, sobered up. Mick just doesn't want to see it."

The arguing stopped, and Mason listened again for a moment.

"You're probably the only person Mick even cares about anymore..."

"He cares about you, Mason."

He shrugged. "Yeah, he does, just not the same way. I'm telling you, so you know where it comes from. His moods, the way he acts. He's a lot like my dad, not the jackass who used to beat the snot out of us, but the part that doesn't take anyone else's shit. My dad doesn't and neither does he. And it pisses him off."

"But I thought something happened at his job."

He arched his eyebrows. "Something did. Even though I've asked him a few times, he won't open up and fill me in. It's never been this bad. He's a good man, Alisa, smart as hell. I wouldn't have anyone else at my back in a pinch. But he won't let anyone fuck with him. I'm telling you, because I can see where he's going with you. He won't ever let anyone fuck with you either. No one, not even me."

"He's kind of said that, but I thought maybe he was just being protective."

He squeezed my hand. "You're the best thing that's ever happened to him and I'm glad to see it. You make him happy, or at least as happy as that stubborn ass can be. I'm just letting you know, that there's going to be a day when you may not understand some things. Just remember he's a fighter and you're his reason for fighting now."

I nodded, not entirely sure what Mason was trying to say, but appreciative of his thoughts nonetheless.

"I'm going to go. Have a few things I need to do for Mick. The guy in the corner is your new bodyguard."

My face scrunched as I looked at the hulking man reading a magazine. He glanced at me and gave me a tight smile. It wasn't exactly friendly, but it wasn't unpleasant, just professional I presumed.

"His name is Paul, and he's a good friend of a friend. Anyway. Just remember what I said about not understanding Mick. Let him do this for you."

"But I don't need one, Mason. I don't want him to spend the money on something that I don't need. It was just a random act of violence. That's it."

He chuckled. "You're cute. That's why I like you. Don't ever worry about funds, Mick can afford quite a bit. See you soon, Alisa. Just get better, okay? Without you around it's not quite as fun to fuck with his sorry ass."

I giggled then winced from the wound in my side. "Thanks, Mason."

"Anytime, sis."

Frowning at the term he used, he chuckled again as he left the room.

I eyed Paul, wondering what the hell I was supposed to do around him. Or what he should be doing around me. He seemed relaxed enough flipping through pages in his magazine.

A bodyguard. Not something I would have ever imagined in my life. Paul was a brick wall to put it mildly. Although not particularly over muscled, he had a broad physique and looked quite a bit like several bouncers I'd seen through the years. The difference lay in the serious expression in his brown eyes, the way they scanned the door every few seconds and the way he carried himself. As if his tall body was poised to take immediate action, but hiding that fact, by looking seemingly relaxed, even if he wasn't.

Mick and Alex both entered the room at the same time. Alex's face fell when I smiled at him. My eyes slid to Mick's and I saw something, a small glimmer of rage, before it was wiped from his face.

"Hey, baby," Mick said as he placed a small kiss on my forehead. "Feeling okay?"

Nodding, I gave him a small smile. "Yeah, just a little groggy."

Alex took my hand and kissed it. "Just glad you're okay."

I looked between both of them as their eyes slid away from me.

"Uhm, what's going on?"

Alex gave me a tight smile as he squeezed my hand. His expression was one that I'd seen a few times with clients when he was trying not to say something, but he had plenty of opinions rolling around in the back of his head.

"Nothing. It's just unfortunate that you two were attacked so randomly. When Mick called I nearly lost it."

My head turned toward Mick on my other side. Unlike Alex, who I could read fairly well given our relationship, Mick's expression was blank. I wasn't sure if it was the blank stare he was giving the wall, or his non-response that scared me more. The fact that Alex hadn't commented on Paul's presence in the room also said a lot. It was if they both suddenly were in complete agreement about something that they were trying to hide. Alex, with his ability as an attorney to lie, and Mick with his dark, moody eyes.

"Right," I said with a sigh. "Then Paul isn't really needed here if that's the case."

Paul looked up at me with an enigmatic expression before he scanned the doorway again and went back to pretending to read.

"He's not going anywhere for now," Mick replied in a flat voice. "Just a precaution."

I rolled my eyes. "So, if it was a random attack, then why the precaution? Have they caught him? Did they pull the cameras? Why was your dad here?"

Alex glanced at Mick. "I told you…"

Mick dipped down to kiss me on the forehead again. "You should rest. I want him here because it makes me feel better."

I groaned at his response. "Really? That's all you're going to say? Then he can stay with you."

He leaned over ran his hand over my jaw before taking hold of my chin. "My father is the Chief of Police. He was here to take a statement, it's his job. They haven't caught the fucker yet, and Paul is a deterrent just in case. He's staying right where he is because I fucking want him to be here."

"You're being ridiculous," I hissed.

His eyes scanned my face before he replied. "Remember when I said there were some things I wouldn't tell you?"

I nodded.

"Well this is one of them. So, get used to it."

Alex mumbled something to my other side drawing Mick's attention.

"We have some things we need to do," Alex said as he gave a nod to Mick. He leaned in when Mick retreated and held his head against the side of my face. Before he moved back, he kissed me on the temple and gave me a genuine small smile.

He left the room, leaving me with Mr. Personality Paul and Mick.

"Do you have to go too?" I asked as I glanced at him.

He nodded slowly taking my hand in his. He studied my palm, running his thumb over my fingers. When he looked back up at me he gave me a tight smile.

"I'll be back later. You'll probably sleep for most of it, your eyes look tired."

I shook my head as I yawned.

He chuckled. "Stubborn."

"Jerk."

He smirked and leaned over me before peppering my neck with small kisses.

His mouth hit my ear and I shivered. "Yeah, but I'm your jerk. I'll be back, I love you."

"Love you," I whispered sleepily as he stepped away and gave me one last glance.

He looked at Paul, who nodded and shut the door behind him.

Letting out a sigh, I turned to Paul and his fake reading expression. "Do you play cards?"

He smirked. "Yeah. Sleep, we'll play after."

I narrowed my eyes at him and he gave me the same look. His was a lot scarier than mine was, so I gave in and closed my eyes.

CHAPTER FIFTEEN

Mick

Angry, didn't describe my mood a week after the attack.

Furious, filled with rage might have come close. Whatever it was, it'd settled in my chest ready for a long, unwelcome stay.

It didn't take a genius to figure out that there was a connection between Alex's house getting broken into, Alisa's car being vandalized, and the man in the elevator with the knife. Something that Mason, Alex and Jack all agreed on. My father was a different story and other than placating my temper, he seemed indifferent to what happened.

While I let the police search for the man on the video feed, I stewed, burying myself in the club's financial records and accounting. It was tedious and mind-numbing, but prevented me from storming my father's office again.

Meanwhile, Mason and Jack were doing their own search for the attacker between chasing down things for Alex. Although it hadn't produced any results, one benefit had been networking with people that had the same idea we did about the King family. They were dirty, and at least half the city agreed when they talked to him.

Their crimes didn't just include the one against Alisa. They were far reaching. Extortion, bribes, threats, and alleged murder were just a few things Mason had heard. He'd laid it out in the kitchen the first night Alisa was in my bed, but the more I heard, the more tangible it became to me. They had an organization, a system, and links to crime after crime all while looking like they were the city's elite.

I moved another invoice in front of me to a folder and grabbed the next one.

The large mahogany desk that was currently piled with papers and my laptop, was left over from the previous owner. It was the only thing that survived the purge of old, ratty furniture when we cleaned out the back rooms.

A cursory look at the man who'd sold the place to us, was enough for me to know that he'd been as shady as the lighting downstairs. I knew at a glance that he'd been using drugs and had more than likely been dealing out of the club. Rumor from the staff was that he was as free with it as he'd been with his dick when some club patron was stupid enough to think he was worth visiting.

The manager, a fiery woman the staff called, "Satan", but was otherwise known as Holly, had clearly been the person in charge of the staff. She'd handled most of the club's daily operations, while her boss snorted, injected, smoked or sold whatever was earned. The club itself, was running at a profit, a huge one. The amount of money they earned versus what they spent was phenomenal. But it was hard to tell how much they'd had year after year by the books the owner had been keeping. Although Holly had cleaned up most of the confusion in the last week by the look of it, unfortunately there was a mountain of missing payments and data.

The door opened, and Alex strolled in, drawing my attention away from the confusion of the last liquor shipment that had been delivered.

I gestured toward the new set of leather chairs in front of the desk. "Come in, have a seat. Isn't it a little early in the morning to be slumming it here?"

He gave me a wry smile and dropped a thumb drive on the desk before lounging in the nearest chair.

Glancing at it, I raised my brows in question.

"That's a gift from Reid Thomas."

I steepled my hands and shrugged. "You mean the dipshit that was flirting with Alisa at the gallery? Why would I care?"

Alex chuckled and surveyed the office. "This place isn't as bad as it seems from the exterior."

"We had it repainted, I've been huffing fumes since we signed the papers. New furniture, new look. Hopefully the cocaine on the floor got mopped up."

He smiled. "Ahh, yeah, I heard from Mason."

"Reid Thomas?"

"Yes, well he's an old friend of mine. Works around Malcolm King, when he shows up for City Council meetings. He owns the art gallery we were at and just happens to be as paranoid as I am."

"Still not hearing any reason why I should care."

"Get over it, Mick. He's known Alisa for a long time and he wasn't pissing on your territory. He's like that in public with every woman."

The door opened to the office and Holly strode in without glancing at Alex. She laid an invoice on the table and turned to leave.

"What's this?" I asked.

Alex's eyes slid down Holly's frame with no indication of what he thought of the leggy woman who was sporting dark blue coloring in her normally brunette hair. Her hair was pulled back in a ponytail, and she wore cut-off jeans with a black shirt that looked like it had gray paint on it. She was younger than I'd imagined when Mason told me about her. I was half convinced that Mason was afraid of the little firecracker by his initial descriptions. It still didn't prepare me to deal with a girl in her twenties with so much ambition and spunk.

"Liquor delivery, boss," she said sarcastically. "Thought you might want it for your pile of paperwork."

I leaned back in my chair. "It's Mick, we've been over that. And it's not just my pile of paperwork, it's ours. As soon as I go through it, you can have your folders back."

She shrugged with a slight expression of indignation and hurt on her face.

"Holly, you're still the manager, we just need to see what we're dealing with."

"Yeah, whatever. You want to know then just ask."

I grabbed the invoice from the edge of the desk and flipped it over. I frowned at the name of the delivery service. *Martin's Shipping* had come up on a few items that I'd flagged to talk to her about.

"We'll talk about this one later," I said absently. "This is Alex. Alex, Holly."

She glanced at Alex for a moment, who gave her a tight smile. She nodded at him then left the office.

"Alex, you can wipe the drool off the floor. How's Heather?"

He narrowed his eyes at me before looking away. "Probably thinking about her next plan of attack to get me to marry her. I'm assuming she's doing what Heather does best, getting a tan, living off her daddy's money and spending loads of time talking about herself to anyone that'll listen."

I whistled. "Hmm, you're not as dumb as you look."

"Her father's a mutual acquaintance of the family. Owns a very large bank with Warren King. To whom I owe a bit of money on a loan I took out to open the firm a few years ago."

"I see. So, you're dating her to extend the loan? Or is it your dad pulling the strings? This is exactly why I question your loyalties, Alex."

"Alright, Mick," he said as he leaned forward, giving me a scowl. "You want to know a few things? I'm a King. When your dad suggests taking the daughter of a wealthy man out to dinner and maybe give her a healthy fuck on occasion to placate your uncle's business partner, you do it. Why? Because as far as they're concerned I'm dedicated to the family. Not only that, but it helps me stay in business, so that Heather's dad, doesn't convince Warren to demand the full amount of my loan to him with a month's notice."

"How much do you owe?"

He chuckled. "Initially a lot, but I'm getting it down. Meanwhile, I work so many late nights that it makes it nearly impossible to see the bitch except for a random date or two or when she shows up at the office."

Alex's hard glare dared me to say something about it as he leaned back in his chair. The urge to prod him and piss him off was on the tip of my tongue until I thought of Alisa. She respected her brother, even if I found him annoying, and unfortunately that alone made me hold my tongue. If he ever fucked her over, it'd be a different story.

Grabbing the thumb drive off the desk I held it up. "What's on this?"

"Reid wouldn't say. Just that you might find it interesting."

I threw him an irritated glance and plugged it into my laptop. There was one file, a video, that I opened. When it began to play, I wasn't sure what I was looking at. An alley, much like any other in the city with few lights and dark shadows.

I shrugged and turned the screen to let Alex watch. "What am I looking at?"

He frowned at the footage as it played. "Not sure."

We watched for several minutes then caught movement just outside the light of the darkened alley. Two figures became visible as they walked toward the camera. Both men, one shorter than the other, but they were both very clear when they stopped just shy of walking out of the frame.

"Son of a bitch," I mumbled. "That's the guy from the elevator. The shorter one on the right. Why and how did Reid not only film this, but also know who we were looking for?"

Elevator guy's arms moved out of view as the other man leered at something they were looking at. When the shorter man stepped back he had a bulging square package in his hand that resembled an envelope. He handed it to the taller man, said something to him, then both walked back in the direction they'd came.

The video cut to a black screen then to a video feed of the gallery. It was a recording of the gallery opening. I spotted Alisa walking away from Reid's table with me, then Alex holding me back as we had words.

Pausing the video, I scanned the room.

"What are we looking at?" Alex said to himself.

"More like who are we looking for. I can't imagine that the videos aren't related."

Alex pointed to the top left of the screen. "There, shorty."

Playing the video again, the man watched us leave, then followed shortly afterward before the video ended.

I sat back, staring at the blank screen. "How does this play into our theory about your family making threats? We can't see who's in the alley with them. The art gallery? He saw me kiss her, but was he already following us?"

Alex ran a hand through his hair. "Good question. But I think what we talked about still fits. I'm not a detective, but the way I see it, my family, at least my dad, thought she was with me. Maybe he hired someone to follow her and then he realized she was with you. Your kiss in the gallery confirms it, but since he doesn't think I'd lie about where she's staying, he had someone break in?"

"Hmm," I said as I tapped my finger on the desk. "Something is missing. Why go after her at your house if shorty followed us to the hotel?"

Alex shrugged. "I don't know."

"Do you have Reid's number?"

Alex pulled out his phone and tapped a few buttons. He laid the phone on the desk on speaker as it rang.

"Hello?" a smooth male voice answered.

Alex opened his mouth, but I cut him off.

"You know who this is. Do you have a name?" I asked when Reid picked up.

"Dan."

"Do you know where Dan is?"

"I do," he said with a distracted tone. "Your brother just walked out of his favorite diner for breakfast about ten minutes ago. I've given him the information."

Why the man knew my brother's habits was disturbing. I didn't even know what Mason's favorite diner was, and that irritated the hell out of me.

I picked up my phone and dialed Mason.

"Hey. I'm working on something," he answered gruffly. He sounded like he'd been up most of the night, likely up to his familiar habits with a woman, since he hadn't come home last night.

"Were you at a diner for breakfast?"

"Yeah, why?" he said defensively.

"Relax. Did you get some information about my elevator problem? Can you handle it?"

He paused for a moment. "Yeah. You want him, or you want to give him up?"

I glanced at the phone, knowing Reid was listening to my side of the conversation.

"You know the answer," I replied to Mason.

"Done, give me twenty," he said before he hung up.

"We'll be talking soon, Reid."

"I'm sure we will," he said before he too hung up.

I wasn't sure why Reid Thomas was willing to help me find the fucker, or what he wanted for passing along the information. Perhaps it had to do with Alex's friendship with him, but from his tone, Alex didn't indicate that they were particularly close.

My eyes flicked to the man sitting across from me. He seemed to be contemplating the same thing as he frowned at the phone he'd left on my desk.

"Money?" I asked.

He shook his head. "He has plenty of it."

"You might want to find out."

"Why?" Alex asked as he stood up.

"The man who stabbed your sister is going to have a little talk with me in the basement in about twenty minutes. And I'm betting Mr. Thomas knew that before he gave Mason the information."

He nodded. "I have a few questions for him myself. I'm going to step out and call the office to cancel some appointments."

"Hmm," I responded noncommittally. "You should go back to the office, Alex. You can't defend me if you witness a crime."

He paused for a moment before he reached for his phone and put it back in his suit pocket. His eyes hardened as he stared at me.

"As far as I'm concerned, I stopped by to talk about Alisa and got distracted by the leggy woman downstairs. What happens in your basement stays there."

"Alex, this is going to get ugly," I said, as I leveled a serious look at him. "This isn't a business meeting. It won't be a nice chat."

His eyes narrowed at me. "Mick, you aren't the only one with blood on his hands. I told you there was a line for each of us and I've crossed it so many times, I'm not even sure where it is anymore. So, don't give me a speech about it. Don't even bother. I'm staying to see this through one way or another."

I gave him a small nod, before he walked out of the office and I wondered if he'd honestly feel like that, once things were over with.

Reaching for my laptop I tapped a video program and brought up the feed from our office, which included sound. I searched for a specific spot then played back the part where Alex was talking about his girlfriend.

His stomach for interrogation, the type that I had in mind, was about to be put to the test. And if he couldn't handle it, I'd be forced to use the information about his loan and girlfriend against him. Something I didn't want to do, but wouldn't feel an ounce of guilt about.

Picking up the phone, I called Alisa.

"Hello?" she said sleepily.

"Hey, baby."

"Mmm. Where are you?"

"At the club for a bit. Paul's there this morning."

She yawned loudly. "Yeah, I hear him in the kitchen. He's not exactly quiet."

"Get some rest, just wanted to check on you."

"I'm fine, Mick, really. I'm a little sore, but I'll be okay. You have to stop worrying so much. Come home so we can watch a movie and make out."

Chuckling, I remembered the previous night when she'd almost convinced me to have sex with her before she'd passed out on her pain medication. She was going to drive me nuts if she tried it again.

"You just got out of the hospital yesterday, I think you need some rest."

"Fine," she said, and I could almost imagine her pouting.

"If you promise to be a good girl, rest, eat, shower then I might give you something when I get home. I'll be tied up here for a little while, so it might be a few hours."

"Hmm," she responded in a husky voice. "Do you mean sex?"

My dick twitched at her tone and started hardening at the thought.

"Do you want my cock, Alisa? Sliding into you, making you wet?" I asked with a smirk.

"Yes, please," she whispered. "I'm touching myself thinking about it."

My jaw clenched thinking of her long delicate fingers playing in my territory.

"Don't do anything, Alisa. You're not allowed."

She groaned. "That's not fair."

"Who has control?"

"You. Not—"

"You're mine, baby. That means I own every little moan, every little inch of you. If you disobey, you won't get anything from me today."

She let out a muffled growl and I chuckled.

"I'll make it up to you, just behave," I replied as the door to my office opened.

Holly stalked across the room. "Mick, Mason said to come up and get you. Apparently, that blockhead and the suit think I'm your personal fucking secretary. Which I'm not."

"Thanks, Holly, I'll be down in a minute," I said as I covered the phone. "Go ahead and take off."

Her eyebrows arched. "Seriously? I still have a shit ton to do."

"Yeah, take off. Tomorrow we're going over the books together."

She mumbled something under her breath and rolled her eyes. "Fine."

As she stalked angrily out of the room, I heard Alisa speaking. "—and I don't like that I have to stay home when you get to sit up there. I could just sit up there too."

"Baby, I have to go. I love you. I'll be home later."

"Fine. Love you." she said with a sigh and hung up.

I looked at the phone and shook my head. Pissing off two women in the same day in less than a minute was a record for me. One of them was going to be fun to make it up to, the other was likely going to be a pain in the ass.

I slipped my phone in my back pocket as I made my way down the stairs to the bar. I arrived just as the front door slammed shut.

Alex was staring past me when I approached him, then glanced at me.

"You sure know how to piss someone off."

"She'll get over it, I'll give her a bonus or something. The way you're looking at the door, though, I'm thinking you might want to give her something too. Feel free, make my life easier."

He shook his head. "I...no. I was just wondering if she locked the door."

"Right, whatever," I mumbled as his eyes darted away. "We'd have to worry about Mason locking the door. Holly, I'm not worried about. But if you want to go chase her down to ask, then I won't hold it against you if I don't see you the rest of the day. Didn't know blue hair did it for you."

"Fuck off."

I smirked and made my way through the club to a staff entrance, that led to a long hallway with two breakrooms, a door to the unused basement and the staff entrance door.

We descended the stairs to the basement together, finding Mason and Jack scowling at a man that sat tied to a chair. His hands were bound by a pair of handcuffs behind the chair and his legs tied with rope.

Mason glanced up at me as I walked around the man I understood was our attacker, according to Reid. He glared up at me as I came to a stop in front of him.

It was him, without a doubt. The one that nearly fucking killed Alisa. That nearly ended every hope I had of happiness.

"Hey, fucker. Remember me?" I asked as I swung at his face and landed a blow to his jaw. His head flew to the side and he groaned. "Hope you didn't have anything planned. I'm about to break every bone in your miserable body."

I swung at him until I saw blood spew from his nose as a result of breaking it, then I went for his ribs. His groans turned to outbursts of pain. When I looked up eventually, I met three sets of eyes, and none of them had an ounce of judgement in them. They knew when they stepped in here what they'd see and help me do. What secrets they'd have to keep.

Alex shrugged off his jacket and rolled up his sleeves as Mason stepped forward. Jack flexed his hands.

I thought of Alisa at home. Stitches in her side, several bruises along her body from being knocked around. Her sweet, beautiful face that always looked at me like I was a goddamn hero when I knew I wasn't. My chest constricted thinking of what could have happened. She was the one person in the world who saw a sliver of the man I used to be. She owned every part of me whether she knew it or not. The good, the bad and the ugly.

The night we were together swam through my head. Not pulling out fast enough. Even knowing that the possibilities were slim that she'd gotten pregnant, the thought that she might be, the thought that I wanted her to be, fueled my rage as I glared at the scumbag in front of me.

When the man's angry eyes met mine, Alex pushed me to the side, took a swing like a professional boxer to the man's ribs and started asking questions.

CHAPTER SIXTEEN

Alisa

It was late in the day when my phone rang. My father had been trying to reach me a few times, and calls to Alex and Mick were going to voicemail. I needed them to deal with him.

I felt like a coward, unable to deal with him myself. In truth, I really was afraid of the man. He'd hurt me too many times for there to be even a chance at reconciliation. I wanted to take a stand, wanted to tell him he was now cut off from my life but the possibility of a verbal, if not a physical confrontation made me hesitate.

Mick and Alex were my life. The only two people that really meant something to me now. I knew they'd bring justice to my father eventually while trying to fight the corruption in the city. I wasn't aware of how deep that ran, but I knew it was enough to warrant their mutual agreement on the subject and I was all for it. If I could help, I would, if only to prove I was just as much of a fighter as they both were.

My phone rang again while I was sitting in the living room reading. Paul glanced up at me from the couch and turned the volume down on the basketball game he was watching.

"It's my dad," I said shaking my head. "I don't want to answer it."

"I can answer it for you, but I'm not sure he'd like what I have to say," he said in his deep voice. "I know what he did. Fucker."

I blushed, embarrassed that he knew anything at all, but not surprised that he'd been filled in on the background.

He glanced at the phone as it stopped ringing then back up at me. "Your call."

"I'll deal with it," I said as the phone rang again. "Shit."

Paul nodded, averting his eyes back to the T.V.

"Hello?" I answered.

"It's about time you answered. If I call, you need to pick up. That's not a suggestion, Alisa."

"Hey, Dad. I'll answer when I want to. What do you need?"

"Don't be impertinent, you don't know how to pull it off with any conviction. Stick to what your mother knows and we'll all get along."

My anger grew as he continued.

"I stopped by the hospital for a chat, but was informed you left with Mick Galloway. Apparently, you were also with him at a gallery event over the weekend. He's not our type of people, Alisa. I don't care what you're trying to prove to everyone. You can fuck who you want, but don't make it public. You need to get back in line with what the family values."

"Like what?" I asked. "Beating their children and making drunken whores out of their wives?"

"That's enough," he hissed in anger. "You can spread those legs for him all you want but you will toe the line in this family unless you'd like to be cut off, or have that loser hurt. I will hurt him. I'll make it my mission in life. When you get married to someone more appropriate..."

"I'm never, ever going to marry someone that you want me to. And I'm never going to do what you want. You can cut me off, you can beat me, you can call me a whore, but you're never going to get what you want from me."

There was a loud noise in the background before he responded. "When your mother told me she was pregnant, I thought about beating you out of her. The only thing that saved you was being the child of one of my brothers. A King regardless of who fucked her."

My mouth dropped open and all the air left my lungs. Speechless over his announcement.

"Which one?" I shakily whispered.

"One of three, take your pick, sweetheart. She learned her lesson after an affair with our realtor. Keeping it in the family and doing what she was told wasn't a question after they all had a go at her. And then you came along. I claimed you, fed you, gave you a house to sleep in. Now you owe me and I'm getting impatient. I'll ruin that son of a bitch unless you come home, Alisa."

Paul studied my face with alarm as he moved closer to me. He shook his head and reached for the phone.

"Fuck off, Denny. You're no family of mine."

Paul grabbed the phone, hung up, then turned it off.

Taking a few deep breaths, I stood up, hands shaking and hugged my stomach.

Paul's hand on my back registered as he spoke. "Don't you believe a word of what he said, Alisa."

"You heard?" I whispered.

He nodded. "He's disgusting, don't let it get in your head. Mick can take care of himself. He's just bluffing to try and control you."

Tears form in my eyes and slide down my cheeks. "He could really hurt him, though."

He tilted his head and smiled. "Not Mick. See, Jack and I have been friends for a while now and when Jack says he'd rather be back on the vice team, dealing with narcotics and gangs, than face Mick in a dark alley, that says a lot to me. And seeing him now? Yeah, I'd hate to be on the wrong end of anything with him."

I blanched as I wiped at my tears. "That's insane. Mick's nice, he's just going through some things."

He chuckled. "Girly, you must have it bad for him. That guy has some demons lashing him on a straight trip to hell and back. That's just how it is. You and Mason are the only people he cares about, and Mason would come in second if he had to choose. Don't you ever worry about Mick."

"Okay, but you're wrong. He's just dark sometimes."

"Alisa, I like you, so I'm going to say this once. Mick and Mason are building something here. You may not want to see it, but I'll tell you what everyone else sees. They're organizing, getting their shit together. This isn't some hobby for them anymore. After you got attacked, I got hired and saw it, even after Jack told me about it."

"You saw what?" I whispered as confusion settled over me.

"Mason said they started with a purpose in mind. To catch some of the Kings in shady dealings. But since then they've been making some friends. It's not hard to see if you want to. The Galloway brothers are starting to get a reputation. You're going to have to accept that."

I sucked in a shaky breath and gave him a curt nod. I wasn't quite sure what he was talking about. That wasn't what I saw at all. Mick spent time cleaning up the club's records and Mason worked for Alex. There wasn't anything else regardless of what Paul assumed.

Mick could be a force of nature sometimes in both the way he loved and expressed his anger. Both emotions were either on or off and I was thankful that the love he had for me was permanently on. There were times, though, that I saw the anger pacing behind his eyes when he helped me with my bandage. It was there and if I could see it, then Jack or Paul might recognize it as well.

Dismissing Paul's paranoia, I said, "I think I need to relax."

"I'll be around," he said as he made his way back to the couch. "And can we not mention that I rubbed your back? I don't want my fingers broken."

Shaking my head, I made my way to the bathroom, intending to take a long bath, then remembered my stitches. I needed Mick, needed to tell him to be careful, and warn him about my father's threats. With his phone going to voicemail it was impossible to do that. A sick feeling settled in my stomach that perhaps my father had already gotten to him and he was hurt somewhere. I wasn't sure if he'd meant financially or physically when he'd made his threats.

Entering the living room again I grabbed my purse and car keys.

"Alisa, where are you going?" Paul asked as he stalked across the room.

"I need Mick, he's not answering his phone."

Paul took my keys and headed to the door. "You know the drill, you can't go anywhere without me. Let's go."

We arrived at the club thirty minutes later, with dark clouds gathering in the sky. Paul opened my door and I climbed out. The front doors were locked, prompting Paul to direct me around the building to another entrance that read "Staff Only".

We entered with Paul holding the door for me and walked down a long hallway to the main room. Seeing the club again in the daylight was surreal. It looked far less mysterious and intriguing with all the lights on. Looking around, I didn't see anyone and there was an eerie silence to the place which was normally so loud.

I wandered over to a table near the entrance and saw a backpack on the table. Someone was here, I just didn't know where.

"Where's the office, Paul?"

"Through that door," he said as he pointed across the room. "Up the stairs. Jack's here somewhere, that's his bag. I'll check in the back."

Paul entered another staff only door, then I heard him talking with someone. Presuming it wasn't Mick when he didn't emerge immediately, I headed upstairs.

The landing at the top led to three doors, none of them marked. Checking the first, it led to a small office with a cluttered desk. A poster of a Rottweiler dog hung on the wall, while a shelf had toy hula girls that bobbed as the air from the vent hit them.

Shutting the door, I went to the second one. Another office, but much larger, with only a small desk and several filing cabinets along the wall. The last office was far more polished and smelled of fresh paint. A leather sofa was against one wall with a coffee table. Two chairs with black leather seats sat in front of the largest desk I'd seen in a while.

I walked in and heard water running from a room to my left. The door was propped open slightly and I could see Mick, shirtless for some reason and washing his face. It made me pause for a moment wondering why.

"Hey," I called out to him.

He turned toward me, water dripping that made its way through the scruff on his chin down his neck and pecks. He looked surprised to see me and grabbed a towel to dab at the droplets.

"Hey, baby," he said as he opened the door wider. I could see a small square shower in the back that looked like it'd been recently used.

"Those aren't your sweats," I remarked indicating the jogging pants that hung off his hips. The curve of the band dipped in the middle to show the V of his muscles and the hairline to things much lower. I squeezed my thighs together under my skirt as I regarded him. How one man could look so good was beyond the laws of nature.

He sauntered out of the bathroom looking around the room. "Where's Paul?"

"He's downstairs. Went into the back to find Jack, I guess. Did you take a shower?"

"Yeah," he nodded. "Small mishap with lunch. Spilled my drink."

Giving him a small frown as he came closer, I inhaled the musky scent of him mixed with the soap he'd used.

"The shower must be convenient up here I guess, although strange."

He shrugged, his eyes never leaving my face. "A perk I don't mind if it means I'm clean when you show up. What are you doing here?"

"I missed you and..."

His arms were around me and my face against his chest before I finished.

"Hmm, I missed you too. But I thought I told you to relax at home."

"Well, I just couldn't. I had to tell you something."

He took my face and tilted my chin up before his mouth descended on mine. The smooth texture of his lips warred with the rough kiss he was giving me. His tongue ran across my parted lips then dove in.

When his hand slid around my waist then down to my ass, I let out a small moan.

He leaned back only slightly to whisper my name before he was moving me backwards.

"Can it wait?" he asked.

I nodded, my news about my father fading in importance compared to the heated look in his eyes. I suspected that things would always be this way. He'd always come first, over whatever troubles plagued me.

Destination unknown, I let him guide me as I kept kissing his bottom lip. My teeth scraped against the side of his neck when my legs finally hit something solid.

"Mick," I whispered as my hand slipped down to the bulge between his hips.

"Shh," he said as he helped guide me down to the leather couch.

When I was finally sitting in front of him he stood back from me, gazing at my face. My hand wandered over his pants, fingers hooking the band and pulling down. The head of his engorged cock sprang free and the expression on his face changed from one of fascination to hunger in an instant.

I licked my lips as he shoved his pants down and stepped out of them. When he came closer to me he grabbed the base and squeezed slightly. My fingers slid over the soft skin where his hand held it in place. Squeezing him, I looked up to see him watching me closely. His eyebrow lifted almost in challenge as I leaned forward to take him in my mouth.

My eyes closed as he stretched my lips apart, very gently sliding into my wet mouth. I sucked at him, glancing up once to see his face had changed to one of both pleasure and pain. He didn't move as I pumped my mouth over him, sucking, licking, teasing the head.

The taste of him hit my tongue, salty and sweet, his scent filled my nose. He massaged the base of his dick where my mouth couldn't reach. His other hand grabbed my hair, knotting it up in his firm grip.

Groaning he began thrusting gently, in and out and a little further each time. When he hit the back of my throat, I struggled as I gagged, but he held me in place before he pulled back to do it again.

He grunted as he pulled out, still holding onto my hair.

"Alisa, get on your knees on the ground and turn around. Face the couch."

I slid off the couch, my knees encountering the small rug that was placed in front of the couch. I peered up at his face, wondering if I'd done something wrong.

His hand kept working the base of his cock as he watched me. His face was somewhat smug and pleased at the same time as I turned. It was Mick in control again just like the first time. It made me wet thinking about it today.

If he wanted to dominate me, needed to have control, I didn't mind. It was something that I knew with certainty I'd gain pleasure from if I complied.

I trusted him, loved him and wanted whatever part of him he could give me. I knew it wasn't everything, knew that he held back. I could have most of him, and for now it was enough.

He gently pushed my face onto the leather seat, taking hold of my hair again. He crouched behind me and his hand slid up my thigh until it reached the hem of my skirt. The cotton material slid over my skin as he pushed it over my hips. My ass rose up toward him, exposed as his hand ran over my panties then tugged them down forcefully.

"You want me inside you, beautiful?" he asked as he rubbed the head of his cock around my wet opening.

"Yes," I whimpered as he inched forward then retreated.

"Are you going to listen next time I tell you to stay home? Listen when I tell you to rest? You won't get this next time if you don't."

He drove into me suddenly and forcefully in one motion, causing me to cry out. My hands grabbed at the leather that provided nothing to hold on to.

He stretched me to the hilt and didn't move as he leaned over to kiss the back of my neck. His hand worked to move the cloth away from my shoulder as his mouth burned a path across my skin.

"Today wasn't a good day to surprise me with a visit, Alisa. I had some things to do that I didn't want you involved in here. I didn't want to see you while I was still angry about it."

I opened my mouth to ask what he was referring to, but any thoughts of protest were forgotten as he slid nearly completely out then slammed back into me.

My walls clenched around him with the movement, loving the control he had over my body. I needed more of him, wanted him to sink so far into me that he'd never leave.

His teeth skimmed across my neck before he spoke. "I was going to be gentle with you at home, show you how much I missed you. But right now, I need something else, something rough. Tell me to stop, Alisa."

I licked my lips, my breathing labored in anticipation and slight trepidation. In the madness of wanting him, full of need and the headiness of pleasure as he ground his hips against me, I didn't want to be anywhere but here.

"Mick, I'm yours," I breathed.

He growled against my ear as he started to move. One of his hands wrapped around my throat, squeezing gently. Not enough to make me panic, but enough to know my life was in his hands alone. His strong palm, long fingers, and grip could strangle me in an instant, but it felt good knowing he had that control either way.

His hips pummeled into me and the slap of his skin against mine echoed in the room. I moaned when he grabbed my hip to change the angle, the frenzy of his thrusts stretching me even more. I couldn't move as he held me in place. Taking me the way he wanted, meant my total surrender to him. It was what my mind and body wanted.

I moaned on each thrust as his rhythm increased. My slick and needy walls tightened around him, the tingling sensation in my belly slid south. His fingers roughly massaged my clit, and he let go of my throat, causing relief. I came suddenly, explosively, with such euphoria that I nearly passed out as I screamed his name. My body was no longer on the couch, no longer with Mick, but somewhere high and drunk on the ecstasy of his continued passion.

He'd been seduction incarnate from day one, the epitome of everything I didn't know I even wanted. His admitted obsession, and my curiosity brought us closer to a moment like this. Where nothing existed but him, the sounds he made, my pleasure in both giving and taking what we both needed.

I clenched around him again as he worked my clit with his fingers and let out a loud cry. He thrust into me faster, his hips pummeling me into the edge of the couch and causing a little bit of pain.

Then he roared as he buried himself to the hilt. He pulsated near the edge of my body's limit to accommodate his size. He didn't even try to pull out of me this time and I didn't want him to. His hot seed shot into me, his continued groans of pleasure washed over me. As his hand pulled at my hair and dug into the flesh of my hip, I shut my eyes and savored every inch of him.

Still thrusting, he leaned over and sucked at my neck, making his way to my ear.

"Tell me you want me, Alisa."

"I want you," I whispered.

He kissed me gently along my jaw. "Tell me you still love me, baby."

"I love you, Mick."

"You're mine, you're mine, you're mine," he whispered. "No matter what happens, you'll always be mine."

As he slid out of me, his hands wrapped around my waist and picked me up. He laid me down gently on the couch, running his hands over my body, adjusting my skirt and panties.

I gazed up at him and turned his face so he'd look at me. There was something like regret in his eyes as if he felt bad about what we'd just done. He kissed my palm and stood to put his pants back on, then kneeled beside me again.

Peppering my face with kisses, his fingers caressed the side of my cheek.

"I'm sorry."

"I'm not," I whispered as I watched his face.

He sighed with a heavy expression on his face. "Not about that."

I smiled up at him. "Then what are you sorry for?"

He hesitated for a minute, his eyes dropping from mine to land on the couch. As he debated on what he was going to say, I saw a myriad of emotions play havoc across his face. Pain, anger, guilt, determination.

"What is it?" I whispered. "What happened?"

His eyes snapped back to mine, boring into me, telling me without words that whatever it was he was going to say, he needed me to accept.

I leaned up and placed a gentle kiss on his lips before withdrawing.

"I killed a man today for a good reason. And it wasn't the first time I've killed someone."

CHAPTER SEVENTEEN

Mick

Her mouth opened, then shut. Blinking at me, as she tried to process what I'd admitted, I watched her face. She hadn't turned away, hadn't looked at me in disgust, only stared at me with those beautiful blue eyes of hers.

"Are you trying to push me away again?" she asked. "After what we just did, you're trying to scare me again?"

I pursed my lips, hesitant to repeat what I'd just admitted to her.

When she sat up she winced, but when I tried to help she pushed my hands away.

"I thought we were over this, Mick. I just thought…"

"Baby, listen to me."

She shook her head. "No, for once you're going to listen. The reason I came up here today was to tell you about a call I got from my dad."

My jaw tightened, and my anger started to rise again.

"He said the most awful things. He said I wasn't his biological daughter, and I think his brothers raped my mother. Then he said he'd hurt you if I didn't go home."

"What?" I hissed. "What the hell are you talking about?"

When her legs swung off the couch I tried to gently cage her in. She pushed at me, but I held tight to her hips. Her turbulent eyes wouldn't meet mine as they scanned the office.

"He's a powerful man and I thought I'd come and warn you. To be honest, I thought, maybe for a minute, of going back. I can't handle the thought of what he could do to you. And telling me this, Mick, I don't even know what to think."

"Stop—"

"No," she said, her angry eyes meeting mine. "I can only deal with so much hurt in one day. And although I absolutely hate him, and don't understand why any of them would even want me in that family to begin with, at least they don't try to scare me away. I'm already scared of them."

My hands squeezed her hips and drew her closer to me. The expression on her face was almost like the one she'd had in the car weeks ago. Hurt, sadness but with quiet acceptance. She looked exhausted, and what I'd just done with her in the office added another reason to feel guilty today. I should have shipped her home to sleep.

"I love you, Alisa. That's not what I'm doing."

Her eyebrows shot up. "Really? Telling me you killed someone is pretty high on my list of scary things I don't want to hear. It feels like you're pushing me again. And after what we just did…"

Grabbing her shoulders, I held her at arm's length in front of me. "Alisa, I killed the man that stabbed you."

She shook her head, tears forming in her eyes. "No, don't tell me that. It's not true."

"Look, you want me to tell you things, I am. I'm not the saint you want to see. I needed to tell you. I don't want you to wake up tomorrow and wonder who I really am. You're never going back to that family and I'll never give you up. But I thought maybe you should understand the choice you've made."

"You couldn't have. You're not like them."

My eyes narrowed at her as I stood up. She didn't believe me or didn't want to. She wanted the man that I could never be again. The man she'd never met, whose ideals and morals had walked a straight path through hell for most of my time at the FBI. She said she loved me, but I wondered some days if she knew what that meant.

What I'd done today, what we'd done, had crossed a line I never thought I'd see again. There was a difference between shooting someone like my partner, and torturing someone in the basement for answers.

Especially when the torture had involved breaking several bones, by using someone as a punching bag, causing massive internal bleeding. Not to mention, when I took a hammer to his hand when he refused to give up who'd hired him. We'd all beaten him until there was nothing left but a twitching man on the floor, still tied to the chair, that had splintered into pieces when my brother kicked it over. The anger had swallowed me, my mind welcoming it, and I'd savored my revenge. All the while, telling myself that in the end it was done to protect her, to find out who wanted her dead.

One word swam to my mind. *Corrupted.*

Something morally depraved or the state of being so.

In a single act, I'd become the same thing I'd despised and tried to resist. Events, either out of my control or manufactured by my own hand, had led to it, but I'd acted on it.

Turning to the idea of faulty justice, was a slow and measured campaign on the mind. The lines of morality became blurred. The justification for what I thought were flawed but noble deeds, didn't matter.

Whatever part of me that existed before crouching in an open field beside my partner next to a dead body, was gone. The man that was left, dreamt about those cases. Women that I couldn't save. Lives lost because I didn't see what I was supposed to.

Even though my mind couldn't let it go, I'd never regret what I'd done. My life, my choices had led to her. Both of us moving back here, a chance meeting in a bar. Her gentle nature to my turbulent one. The one woman that could bring me to my knees with a look and make me worship on her altar. She could break me or save me with a word.

It'd been her choice to be with me and now for both of us, it wasn't a choice at all. She wasn't weak. She was the siren to my soul, a broken one now, but the only person I'd ever consider loving.

She had a beautiful, strong spirit and to hear she'd felt unloved, abandoned by the people that should love her most, nearly gutted me. She'd just lumped me in with them in a way and that burned.

Not like *them*? Like her family? God, if she only knew the lines I was willing to cross. I needed her to understand who I really was, what she meant to me, but she also needed to know what it was truly going to take to fight against her family. This wasn't going to be an easy road. We were going to have to jump off a cliff together and hope for the best, but I wasn't sure if she could even handle the truth of it at this point.

The man she thought I was, didn't exist anymore. What remained, was a man obsessed with her, tangled up with her, willing to be shredded by her just for a glimpse of her devotion.

Walking over to the desk, I grabbed the shirt that Mason had brought me earlier and pulled it down over my bare chest. Snatching up the tumbler of whiskey, I tipped it back until I drained it. The burn of it sliding down my throat made me feel something physical rather than emotional. I needed those precious few minutes before I spoke to her again.

She was still sitting on the couch, staring at the wall when I glanced back at her.

There was a knock at the door before I could vocalize a response to her comment.

"Come in," I called out.

Paul's large figure filled the door. He glanced at Alisa before he looked at me. I knew I'd made the right choice in hiring him as her bodyguard when he shot me an angry glare. I deserved it for the sad expression on her face, the vacant look that I'd put there.

I'd told her the truth. I killed a man today. She was either grappling with that truth, or still thought I was pushing her away. Either way, she was bound to me like every cell in my body. I meant it when I told her that I'd never let her go.

"Can you take Alisa home? She needs to rest," I said in a flat voice as

I sat down behind the desk. Our talk could wait, she needed rest after her ordeal and my rough use of her body to shake my demons.

He nodded and offered his hand to Alisa when he made his way to the couch. Shaking, she took it, avoiding my eyes.

"Take her to the apartment, Paul. And I need you to look at the setup there since you'll be keeping her company."

Alisa sucked in a breath. "The apartment?"

I nodded. "Yeah."

Before she turned away completely, there was a small frown that passed across her face, confusion perhaps, but she didn't voice what was on her mind.

I wanted to hold her, wanted to spend the rest of the afternoon trapped in her arms with her giggling against my chest. I wanted to be the man that put a smile back on her face right now, but I needed some time to calm down.

She exited the room with Paul, and I ran my hands down my face in frustration.

Another knock sounded at the door and Mason strolled in.

"What happened?"

"I'm a jackass."

He shrugged and sat down in a chair in front of the desk. "You are, but why does Alisa look like you've just killed her favorite pet and danced in the blood?"

I pursed my lips and shook my head.

"Okay," he said as he scratched at the beard on his face. "Couple's fight. Fine."

"Paul's taking her to the loft. I told you about that weird room that was separate from the main apartment?"

"Yeah, some building code thing on that floor?"

"Right, it was part of the deal. Not something we'd use, but it has a separate kitchen and it's huge. If he still wants the job, he can set up easily in there when he's with her. He looked like he wanted to murder me in my sleep when he left, so I guess we'll see."

Mason snorted. "Oh, so it'll be like living with me again. Did you tell her?"

"About the apartment? No, I think telling her that she's moving in with me, finding out that her father isn't her father, and that I killed a man all in the same day might be a little too much."

He narrowed his eyes at me. "What the fuck? Okay. Wait, you told her?"

I nodded. "Yeah, Mason, I told her. I told her about some other things too. I don't want to lie to the woman that I want to be with for the rest of my life. If she finds out about it later, what then? She thinks I'm trying to push her away. If I'm not honest with her now, then I run the risk of her leaving over something I should have told her. She thinks I made it up, and short of dumping the body in front of her, she doesn't believe me. She needs to, though, because I'm not going to change at this point."

"Alex is going to kill you."

"I didn't mention the three other people that were in the room. Just me, I delivered the final blow."

"Mick, we all share that. It wasn't just you. All three of us went there today. And the fucker deserved it. No one touches that woman without consequences."

That excuse grated on my nerves for a moment. It was yet again another argument to justify what we'd done.

"What are we doing, Mason? We were in law enforcement. Our father is the Chief of Police. What the fuck are we doing?"

He rolled his eyes. "Well maybe he'll call you in on the case."

"Mason. Jesus."

He pinned me with a serious look. "What we're doing is fixing this city. If that takes killing every last one of their henchmen that comes after us or someone close to us, then they're going to have a lot of dead bodies on their doorsteps."

"You're the one that wanted me to stand down the day I wanted to shoot her father's hands off. You're the one that balked at it. And now what? You've suddenly changed your mind?"

He gestured toward the door angrily. "You want that guy out on bail and hunting down Alisa again in a week? That's how this works. Sometimes you have to commit a crime to fight crime. She's been through enough and they don't get to hurt her. She's family now. If he was as connected as he said he was when he was spitting up blood, then that's what the reality would have been."

"I heard him. The last part...I wonder how much he took for the job. I think he said she was worth a mint."

"Yeah I heard that. Worth a fortune dead? What about the father thing?"

Shaking my head, I sighed. "No idea, she said it when we were arguing. I should have asked, but I was angry. He insinuated that her mother was possibly raped by the brothers. It may have just been how she took it."

"Jesus," he said, looking horrified.

"The thing is, she has no idea that she's trading one shitty life for another with a man that literally can't go a day without being insane around her."

"It's better than feeling nothing. And don't try to tell me that's not where you were before she came along. You're my brother, always will be, but watching you burn yourself down was like watching you try to kill that too. Whatever you did, fix it and if you can't, I don't give a fuck, do it anyway. Her life with you means I have a life with you."

I groaned and ran my hand over my jaw. "Have you ever loved something so much that you couldn't give it up? But you knew there would be a day that you might tarnish what you loved? That's how things have been for me."

"Figure it out, man. Before she decides you're not worth it. Right now, she thinks you are, and something like that doesn't come along every day."

Eyeing him, I nodded without comment and changed the subject. "How's Alex?"

He knew what I meant when he gave me a shrug. Of all the people in that room, Alex was the least likely to take what we'd done well. He hadn't shown an aversion to it, but it didn't mean when he got home and crawled in bed tonight that he'd be happy with it.

"He'll be fine, I don't think you give him enough credit. Or maybe you do, and you can't see that he's just as bought into this as we are."

"I think he's going to crack."

"You're not the only one that owns a share of anger issues, Mick."

I withheld my opinion on it. "The body? Clothes?"

"Jack and I will take care of it later. You sure you want to do this?"

Giving a brief nod, I said, "It's too late to change direction now."

I pulled out some paperwork. Talking about bodies just made me think about a past I knew I couldn't go back to and haunted me nightly. There was a deep yearning in me to leave. To go to Alisa and kiss away whatever hurt I'd inflicted today.

"I found some discrepancies with some of the receipts. Things that would be questionable if we were ever investigated. Granted, they're not our mistakes, but we're about to adopt them."

Mason leaned forward to look at the invoice I laid in front of him. He frowned at it for a moment then picked it up.

"So, we're paying for liquor from a local distributor?"

"Distributor would be a nice word. It's a family run business. If he'd gotten caught they would've taken his liquor license. And by the look of it, he was paying them half of what the shipments were worth. I was going to ask Holly tomorrow, but…"

He tapped the sheet and looked like he was considering something. "Let me look into this. Don't stop the shipments yet, though. I think I know what's happening with this family. Long story, but I think they're one of the businesses here locally that the King fuckers on the force were extorting money from."

"Why would they do that?"

"You're seriously asking me that? They're the King family. They do this to half the city, and if I remember correctly, for some reason they came down on these people pretty hard last year. I'll deal with it."

I waved it off, as I grabbed my keys from the edge of the table and eyed them. They'd been an instrument of torture when I'd slammed them into the fucker's face earlier. I'd gotten the blood off them more than an hour ago, but they still looked dirty to me. They always would now. Grabbing my laptop, I headed to the door.

"I'm headed to the apartment," I said over my shoulder as I left.

As I drove, I tried to wipe away the events of the day. The ugly feelings that still churned in my chest about everything. It shed from me, piece by piece, as I drove through the darkening city streets. A light drizzle of rain came down, washing over the windshield. City lights came on bathing the sidewalks in a faint amber glow.

Twenty minutes later, I was there. As I drove by the four-story building, in the heart of the city that I'd started renting the week prior, I wondered what her face might have looked like had I brought her here in different circumstances. Together, as a surprise. Whether she would have been happy.

While she'd been at work, I'd been busy. It didn't take long to find something that suited what I thought she might like. Four bedrooms, open layout and very close to her brother's office. I'd had my furniture removed from storage, bought a few more things I hoped she liked.

It was assumptive on my part to think she might want to live with me for a while. I'd been hoping that maybe she'd choose to on her own given enough time. We couldn't continue to live with Mason, regardless, and I wouldn't let her live with another King, including her brother. On her own, in the apartment she'd rented, I would have worried, would have spent restless nights likely camped out in front of the complex. I'd had Alex's secretary bring her things here instead, telling her that it was what Alisa was insisting and rather than talking to her brother about it, needed her to do it privately. I told Alex while she was in the hospital and hoped that she'd stay.

When I parked beside Paul's vehicle in the garage, I thought of her upstairs exploring the place. I needed her and yet, I hesitated. As much as she said I scared her, she terrified me.

I chuckled and turned off the car. She'd probably tell me to fuck off if I told her that. That was, if she was still talking to me.

Entering the building I looked for the doorman but didn't see him. He was nice, and supposedly part of the security feature of living in the building. I doubted the truth in that, given the dopey eyed look he gave me when I'd met him.

When the realtor had shown me the area and property, she'd mentioned several times that the balding, middle-aged man, named Bill, was a deterrent against unwelcome guests. Unknown to the realtor,

I did my own background search on Bill before I put any money down. Nothing. Bill was clean. He still wasn't much of a threat though, and clearly, "guarding" four lofts, was too much for him if he couldn't stay at the desk to watch the front entrance.

Taking the elevator up to the fourth floor, it opened to a long hallway that led to our apartment, and a bit further down the hall there was a door to Paul's studio apartment, if he wanted the job long term after today.

I grabbed my phone out of my pocket when it began buzzing. Mason calling.

Frowning I answered. "Hello?"

"Hey, heads up, we're clean, headed to a place Jack knows minus his right hand. We'll dump that on daddy's car on our way back."

"Careful," I replied while eyeing my door.

I noticed a scuff mark on the wood. I regarded it before I tried the handle. It was unlocked. Something I'd have to talk with Paul about. With a lazy employee downstairs and no specified codes on the elevator, it was a security risk. Something I'd be bringing up with management soon enough.

Stepping into the house, it took a moment to process the scene in front of me. The once inlaid glass on my entry table laid scattered in pieces on the wood floor.

"Mason," I said.

"Yeah?"

I scanned the living room, setting my bag down quietly. There was groaning coming from my right. When I stepped into the kitchen, I saw Paul laying on the floor. Blood coated his shirt over his shoulder. I rushed to him, crouching down to look. He'd been shot, but hadn't been killed, a minor wound as shots went. His head turned to the side as he let out another moan, likely from the welt on the side of his head.

"Alisa..." I started to ask, before I heard something further into the apartment. A banging sound like a rubber mallet on a wall.

"Come here. Emergency, Paul's down but breathing," I said as quietly as I could then set the phone down on Paul's chest.

Grabbing a knife from the holder on the counter, I cautiously made my way toward the sound. When I rounded the corner to the hallway that led to the master suite my eyes fell on Bill's unmoving body.

Then I heard it, a muffled sound and water splashing.

Running down the hall, I checked the bedroom quickly, an open suitcase lay on the bed with clothes strewn on the floor. Another pounding sound to my left and I barreled through the bathroom door.

A man, dressed in black, with shoulder holsters, was bent over the bathtub. A small hand flailed against the side in desperation and a leg kicked out. He was holding her down in the water, drowning her as she struggled against him.

In a rage I tackled him, knocking him down to the floor. He cried out then tried to flip over to face me.

Alisa's body came out of the water in a rush, her face red, gasping for air. She was coughing, spitting up water and crawling out of the water as fast as she could. When she hit the floor she scrambled away, her naked body slick with water, skidding across the tile as she tried to escape.

I flipped the man under me, as I snaked my arm around his face. He threw his head back connecting with my jaw. Twisting him again, I wrapped my legs around his like vice grips, preventing him from moving any further.

Alisa sobbed in the corner, knees curled up as she looked on in horror.

The knife I'd brought with me had fallen to the ground inches from us. I grabbed it as the man started to once again, twist out of my grasp.

Every muscle strained as I held him in place. Everything in me felt molten hot with anger that I couldn't control. He'd tried to murder her in the bathtub. Tried to drown her for me to find no doubt. In the unclothed state she was in, I had no idea what damage he'd done before he'd attempted it.

Rage filled me before I brought the knife to his neck and cut so deeply that the arterial spray hit the floor, my clothing and dripped down my arm as I held him. He struggled, making gurgling sounds as he tried to breathe through his open windpipe. I roared my anger into the tiled room as he jerked against me, roared from the adrenaline, and Alisa's terrified face.

Only her sobbing reached me as I felt the intruder go limp against me. Only her tears tamed the ugliness that overwhelmed me.

"Alisa," I whispered as her beautiful blue eyes met mine.

CHAPTER EIGHTEEN

Alisa

I SHIVERED, my body wracked with terror at what had just happened. Crouched in the corner, as the man that had tried to drown me had his neck split open by the man I loved. I cried, convulsing with shock as Mick's roar of anger filled my ears.

When he looked up at me, for the first time I saw the depths of what he'd warned me about. The thing that Paul said he saw, the thing that Mason knew, slithered behind his raging black eyes.

This man, the man I loved with everything in me, was wild with something I'd never seen. He was showing me, what it meant to be loved by him, what I could never in my life define before now. He wasn't evil, even now, covered in my brutal attacker's blood, but he was, to the depths of his core, willing to skirt along those edges to protect me. He could have taken another course, but as I looked at him, I knew if he'd let the man in his arms live, Mick's demons would have haunted him.

Catching the guy, turning him in like he should have, would have rankled and soured with his inability to mete out justice in his own way. He killed for me, because of me, and maybe a little bit for himself, so that he could sleep at night knowing that he'd done all he could to remove any threat.

It was so wrong in so many ways to take the man's life. Everything about this screamed that, as much as I feared my father and family, he was equally capable of the same cruelty. Instead of being turned toward me and taken out on me, though, it was for me. To protect me. I didn't know if that made it better or worse to see it as acceptable. Or if I was just as fucked up as he was for seeing the sanity behind his insane actions.

I saw the truth of him now. There was no denying it when he whispered my name. He worshipped some part of me, called out to me, needed me in a way that would be impossible for him to let go. I was his and he was mine. It might have been twisted to think that way, but I couldn't help being drawn into his soul as he gazed at me.

He dumped the body to the side like a ragdoll and crawled to me across the blood streaked floor. His eyes examined my huddled form as he got closer. He ripped the now blood-soaked shirt he'd been wearing off his chest and tossed it aside. His arms were covered in the crimson liquid of a man's now extinguished life.

Maybe he saw my involuntary flinch as he tried to touch me, or something registered in his mind. He looked down at his hands and sneered as he stood up, turned then plunged his arms into the clear bath water. He washed, then washed again, slopping water on the floor. The soap turned red and he furiously cleaned himself, his arms turning the same color as he scrubbed himself raw. He bent his head at last and stopped, breathing heavily when he did.

"Mick," I whispered.

His eyes met mine again with a tortured look.

"Did he hurt you? Before he tried to drown you? Did he..."

I was confused about what he was asking, and my lack of response had his anger returning.

"Did. He. Do. Anything?" he growled.

I shook my head, understanding dawning on me at last. He meant had he assaulted me. Lucky for me, it hadn't been his intent. "No, I was already in the bath. He just shoved me under the water."

"Thank fuck. God, I'm sorry, Alisa. I'm so sorry, baby. I had to do it and now I can't touch you. I had to. Fuck. He tried to kill you. I can't live without you and now I can't touch you."

"I need you," I whispered as I began sobbing again. "Please, Mick."

I could see the debate slide over his face. "I'm a monster, baby. How can you want these hands on you? I'll ruin you."

I uncurled from my position, watching him as I inched across the floor.

"Mick, I love you."

His eyes swung up to mine and he hissed as he put out his hands for me to stop.

"Baby, you're going to get blood on you. Please."

I reached out and he flinched as my hand landed on his arm. One touch, my touch and he was wrapping me up in his arms, carrying me away from the scene in the bathroom.

Shuddering as he walked to another room, he set me down in the bottom of a shower. He turned the water on, letting the warmth of it spray over me before he crawled in with me, still clothed in his sweats and shoes.

He lay there against me, holding me, lips caressing my face and repeating his apologies. When I began to cry, he let out a muffled grunt and pulled me into his lap as his chest began to shake with his own sorrow.

My arms wrapped around his neck as he cradled me. When I looked up, his face wore a mask of pain as he let me see his sadness. He stroked my face wiping droplets of water and tears from my cheeks and I returned the gesture.

"I don't know what I'd do without you. I can't imagine what I would have done if he'd killed you, if he'd touched you. I'm so sorry."

Nodding, I laid my head against his neck as he stroked my back. My fingers skimmed down the side of his neck in comfort for both of us.

After a few minutes, we heard someone yelling in the loft.

"Mick!" Mason called as his voice got closer.

He stumbled into the bathroom, took one look at my nude body in Mick's arms and turned away to stare into the bedroom.

Mick's arms tightened around me, then he reached up to shut off the water.

With his back to us Mason asked, "Okay?"

"Yeah," Mick grunted, his arms still holding me against his chest. "Check the other bathroom. How's Paul?"

"A graze on his shoulder. Jack has him. Says he got hit with something after the guy shot at him and lunged. Says there were two of them."

"Bill maybe? Doorman?"

"I'll have Paul confirm. Sounds right, but why would the other guy kill him?"

"Witnesses. I need to get her out of here. Guy in the room tried to drown her."

"Fucking shit!" Mason yelled as he stalked out of the room. We heard him lumber through the hallway as Mick picked me up and carried me to the guest bed. He wrapped me up in the comforter and stripped down, throwing his soaked clothing on the floor of the bathroom before he too walked down the hall completely nude.

I laid there for a minute listening to a muffled conversation, trying to process the events of the last hour.

I'd been both furious and hurt when Paul had escorted me out of the office earlier. Livid over the assumption that he was driving me to the apartment that Alex helped me with. Coldly dismissed based on my words to him. I was harsh, blunt, but truthful in what I told him.

Thinking that he was pulling out a huge, terrible lie to make me run, I'd overreacted, but with good reason. I'd assumed he was just playing one last card. And after the rough sex we'd shared in his office, it stung. One last fuck before he delivered the final push. I'd felt used in the most awful way.

Then we arrived at this place. Furnished and clean, smelling faintly of fresh paint, with items that I liked arranged on countertops. His boxes along the wall in the bedroom, my clothing in the closet. Yet I'd been pissed, so miserable, I'd started packing a bag to leave for Alex's house. But I'd wanted a bath and some time to think first. Screw the stiches. I needed some solitude and I knew he wouldn't be home anytime soon.

As I lay there in the warm water, I heard a crash, then yelling. Two loud sounds and then the man had barged in and went straight for me. I'd had no time to think, no time to react. I screamed and fought, thinking of only one thing. Mick.

Shuddering, I pushed the memory aside, Mick had gotten there in time. But what he'd had to do...

Jack's tall frame walked past the door. He turned toward me, his face so closed down that he barely registered any reaction. I'd met him a few times and his expression was always the same. He was like Mick sometimes. Cold, but I could tell there was something behind his strangely sad eyes.

Mick walked in and shut the door behind him, dressed in a pair of jeans and a tight black shirt that hugged his muscles. I blinked up at him as he came to rest on the side of the bed.

"Hey, baby, sorry to leave you alone. I brought some clothes for you. I wasn't sure what you wanted to wear so I took them out of your suitcase."

He helped me sit up and slid the blanket off my shoulders. His hand caressed the side of my arm before he started handing me things.

I dressed stiffly as he watched my movements, repetitively glancing back at my face. When I finished, I sat back down beside him in my knee length skirt and blouse.

He sighed and ran a hand down his face. His eyes avoided mine as several emotions rolled across his face.

"Do you want to go to Alex's house? I don't want you to, but right now I can't think. If you want to go, I'll take you. Or I know some people, they live south of here. You'd be safe. Your choice."

"No," I replied, reaching for his hand. "I want to stay with you."

His eyes met mine before he looked down at our linked hands.

"You'll have to talk with some detectives about what happened. With Bill being an employee of the realtor and the cameras, we can't hide this. I don't know what you want to tell them, but we're doing something here that will make you an accessory to a crime if you stay. Fuck."

"What are you doing?" I said as I squeezed his hand.

His eyes briefly slid to mine then darted away.

My hand reached out to his jaw and turned his face toward me. "Mick, I told you. I love you no matter what. I just didn't know what that meant when I said it."

He held my hand to his lips as he placed a kiss in my palm. He pulled it gently away and stood up pacing toward the bathroom.

"Well, you do now," he said with his back turned toward me. "I don't want you to go but..."

His voice trailed off and I prodded. "Talk to me, Mick. But what? I'm trying. What happened...I don't care. I mean I do and I don't. But the thing is, I'm not thinking about that guy in the other room, and that should make me a monster too. The person I'm thinking about is you."

"I'd never give you up, Alisa. Not in my heart. You'd always be there. But things have gotten complicated. You see what I'm capable of. How can you love that? How can I let you? It's been the main debate in my head since the first time I saw you. You're such a beautiful person and I never wanted any of that part of me to touch even one inch of you."

I let out a mirthless laugh. "Well I've seen it now. The other thing I saw? You. And the thing is, what I saw, wasn't terrifying in the way that you think."

He stalked back to me, dropped to his knees and embraced me with his head in my lap. My hands ran gently through his hair, pushing the thick, dark locks away from his face.

"What did you see?" he whispered.

"The very edge of what you could be versus what you are. I didn't see some things before. What you did...it was for the right reason, no matter what twisted origin it came from. I saw you. I know you struggle with doing the right thing, while doing something that seems so wrong."

"I'm as corrupted as your family, Alisa. I'm not clean."

My hand ran down the back of his neck as he buried his face against my leg.

"Why would you say that?"

"I killed my partner on a case," he mumbled. "I won't go into details, but he was responsible for the death of four women by the time I ended him. He'd been my friend and so was his accomplice. I shot his friend, then put a bullet through his head out of anger. I should have arrested him. Had the ability to, and I was close enough to take him down, wound him at the very least. But I put a bullet in his brain. Then I lied about it."

I frowned, unsure of what to say.

"I stood by his family, held the hand of his little boy at the funeral, wondering what would have happened had I only arrested him. There was an inquiry, they cleared me. But it was a lie. I killed him, no regret. And the thing is, the really fucked up thing, was that I didn't do it because he was reaching for his weapon. I didn't even do it because of his victims. I was just so tired of seeing that kind of evil in the world. And now look at me."

I slid onto the floor with him, straddling his hips and held him. "You're not evil, Mick. You didn't do it out of compulsion. You did it for me, and there's a part of me that wanted you to. So, I'm just as evil."

"No," he whispered as his arms held me tightly against him. "No. You're my life, there's not a cruel bone in your body."

"I'm a King, Mick. It's written into my genetics that I'm something different. Maybe not cruel, maybe not evil. But my darkness sees yours and I'm not afraid."

His hands grasped both sides of my face as he gazed down at me. Time was suspended for both of us as we explored the depths of each other's eyes.

"I know," I said to his unspoken words. "You love me. What do you want me to say to your dad? Or the police?"

"What do you want to say? I'll do whatever you want me to do, Alisa, even if you want to send me to jail, I'll do it."

I sighed, knowing he meant every word of it. He wasn't a man that dealt in grey half-truths most of the time.

I could send him to jail, tell him to fuck off, and sign a movie deal about it. And he'd do it for me. Oddly, it made me feel powerful. As a person who'd had no power over the course of my lifetime, the feeling was heady. I appreciated every bit of what he was giving me, and might use it to my advantage at some point if we were in an argument someday. But not for this. I'd never take the one person out of my life that gave me that sort of gift.

"No, Mick," I whispered. "I want to be with you. Just tell me what to say."

He chewed his lip. "Two men broke in. They assaulted Paul, and in the scuffle, one shot the other. One fled, Bill died. Do not mention a dead man in the bathroom. He fled."

My mouth opened then shut again, hesitant to agree outright and trying to think of a different way. "He tried to kill us, Mick. Couldn't I just tell them that they broke in and tried to murder both of us?"

He shook his head. "If they find that body in the bathroom, they'll know it was me. Fibers, hair, the force of my cut. They'll know. More importantly, I want whoever is behind this wondering where his hitman disappeared to."

I nodded. "What about the body? Won't there be evidence anyway?"

He smirked. "There's always some evidence. Two ex-law enforcement officers and a retired FBI agent? Believe me, we can handle it, but why would we lie? And you're a King, why would you?"

My eyebrows shot up. "For once my name is convenient."

He nodded, looking at me softly. "When this is done, Alisa, I want you to be a Galloway. Not a King."

It was my turn to smirk. "It'll never be done, Mick. Better just set a date."

His lips pursed before he spoke again, letting my remark hang between us. "Is that a yes?"

I nodded, giving him a small smile.

His lips crushed mine in a rough kiss. His tongue slid in when I opened to him and he slanted his mouth over mine. It was a deep kiss, the type that lingered and wasn't hurried. It seemed like one of possession and affirmation that he was more than happy with my answer and better still that I'd accepted who he was.

"Tomorrow," he whispered against my lips. "Right now."

"Mick, go do what you need to do. I'm tired and I have a feeling that the day isn't quite over yet."

He grimaced and touched his forehead to mine. "I have no idea why you're still here."

"You know. Hurry."

He nodded and slid me off his lap. I sat on the edge of the bed as he turned toward the door.

"Alisa?" he said as his hand landed on the doorknob. "We'll have to go someplace for a few days while they go over the evidence. But do you want to keep living here? Were you happy when you walked in?"

"No, I was pissed at you. But I do like it. We can talk about it later."

He nodded. "I'll pack a few things for you. Just don't leave the room."

I wasn't going anywhere. The last thing I wanted to see, or know, or hear about was how to get rid of a dead body and a few pints of blood.

CHAPTER NINETEEN

Mick

I PINCHED the top of my nose as I sat with Mason and Holly going over the receipts and expenses.

"Look, it's not rocket science," Holly said. "The reason why we're saving money is the back-alley deals Randy made. The question is, are you going to keep those deals?"

Mason looked up at me from the three invoices we'd been talking about for the last hour. Any other time I might have been interested in discussing it as a distraction, but my eyes kept drifting to the couch and thinking of Alisa. She was due back any minute and I was in a mood.

Three weeks had passed since the police were called to our house for a report of a home invasion. Fortunately, Bill the bumbling killer had done us a favor by turning all the cameras off in the building before he'd led his accomplice upstairs to kill Alisa. One item that we hadn't had to worry about. All the "evidence" pointed to a burglary gone wrong and with Alisa's sterling name and statement, it'd been the shortest investigation I'd ever seen.

It also helped that our father showed up, took one look at Mason and me, and sped things along. He knew. I could tell from his expression that by some sort of cosmic magic, he recognized when his sons were lying. It was a strange phenomenon I assumed, that nature had given parents the ability to see through their offspring's attempts at deceit.

He could tell since the day we were born when we attempted it. And if I had a guess, he was the one that stood between an actual investigation and our freedom. I didn't understand him, didn't particularly like him, but I had to admit that he might have done us the world's biggest favor. It still put a bad taste in my mouth when I thought about it. Mason said he was clean, didn't take bribes, fine. One part of me wanted to tell him that I wouldn't have let us go as easily, just to be a dick, but the other part felt indebted and relieved. Either way, I still didn't like him.

"We'll keep the deals," Mason replied as he handed Holly back her precious paperwork. She stuck it in a color-coded folder that would go back in her color-coded file cabinet that Mason and I had yet to figure out.

"We need to pay the Andersons more for their shipments. We can't just keep paying them bare minimum. One of these days, if they get upset enough, they could turn us in."

"You know they wouldn't do that, Mick."

I gave Mason a flat look. "Do I? I've met them, they're nice. But from what you tell me, the King family has been pressuring them for more money. If we tell those two idiots that come around that they're working with us as a main source of liquor, do you think they'll back off or pressure them more? How long do you think it'll take for the Andersons to flip if they were threatened? Pay them more."

Holly rolled her lips between her teeth and tried to look distracted.

"You disagree?"

Her eyes snapped to mine. "No, I completely agree. Randy was a douchebag, you guys aren't. Tried to tell him that a year ago. I know it's illegal, but it just seems like the right thing to do. They're happy with what they have right now, you pay them more, they'll be loyal."

"Okay, settled. Agreed?" I asked between Mason and Holly. They both gave me a nod.

"I think we're agreed on everything else," I said as I glanced at Holly. "But I need you to tell me about the two brothers working on staff. Are we going to have any trouble with their extended family or them?"

"Ben and Eli?" she asked. "Not that I know of."

"Mason?"

He shook his head. "They're fine. Jack said the gang canvases this neighborhood and Randy apparently bought protection by employing them. Their brother wanted to see them do something other than work the streets, I guess. Jack said they were clean as far as gangs go, but mean as hell about their territory. They have family here."

"Hmm," I said as I tapped my chin.

"What are you thinking?" Mason asked.

"Holly, did you say we were over in budget on bouncers?"

She flipped open a green folder and pulled out a sheet. "Yeah, we've got too many, most of them are looking for more time. Rotations are good, but we'll lose a couple if that doesn't loosen up."

"Tell Ben and Eli I'd like to personally hire them for some work."

"What?"

"I'd like them to work with Paul. He's got a life, and he's going to burn out if he's on constant security."

"He loves that woman," Mason mumbled.

"I realize that everyone loves my fiancé, but he needs a break from time to time. And frankly, I think we both need some protection too."

Mason shook his head. "No way, I don't need a bouncer driving me to the club."

"Didn't say that. You can drive yourself to the club. But if you get in a pinch one of these days and Jack is having an off day, then you can call Ben and about fifty of his posse will show up. Understand?"

"Are we taking over a gang now?"

"Didn't say that," I responded again. "I don't know what they're into and don't want to know. We give Ben and Eli a boost up, though, better wages, and maybe their brother would consider it a sign of deep respect and gratitude. They work for us, and if the need ever arose, I'm sure they could call in a favor."

"Paul takes care of them?"

"Yeah, he'll give them plenty of work, so will I. I'd like that to start tomorrow, Holly. I want Eli posted in front of the entrance to this office downstairs. No one gets up unless he clears it. Obviously a few people with priority status. Make a list."

"You gonna put them on Alisa?" he asked.

"I'm going to get to know them first. So are you. Take Ben everywhere for a while. Do we have any tech for them? Earpieces, phones and whatnot?"

"I know someone who does," Alex said as he strolled across the office.

"Holly, make sure Alex isn't on the list," I said as I eyed her notes. She scrunched up her face at me and didn't write it down.

"Tech gear?" I asked as I rubbed my temple and looked at Alex.

"Reid," he said as he watched Holly stand nervously, gathering her folders. "Sit back down, Holly. I don't need the seat."

"Uhm, no, I'll just be going," she said as she gave me a tight smile. "I've got your lists and they'll be in my office. Don't fuck with my lists, gentlemen, I'll murder you both if you go in there again. You need something just ask. Let me know about this Reid guy. Do you want me to call him?"

"No," Alex answered quickly. "I'll call him. He's not a great person."

"Oh," she said with her eyebrows raised, backing out of the office. "Okay."

I frowned at her retreating back once she made it to the door. She shut it behind her with some force.

Mason and I turned to Alex. "What was that about?"

He shrugged and slid into her seat.

"Are you fucking her?" Mason asked as he leaned toward Alex.

"No. I have no idea what that was about. I have a girlfriend."

"I want to fuck her. Think she'd say yes?"

I rolled my eyes. Mason didn't want to do anything of the sort. He and Holly fought like siblings with absolutely no attraction to each other.

Alex's jaw clenched for a moment. "Do whatever you want, Mason, it's none of my business. Heather and I have been dating for a few months so I'm not on the market."

Thinking of Heather made me cringe. Alex was backed against a wall by his father with that one. According to Alisa, she'd been up to the office a couple of times this week and I wondered if Alex's plan to ignore her as much as possible was truly working or backfiring. He was attracted to Holly, there wasn't a doubt in my mind about it, but Alex would play their game if it meant flying under the radar with his family. It made me feel sorry for him in a way, but he made his own bed and it wasn't my problem.

Alex threw Mason one last look before turning to me. "Reid has your tech, Mick. He sells a lot of it, it's how he made his money."

"Cameras in alleys?"

He nodded. "Yeah. Something like that. I need your help," he told me, changing the subject.

"What's that?"

"Alisa and I had a talk about my mother. I'm assuming you know about the conversation she had. She and I both want her out of that house and put into rehab. Might be a bit tricky since she has to be willing, but at this point we wanted to offer it to her."

"She didn't say anything about it."

He shrugged. "We had a talk at work yesterday and she was going to give it some thought. Regardless, I'd like to move ahead anyway."

"Okay, so what can I do? I don't see how I can help."

"I'd like you to go over there with me."

Mason whistled. "That's going to go over well. You remember the "I'll shoot his hands off" conversation, right?"

Alex frowned. "I realize it won't be the most comfortable situation, however, I also think it would be a good opportunity for Mick to draw a line for my father. Spell it out in plain terms that he needs to leave Alisa alone, or face a united front from his son as well."

I smirked. "Sure you want to do that? He'll probably disown you."

"He won't. I'm his only heir if nothing else. He won't want the fallout."

"I'm not there to get his approval. And to be honest, I'm not sure I can keep my temper in check. Although we can't prove it, he's the most likely person pulling the strings on these threats against Alisa."

Alex nodded. "I thought that too, but why would he want her home under his roof, ripe for marriage, if he wanted her dead?"

"The mentality of a madman."

"You'd know more about that then I would. I'm asking, your choice but I thought you should know that Alisa was also concerned about it. Neither of us hold much affection for her, but she's been through enough and neither of us want her to suffer any more than she already has. He may not even be there."

Alisa walked in chattering with Holly and I sat up straighter. She was beautiful in her pencil skirt and blue blouse that matched her eyes. Something I thought every day when I got home or saw her after more than a few minutes. Days like today when we'd both been at work were torturous for me. I craved her company.

I glanced at Alex, annoyed that his errand made sense and even more annoyed that I wouldn't be able to repeat an office interlude with Alisa, unless we kicked everyone out and made it quick.

I smirked at the image that played out in my mind.

Standing as she made her way around my desk, I kissed her quickly making her smile.

"Hey," she said. "Uhm, can I cancel lunch? For now? Holly and I want to stop by the mall really quick."

Frowning, I studied Holly, who looked like a child with the pleading smile on her face. They were about the same age, and Alisa didn't have any friends, so it wasn't completely surprising that they'd be drawn to each other. I didn't know about Holly's personal life, but if the amount of time spent at work was any clue, I'd assume she didn't have many friends either.

"Sure, baby. But no blue hair. Or any other color hair. I like your hair. I'm headed out with your brother anyway."

The smile she gave me was worth skipping the plans I had for her on the couch. I always had later.

She eyed Alex, who was in deep but quiet conversation across the room with Mason. He looked pissed and I could only guess at the subject.

"Oh, my mom?" she asked as she looked down.

My finger slid under her chin tipping it up until I could look at those blue eyes of hers.

"You know you could have told me. I would have listened."

"It's just embarrassing, and I needed to think about it."

"Okay. Just make sure you clue me in, even if it's just thinking about it. I hate to find out your brother knows something I don't."

She rolled her eyes and whispered, "Go with Alex, don't be an asshole, and try not to hurt anyone."

"Is that an order?" I asked, winking at her.

"Yes," she responded. With a smile, she walked away with Holly and Paul following.

Shaking my head, I grabbed my keys. "Let's go, Alex. I have things to do and I'm assuming you do too. Is there a plan here?"

He gave Mason one last dirty look and led the way to the cars. "We'll see if my mother is there. If she is, then I'll offer to take her today. Easy. If she doesn't want to go then not so easy. My father may still be at the office. If he is, then we'll wait. If not, then we need to go ahead and have this talk."

I looked down at my clothing, wondering why I gave a damn what I showed up in. Slacks and a dress shirt today, no tie. Nothing fancy, but I thought it might set a standard at the club if the boss didn't look like he just rolled out of bed every day. It was a business and we were slowly changing it.

We rode in Alex's BMW to the nice part of Kingston, where golf courses and designer shops were far more prevalent. It was such a contrast to where'd we just been.

When we pulled up in front of a two-story, colonial home that looked like it could house half the state in sheer size, I shook my head. Alisa's life, although shitty growing up in this hellish home, had been extremely different than the four-bedroom loft in a renovated industrial building overlooking downtown that we were now living in. I wondered if she would have preferred something a little more traditional.

Alex didn't bother knocking as he entered the house. The door was unlocked indicating that at least one person was home. He made his was through a formal sitting room and down a long hallway toward the back of the house as I followed.

Glancing around what appeared to be a sunroom, he frowned. "She might be upstairs, give me a moment."

I strolled into the sunroom and gazed out onto the sprawling lawn and trees. It was peaceful for anyone who spent time in here. I could see the draw to it.

A door slammed somewhere in the house and made me flinch. There were a couple of muffled noises then nothing.

Alex approached me after a few minutes and shook his head. "Not here. She may be at the spa. Was worth a shot, I'll go by there after I drop you off. Did you slam the door a moment ago?"

"No, I thought it was you," I said as I glanced down the hall.

He frowned as I followed him toward the front of the house. The closer we got, the more noises we heard. The sound of a woman letting out several high-pitched squeals, reached our ears before we heard another voice.

"Oh, fuck," the man's deep voice flowed out from behind a door that was partially open by a few inches. "All of it. I know you want all of it."

My eyebrows shot up as I looked at Alex. His face was a contorted mask of fury.

There were a few more groans before everything ceased, then the man spoke again. "Get the fuck out of here. Come back tomorrow."

The distinct sound of heels clicking on the wood floor approached the door. When it opened, a very disheveled looking Heather was adjusting her skirt and scowling.

She froze as soon as she saw us. A look of surprise and panic slid across her face before she plastered on a forced smile.

"Alex! Wow, I didn't expect to—"

"I bet you didn't. Get the fuck out, like he said," Alex growled as he pushed past her to enter what looked like an office.

He glanced over his shoulder at her and sneered. "By the way, Heather, we're not dating anymore. Don't fucking come near me again or you'll regret it."

Heather's face fell, then she turned to me with a leering glance. I shifted away as she passed me and ambled to the entrance of the room. Leaning against the door frame, I crossed my hands over my chest and took in the scene.

Denny was zipping up his fly, and shooting Alex a hellish look from behind his huge mahogany desk. Two couches were on either side of the room and one chair sat in front. Hundreds of books lined the walls. The most interesting thing I noticed was a sculptured bust of the man himself, sitting on a pillar in the corner, in front of a painting of the same subject. He was an extremely vain man.

"What the fuck was that about? You're fucking my girlfriend now?" Alex asked in a disgusted tone. "If you wanted to do that, then I wouldn't have dated her in the first place."

Denny smirked, barely taking any notice of me. "Yeah, son. I've been doing her for a while now. I'm getting done what you won't."

"What's that exactly?"

"Getting her pregnant. Then you're going to marry the bitch."

Alex's face was a mask of shock as his mouth dropped open. "What the fuck? I'm not marrying Heather, you sick bastard."

Denny smiled and sank down into his office chair. The resemblance between father and son was unmistakable. Dark, almost black hair, strong jaw, patrician nose. They both had a wide chest and broad frame. The difference was age alone, and Denny hadn't aged well.

He took out a box of cigars selected one, snipped it and lit it before he looked back up.

"When that whore announces to her family that she's pregnant you're going to do the right thing, Alex. If you don't, you'll be ostracized as a deadbeat and user in our circles. No family worth anything in this town will even look at you or come near you again. It's politics, son."

"Holy shit, you're fucked up. When Alisa told me you'd taken a belt to her, that was enough, but this is just fucking off the charts insane. Let them think what they want. I'll demand a paternity test and go public with a statement that'll have you scrambling for those same friends."

Denny smirked then slid his gaze over me as he smoked his cigar. His eyes roamed for a minute, dismissed me, then slid back to Alex.

"I'll counter that by stating your sister is a child of infidelity and you're too much of a snob to take on a poor pregnant girlfriend and forgive her. Heather can play any part she wants with conviction if it means being a King. She gets what it takes and knows how to get there. Her child will be a King regardless of who got it done."

Alex charged across the room and I unfolded my arms to shut the door behind me. He had his father on the floor behind the desk before I made my way across the room. He was red-faced and sputtering as Alex delivered several punches.

"Hey, Denny," I said as I leaned over them and watched them struggle. Alex had the upper hand, but I was going to get mine today.

Denny's face was turning red when he looked at me.

"I'm Mick Galloway, and I'm marrying your daughter. Came to talk, but I have to say, this is so much better than I expected."

Pushing my sleeves up to my elbows, I bided my time as Alex wore himself out on his father's ribs. I slid the belt out from my pants and wrapped it around my fist a few times.

I bared my teeth in a cold smile.

I was going to enjoy this.

CHAPTER TWENTY

Alisa

Shopping with Holly was an experience. I'd never been to Las Vegas, but in my head, I imagined the old Las Vegas with women in boas, feathers, glitz, glamour, and a certain wildness to everything. That was Holly when shopping.

I didn't expect her to be so frilly when it came to things she liked. Or maybe it was that she liked frilly things on me. She'd handed me no less than twelve nighties with see-through material, mostly in pink and several, if not too many, skirts that either had floral prints or ruffles.

The nighties were my request. I wanted to surprise Mick with them, but I was completely lost on what sort of stuff might be interesting to him. Holly seemed to have an idea of things but noted, to her credit, that just about anything would do.

Paul was trying to ignore the shop we were in but was failing miserably. For such a serious man, he'd turned a certain shade of red since we'd stepped in the store. After a few laughing fits from us, he'd surrendered to standing watch outside. Probably no less red, but at least he wasn't having to try and hide it as much.

"I don't think I need the skirts," I said as I stepped out of the dressing room and checked the time on my phone. It was already late in the day, and we'd been gone longer than I expected. "We should get back soon. I can't believe it's been two hours."

Holly scrunched up her nose. "Really? Feels like we just got here. Were the dresses too much? I can grab some others. Did you like any of the nighties?"

I held up my arm with three of them. "Yeah, I like these. I hope he does."

"Alisa, I think you could wear a paper bag and he'd still think you were amazing. Too bad about the skirts though, they were cute."

She eyed them for a moment before turning away.

"Put them on," I said, holding the door wide.

She spun around and shook her head. "No, they're really nice."

"And?" I prompted.

The expression on her face changed a few times like she was wondering what to say. "They're way too nice for me. I'd just get something on them and ruin them. Plus, I work at a bar, I don't think they'd really be appropriate there, ya know?"

"Holly, just try them on. See if you like them. You don't have to wear them to the club. Wait, there's plenty of women that wear skirts there. Why would it matter?"

She hedged for a minute and I gave her an impatient look.

"Alisa, it's different for you."

"Why?" I asked frowning at the fact that she'd make a distinction.

She shrugged. "You have a guy. And he's scary as fuck sometimes when he's around you. He watches over you and people know you're with him. They respect him, because again, he's scary as fuck, and they respect you since it's pretty obvious who has who wrapped around their finger. Then there's the fact that I work at a club where people get drunk and make assumptions even when I'm wearing jeans."

I blinked at her a few times. Mick was scary, I knew this for a fact. When he was around me, he could go from deadly to playful. Regardless, that didn't have anything to do with me and I wondered why she said it.

"What do you mean by respect for me?"

She moved in closer and leaned up against the stall. Her lips rolled between her teeth as she considered her next words. A small habit that I thought was really cute for Holly, since she seemed so self-assured when she spoke. It was like she got nervous occasionally and that seemed so out of character. There was a definite reason why her nickname was "Satan" at the club. She could bark orders to rival Mick and Mason put together any day.

"Well, look, it's like this. Mick and Mason, they're known around the neighborhood now. People like them, but they also know they're not people you mess around with from what I hear. I don't know why, but I can tell just by working for them that they have a thing. As in, something about them that you don't want to mess with."

Her statement worried me a little. If anyone ever knew just how scary they could be, they wouldn't go near them again. Although I wasn't afraid of either of them, there were plenty of reasons for other people to be nervous. After the assault, I'd struggled with it for a while. I felt safe with Mick and I accepted who he was, but there was always going to be that moment in the bathroom when I witnessed things that no one should ever have to see. He was the love of my life, but he also had the capacity to be brutal.

Mick and I were so deeply entwined that I could no longer identify a life before him. He was everything to me, and I to him. That would never change or be broken. I knew there were still things that he didn't want to share with me about his past. It was something that I'd accepted afterward knowing that it might have had a profound impact on who he was now, but didn't affect how I felt about him regardless.

Other people's opinions, though? Even without knowing much about Mick or Mason, apparently some people had good instincts. What worried me, was wondering if they'd constantly be threatened by people wanting to be just as frightening.

"And Jack? No one wants to go near him since he's a complete mystery. And again, he has that thing about him. Your brother..."

I frowned. "What about Alex?"

She shrugged. "I mean, I know he's a King, but hanging out with those guys and being just as scary, he's kind of respected too. Maybe not scary but, intimidating…forget it. I know he…I know what he does, and people have said some things."

"Like what?" I asked, wondering why she was having so much trouble talking about Alex.

"That he can be vicious in a courtroom, but he defends people sometimes without charging them much. He doesn't try to gouge his clients and people respect that."

"I'm starting to wonder what people you hang out with."

She laughed. "I don't. You just hear a lot of things when you're serving drinks and live in certain neighborhoods."

"And me?"

She smirked. "You could make any one of them do something if you wanted. Everyone loves you. And to be honest, that's kind of scary too."

It was my turn to scrunch my nose. "Ridiculous. I'm nobody, just me."

"And that's why people love you. Not to mention the seriously hot and scary guys you hang out with."

Rolling my eyes, I nudged her backward in the stall. "Try the skirts on. We'll have a girly night and you can wear one. And it won't be to the stupid club."

"Alisa, straight up, they're out of my price range. I'll try them on then we'll do something else."

She looked embarrassed by the admission, and I didn't blame her. Had it not been for Mick, I wouldn't have been shopping in this particular store either. But I did love that he hadn't pressured me into spending his money, although he'd offered. The only thing he'd requested, was that I spend mine on whatever I wanted, rather than worry about any bills.

It was mostly a win.

I made a mental note to get her a gift card to the store sometime between friends. Nothing crazy, just something she could spend to buy some pretty skirts with ruffles if she wanted to.

"How do those fit?" I asked through the door.

"Really, really good. They fit perfectly. Ugh. I love the red one, but I don't like it with my hair."

"So, dye your hair a different color. I'll be back, I'm going to get these."

I stopped by the rack with the red skirt she was talking about, picked out a black one and went to check out. The lady behind the counter took the skirt, as instructed and wrapped it in a box.

"Hey, Alisa, how are you?" Heather's sickly, sweet voice asked from beside me.

Turning toward her, she grabbed my shoulders and did a weird air kiss thing that I absolutely hated.

"Heather," I responded between my gritted teeth. "How are you? What brings you here?"

She shrugged. "Shopping of course. I needed some retail therapy. Better question is why are you here? Something for you or for the man?"

"Yeah, something like that."

"Hmm," she said, then pursed her lips as she looked through the store. "Ran into Monica the other day and she said she hadn't heard from you in weeks. I think she's a little lonely. Especially after, you know, her dad."

"Uhm, I guess," I replied. "What happened?"

"Oh, Alex didn't tell you? I'm surprised, he seems to tell you everything. Well, word is, that he's getting a divorce and remarrying. Something about her mom not being able to have any more kids, and apparently the new girlfriend is already pregnant."

"Really?" I asked with some surprise. Divorces were unheard of in our family. Affairs? Plenty. But rarely divorce. "When did that happen?"

"They're already finalizing everything this week. Lawyers work fast if you're a King, I guess. Alex and I may have some good news. We're talking about some long-term plans. I don't know yet, but I think I'm pregnant."

My stomach dropped. My first instinct was to grimace, which I held back by some miracle. My second instinct was to laugh rudely and tell her she was a bitch. My brother wouldn't torture me with this woman for a lifetime. No way. He would have gotten fixed or had military grade anti-Heather pregnancy condoms on and that was a fact.

"Oh, well, congrats. He forgot to mention that too."

She smiled, showing off her perfect teeth. "It'll be great, we can go shopping together anytime."

I blinked as I smiled, unsure of what the polite thing was to say.

"Oh, yeah, guess we'll see. Well, I've got to go, looks like my friend is ready," I said as Holly made a beeline for me.

"Sure, see you soon," she replied with another dreaded air kiss.

As I walked away, Holly joined me, and Paul appeared, trailing behind us, but not so close that he'd hear anything or look too obvious.

Holly chattered about the things I'd purchased with a smile on her face while I stewed over Heather's news.

Pregnant. Surely Alex wouldn't be so careless.

I felt like a hypocrite for thinking it, since I was waiting on my own body to give me news. I'd been equally as careless with Mick. I was late and that wasn't normal for me. I was like a finely tuned clock when it came to my monthly cycle.

Although I was on birth control, I'd skipped a couple of pills over the last month with my residence change. Luckily, Melanie had been able to retrieve them while organizing my things to move. But those few days I'd skipped them, then my hospital stay, and everything that had come afterward, might have made a difference.

Right now, I was more concerned with Alex and the mega bitch.

I tried dialing his number, but it went to voicemail. The same with Mick.

Hopefully their visit with my mother had gone well. I could remember a time when I was a child that she hadn't been like she was now. She'd been distant, but affectionate at one point, before my father started his abuse. She wasn't the best mom in the world, but certainly not the worst. It was that memory that really made my mind up about helping her. I wasn't sure if my father was lying. If there was any shred of truth to what he said, though, I wondered if she'd truly accepted her fate or was just resigned to it. Maybe a little of both.

Turning to Paul I asked, "Hey, can we go by the pharmacy before we head back to the club? I'm not sure where Mick is at right now, but we were supposed to have a late lunch."

"I'm sure he's fine," he replied.

"Right," I replied. "Still, if he's not answering then I'd like to run one last errand."

"You can have lunch with me if he's not there when we get back," Holly said.

"I'd love to. We can order some takeout or something. There's a deli downtown we can pick something up at, or just eat there."

As Paul drove us, Holly asked, "So who was the bimbo in the store? You've had a frown on your face ever since we left."

I grimaced. "Alex's girlfriend. She's a bitch and I need to talk to him about it. I can't even believe they're still dating at this point."

Holly nodded, but didn't say anything as she chewed on her lip.

Stopping by the pharmacy, Paul followed me until I got to the aisle I needed while Holly stayed in the car. I picked up two tests from the shelf and walked back down the aisle while I read the directions.

"Hell," Paul muttered.

When I glanced up at him he was eyeing the tests.

"I…"

"We should go back to the club, Alisa. Mick's gonna lose his shit."

Shaking the boxes, I gestured toward the door. "They aren't for me, they're for Holly."

"Right," he said slowly in his baritone voice. "Why do I get the feeling that Mick's going to be about ten times scarier if it's positive?"

I frowned as I paid for the pregnancy tests. "What do you mean?"

He shook his head. "He'll get a bodyguard for the baby."

"That's ridiculous and insane."

"You're the one marrying him. You should know."

We climbed in the car and I threw the bag under my feet. Holly watched through the window quietly as we made our way downtown.

I saw the box with the skirt I'd bought her in the retail bag, slid it out and nudged her with it.

She looked down, distracted and in mid thought about something. "What's that?"

"A gift," I said and pursed my lips. "Just for letting me hang out with you today."

"Alisa..."

"I'm not taking it back," I said as I watched her bite her lip. She was a softy, despite her reputation.

She opened it and her mouth dropped open. "Seriously?"

"Well, we're going out on girl's night. You need a skirt."

She smirked at me, the whispered, "Thank you."

Paul pulled to the back of the club where the staff entrance was. Mick's car was still parked in the same spot it'd been, and Alex's car wasn't present.

"Looks like the guys aren't back yet," I observed. "Guess we'll have to get some deli takeout."

Holly smiled as we entered the building and made our way down the long hallway to the main floor. "I'll look up the menu. Do you know what you want?"

"Yeah just call it in. Tell Heath that Alisa needs her sub sandwich. He'll know what you mean. And send Paul to pick it up, it's less than five blocks away. Or tell Heath if he wants to join us he can. He's nice, you might like him. I'll be right back."

Quickly heading up the stairs, I set my bag of naughty nighties on Mick's desk and took my other package to the restroom. It seemed fairly straight forward and after doing my thing, I set the tests on the sink. Fidgeting, I waited on them without looking directly at them. I was nervous about the results. One result would be life changing.

Hearing the door open and close in the office, I grimaced. I was hoping to have an answer by the time Mick arrived back at the club. If I wasn't pregnant, then there was no need to mention it and life would continue as normal. As normal as it'd been anyway. If I was pregnant, then I wondered how he'd react. Either way I was happy just to spend my life with him.

Footsteps approached the door and I swung it inward, blocking the tests.

Heather stood at the entrance holding a gun.

"Well, hello there again, Alisa. Funny how we keep running into each other today."

"Heather," I said glancing down at her weapon. "What are you doing?"

She leaned against the doorframe and smiled. "Collecting on a paycheck."

"How did you get in?" I asked nervously. "Where's Holly?"

"Well, your hired man, was kind enough to leave the building. I followed you over here to take care of what should have been an easy job, but apparently seems to be just a little too difficult for anyone to do. So, what's a girl to do? Get it done herself."

"Holly? Where is she?"

"Is that her name? She's downstairs somewhere with a friend of mine. They're getting acquainted," she chuckled.

I gasped. "God, Heather, don't hurt her. Put the gun down."

"Shut up. You know, it's cost me quite a bit to have you followed. But ever since you showed back up in Kingston, I knew it was fate telling me to get some things done right. I thought for sure that it would only take one drunken night out on the town to speed things along. But when you ended up here with Monica and that bumbling oaf I hired fucked it up, I had to think of something else."

"Put the gun down, Heather," I responded with only a small quiver to my voice. "What are you talking about?"

"Money," she responded. "Is there really anything else worth talking about? See, I thought that maybe you'd just stay away after college. That maybe after a taste of freedom you'd fly away to whatever you were going to do and wouldn't come back. And if you just happened to have an unfortunate accident one of these days, well, who would care?"

She stepped further in the bathroom and I backed away.

"Your brother and I would be married with children. And when you suddenly pop up missing or dead, he'd be the sole heir to your father's fortune."

"He's not that loaded."

She pursed her lips. "On the contrary, your dear old dad has made some extremely lucrative deals over the years. You were supposed to be one of them according to him. He gets drunk sometimes and spouts off about how you were going to be his golden goose when you married some foreign investor. No such luck, though, and I'm impatient."

"Denny sent you?"

She sighed then smiled. "Yes and no. He tried it his way after I begged him. You wouldn't believe the things I had to do for him to get him to agree. He knows I'm dedicated to ridding the world of a little mistake like you. But he couldn't even get this right. There's been so many misses for him. I think the first time I knew he wasn't going to be able to do it was the park. He'd hired some idiot to run you over, and that was a complete disaster, obviously."

She sighed and shook her head.

I glanced at the gun and thought about the black BMW that had swerved to hit me that day. It'd been fortunate for me that I'd gotten out of the way, but I would have never guessed that it was an attempt on my life.

She kept the gun steadily pointed at my chest as she spoke. "You're causing a lot of ripples in the otherwise calm King family. Dating below your worth, dear God, the scandal. You could have had anyone. But, word is the Galloway brothers are making a name for themselves. Building their own little dynasty, gaining a reputation. I didn't think they had it in them. Too bad I didn't find one of the brothers first, I might have enjoyed fucking one of them. And look who's sitting on a pedestal at the top now. You. So, I guess you won either way."

I backed up further when she came closer. Her eyes danced with mirth at my fear.

"You really don't know how much you're worth, do you?" she hissed. "Marry a Galloway and reap the rewards, or marry your daddy's pick and he reaps the rewards. He dies, you and Alex inherit."

I shook my head, trying not to make any sudden movements. "Heather, that's just not true. I'm not worth anything to any…"

"Shut up," she hissed. She regarded me for a moment then her eyes slid to the counter. I knew what she was looking at, but couldn't understand the laughter that suddenly exploded from her mouth.

"You're pregnant, dear. This is going to be the best set up for your precious Mick. The news might say that he got mad and killed you. Poor guy might get the death penalty after you're gone."

The sound of someone moving in the hallway alerted her and she closed the door partially. She grabbed my hair and put the barrel of the gun to my face.

I worried about whoever was making their way through the hall, thinking of Holly, but my worst fear was for Mick. If he found me dead, he'd break.

CHAPTER TWENTY-ONE

~Mick~

The afternoon would either cost us or help us, depending on what Alex's father decided to do. After Alex had a go at him, I'd used the belt on his back a few times to show him how it felt. Vindication was sweet, and vengeance was mine for at least a few minutes. But like the bastard he was, Denny King had spewed threats along with the blood in his mouth as he promised retribution.

He'd threatened Alisa again. The vile things he'd promised to deliver had me wanting to tear his limbs off one by one. But killing a D.A. wasn't something my father could overlook, nor was it something that the city of Kingston would let go of easily. If he followed through on any of the things he'd promised, I'd revisit that thought and carry through without hesitation.

Alex had surprised me. The level of his fury wasn't what I'd expected. It was one thing to be in a room with him and beat a threatening stranger to death in the basement of the club, but this had been very different.

Eyeing him in the car, I knew how he felt in a way. He wasn't blind to how his family operated but facing a father whose sins against you made you question everything about your life, was not an easy pill to swallow.

I'd known the feeling quite well with my own father after I'd found my mother with a black eye. Mason and I had been in high school by that point, but it made me realize just how awful he'd been without ever seeing evidence of it. He'd hit us a few times, and there were times when I felt like we deserved it. Our youth was spent destroying things around the house the way only two rambunctious boys could. But it was his drunken tirades, his verbal onslaught of abuse toward my mother, that I'd never gotten over.

Mason might have been able to look past it, now that my father was clean and sober. But I'd seen my fair share of the demons that dwelled in the man to forget about it and move on. The worst part of it was that he'd been trying to mend things for a couple of years. As if, now that he'd come to his senses, he wanted to wipe the slate clean.

Denny was a completely different person, however, and I felt for Alex now that the kick of adrenaline and anger was gone. I wondered how it would settle in him when he had a chance to reflect.

Rolling my eyes at the thought of wanting to help him, I looked down the small bar we'd stopped at to have a drink. I had no idea when I'd started caring, if that was what this was, about how Alex might function beyond this point.

Glancing at him, I opened my mouth, but he cut me off.

"Whatever you're going to say, save it. I'm fine. He's a piece of shit."

"I wasn't going to ask."

He shrugged and took a sip of his drink. "He deserved it a long time ago and this was just karma coming around."

"How long before we're arrested?"

He looked over at me and laughed.

"What?" I asked, a little surprised at his reaction.

"He's not going to report that shit. Are you kidding? Hundred bucks says he takes off on leave for some unnamed medical or family emergency until some of the bruising heals. Something I learned early on, thanks to my father, was that Kings never show weakness. Never."

"Is that why you've put up with it for so long?"

He took a long drink, draining his glass. "I don't know, Mick, you tell me. You're the expert at psychology, right?"

"Criminal behavior," I said, as I smirked to myself. It was amazing how life changed. "I've seen a psychiatrist a few times. Haven't had much inclination lately. She's a ball-buster, you should meet her. Threatens me every time I visit."

He played with the rim of his glass for a moment, thinking to himself. "Did it help?"

"Apparently not."

He laughed again. "This city is so fucked up. No one is ever pure here."

Taking a drink, I watched the amber liquid in the glass for a moment. He was right in a way. From what I'd seen and heard so far, the long reach of the King family had managed to sour most of what we considered normal business and city functions. Mason had done a lot of digging on his own into things and had filled me in before Holly had joined us this morning.

They controlled through the power of intimidation. If one of them had an issue with someone specific, then one of the other family members would start squeezing them in areas they could control. Their children had married well, their extended family bordered on ridiculously rich and every one of them knew how to do the other a favor.

The main weakness of the King family was hubris. Excessive pride and self-confidence. They thought that no one could touch them, stand up to them or make them pay in any way.

If Mason and I continued with what we were doing, building our contacts and gaining friends, then we'd be well on our way to giving them a little bit of their own poison. It was just a matter of organizing, planning and having enough money to make it happen. One of those relied heavily on the club turning a profit, and it would. We'd be doubling what we were making by the month's end.

I sighed deeply and glanced at Alex. "Your sister is pure, so I have to believe that not everyone ends up choking on the wreckage your family seems to cause."

"Hmm," he said without commenting for a moment. "She's a fighter, she just doesn't know it. She'll be good to you, don't fuck it up."

I tapped the bar for the tab and the bartender brought the bill. "The thing about your sister, is that she has her eyes wide open at this point. She knows what she's getting. It may not always be what she wants, but she isn't walking in blindly."

"Which goes back to my statement about not fucking it up. Or you'll deal with me."

I narrowed my eyes as I glanced at him. "Just when I start to like you, it's back to the threats. I'm too tired to take this to the parking lot at this point. Can we call it a draw?"

"Definitely. I wiped my appointments today and still need to get my mom after I drop you off, so we'd better get out of here."

I checked the time on my phone and noticed a missed call from Alisa. It'd been more than two hours since we'd left the club on our errand.

I called her number, but no one answered. She might have been mad that I'd missed our lunch date. It wasn't like her to ignore an opportunity to lay into me about it, though.

Frowning at my phone, we got back in the car.

I dialed again but it went to voicemail.

Alex was driving through traffic when I started fidgeting with my phone. My next call was to Paul who also didn't pick up.

"What's wrong?" Alex asked beside me. "You look nervous."

"Paul and Alisa aren't picking up the phone. Alisa, maybe. She takes a nap occasionally. Paul knows to pick up."

"Trouble?"

"Get us back to the club."

"Mason," I said after I dialed his number.

"Yeah, what's up?"

"Are you at the club? I can't reach Alisa."

"No," he replied. "I'm with Jack on surveillance. Do you need me?"

"We're on our way there. I'm sure it's nothing."

"Alright, let me know."

I hung up the phone, clenching as Alex ran a red light and careened around a corner.

"I hope he didn't call anyone," Alex growled. "I swear if he called someone out to hurt her, I'll kill him myself."

All the possibilities of what he'd threatened swam through my mind. They may have been idle threats to someone like Denny King, but I'd seen the reality in hundreds of cases. What he'd outlined, rape, torture, murder, made my skin crawl as a reel of past cases played in my head.

Alisa's face suddenly became the dead and I started breathing hard.

"You okay?" Alex asked as he glanced at me, barely missing a car.

I rubbed a hand on my chest and nodded. "Just get us there in one piece, Alex. I'm fine."

We came to a sudden halt in the street with a lurch and ran toward the front door which was partially open. The interior looked normal until we got to the main room. Several tables were overturned, broken glass littering the floor. A man lay unmoving on the ground beside the bar.

We ran over and inspected the damage, but as we passed the end of the bar I stopped. Holly was on the floor, hands tied, gagged and moaning. She was sporting a bruise on her cheek with some swelling.

Alex barreled past me, frantically trying to untie her bindings, when I noticed her jeans undone and pushed to her hips.

"Motherfucker," I growled and ran for the stairs. "Alex get her in the car."

Adrenaline surged through my system as I ran up the stairs. I found Paul at the doorway crouched and pointing his weapon inside the room.

"Boss, she's got a gun on her. Killed some delivery man. Guy downstairs was trying to hurt Holly. Killed him before he did anything I think. There's another guy dead in the hallway that came at me."

I scanned the room and saw a body slumped on the floor with a package laying near his hand.

"Alisa."

"This crazy bitch has her in the bathroom. Door is open, but I don't have a shot. I can see them in the mirror. I got back from getting lunch for the girls and they were here."

I touched Paul's shoulder. "We'll talk about it later. Give me your gun. I have one in the car, go get it."

Paul handed me his weapon and I switched places with him. Looking through the open door to the restroom, I caught a flash of the two occupants, but not enough to see who it was.

"Alisa?" I called into the room.

There was a muffled sound in the bathroom, then Alisa's face passed by the mirror. Behind her was Heather.

I spun and aimed when I heard an unfamiliar noise behind me, ready to drop whoever was stupid enough to sneak up on me. Alex threw out his hands as I lowered the weapon.

"It's Heather, she has Alisa in the bathroom. How's Holly?"

"Scared as hell, I sent Paul to her. He said to bring you a gun. She said she wasn't hurt but her jeans…"

"We'll talk to Paul later. See what happened," I replied with my eyes on the mirror. "I may need your help with Heather. Just get her out of the bathroom. You know how to use that?"

When I glanced back at him, he turned the gun in his hand and took the safety off. "It's been awhile, but yes."

"Okay, hand it to me, I'm going to have it on my back if you need it."

I slipped the weapon in the small of my back and into my jeans. Entering the room, my back was to the wall as I kept the bathroom in view. Alex came in after me but stood a little further in front, nearly blocking my view. He was shit at this, but he was at least here and willing to help.

"Heather?" he called. "Are you in here?"

"Of course I am. I've already told Paul that I want out of here and you're in my way. And now that I know Mick is here, you might want to put a leash on him. If he takes a shot at me, it's bye bye, baby."

Alex moved to the side, blocking my view further so I shuffled to the side and crouched. I'd shoot his knee and drop his ass if it meant a clear shot at Heather.

"Hey, what's this about? Come out, let's talk. There's no reason to do this."

She came to the edge of the door and scanned the room. When she spotted me, she put the gun to Alisa's face.

Rage started to boil in me as Alisa spotted me across the room. With a look of relief on her face she tried to take a step forward.

"Don't move, you stupid slut," Heather sneered as she tapped the gun on Alisa's forehead. "You're my little ticket out of here and I'm cashing in."

Alex held up his hands. "Heather, why are you doing this?"

"Since I've told Alisa, I'll give you the short version…"

As she explained about planning to kill Alisa long before I came along, it sounded like Denny wasn't interested in her whole plan until she was seen with me. It alarmed me how many missed attempts had been made on her life just in the short period of time before I'd really known her. And the dick at the club was one of them.

I shifted slowly to the side, trying not to draw attention. One glance at the camera on the wall told me it was functional and recording.

"So, Denny was behind this?" I asked as I cut her off mid-rant.

"He was involved," she replied with a smirk. "Just like he is with everything else. He's the dirtiest man in Kingston. Bribes, theft, and now attempted murder of his precious daughter."

Alisa strained against Heather's hold. "I guess he didn't tell you that I'm not his daughter."

Heather smiled. "Oh, he did. And he told me in remarkable detail what happened to your mother. Would you like to know who your father really is? He had a paternity test."

She shook her head. "Doesn't matter."

"Well it doesn't now, he's dead. Poor George, didn't see it coming. But you don't run for mayor without Denny's permission. I guess that means you've gained two new half-brothers, J.D. and Tyson. Won't that be fun at family reunions. Cops as brothers and your precious, Mick, mingling together."

"Heather, that's enough," Alex said in a stern voice. "Put the gun down and let's talk."

"I don't think so, not unless we're talking money."

"Whatever you need," Alex replied as he took a step forward. "There's always a mutually beneficial compromise. I'm sorry I was mad at you earlier, but my father explained."

Heather gave him a heated look as I tracked where her gun moved. With every word that came spilling out of her mouth about Denny, she was sealing her coffin and his.

When she tilted the weapon to the side, I stood up and took aim.

Heather quickly ducked behind Alisa as Alex started backing away. When he was beside me I stepped in front of him.

"Not today, Mick," she hissed as she maneuvered the gun down Alisa's body. "Precious cargo aboard. Wouldn't want you to miss."

My eyes swung to Alisa's then down to her stomach where Heather was pointing the tip of her gun.

I felt movement at my back and the gun I'd tucked in my jeans lift away from me.

"Heather, honey," Alex said. "Concentrate. He's not going to do a damn thing. He works for me."

I wanted to laugh at that statement, but Heather's eyes lit up at the possibility. Her main problem was a craving for power and greed. So, instead I gave a short serious nod in agreement.

Glancing at him, I noticed he'd transferred the gun to his back pocket.

Alex held out his hand to her. "We have a lot to talk about, let Alisa go."

She peeked over Alisa's shoulder and gave me a haughty glare. "I knew they couldn't do it on their own. Alex, we have to get rid of them. Your father promised me that you'd inherit everything if she was out of the way and we married. Don't you see we were meant to be together? We have the same friends, run in the same circles."

"I can't get rid of them. That's not how this works."

Her face changed from one of desperate pleading to anger immediately. "You're a fool, Alex. I should have been a King, I understand what it means to make sacrifices no matter what the cost. I can't believe you'd choose them over your destiny. You were made to rule this city, just like your father and uncles. She's the one holding you back."

My hand twitched, wanting to drop her, but still following the movement of her weapon as she slid it along Alisa's stomach.

My eyes slid up to Alisa's as she silently cried. Her hand slipped down to her belly, covering it like it was the most important thing in her life. She'd make an exceptional mother because she was already an exceptional woman. Kind, sweet, attentive, with a backbone of steel. She was my other half, and now she was carrying my baby. Something I'd never really considered in my life. A child. My child and my woman together.

Heather's grip on Alisa tightened as she walked slowly to the side and toward the office door.

"Where are you going, Heather?" Alex asked. "Let's stay here and we can work it out. We'll talk about it."

"There's nothing to work out." She laughed. "If I can't have you then I'll have your father. Simple. But like I said, this bitch is my way out of here. If you don't want her to take a nasty fall down two flights of stairs, then you'll back the fuck off."

Alex wasn't getting anywhere with Heather. He'd made his point clear enough to her at his father's house and by refusing to help her get rid of us, he'd cut off any possible chance of negotiating with her. I could see it in her expression that our lives meant absolutely nothing to her.

Stepping forward, keeping my eyes only on Alisa, I gave her a small smile as I spread my arms to my sides and dropped my gun.

"Mick," she whispered. "No."

Heather's glare swung to me as I kept my eyes on the beautiful woman in front of me. She was my life and she'd be the person to give a wonderful life to our child if Alex could drop Heather. I remembered Alex's words to me weeks ago, and my smile spread while I looked into her beautiful blue eyes.

Recalling his words, the situation seemed ironic now. *You're fucked. Either way someone loses in the end. You or her. Make sure it's you.*

It was going to be me. It always was.

CHAPTER TWENTY-TWO

Alisa

God, what was he doing? My gut clenched when he smiled at me. The moment I saw him in the mirror, I knew he'd save me from this evil bitch.

She was twisted by an upbringing in the most affluent circles, convinced in her self-delusions that she was entitled to things that she desired. She was the epitome of what my father wanted out of me. Immoral, depraved and deviant. She stood for everything that was honestly wrong in my family, and in the city. She was murderous by choice and corrupted by circumstance.

Then Mick had come to get me. The furious look on his face earlier was only a small hint of what the room suddenly felt like. The heat of his stare had nearly undone me when he'd looked at my stomach. He wanted this baby as much as I did. Which meant he'd do anything to protect us. I knew he'd kill her then, and oddly, the thought didn't even bother me.

But now, I was worried. He raised his hands to hip level and dropped his gun while he stared back at me. Then he moved forward, keeping his eyes on me the entire time.

"Mick," I whispered, when I realized what he was doing. "No."

Heather's grip on my arm tightened and the gun swung toward Mick.

He kept moving forward toward me then gave me the widest smile I'd ever seen on his handsome face. It was genuine, honest, like nothing I'd ever seen. He was happy.

Not in the way that he normally was. Not the subdued laughing, the soft loving smiles. This was Mick letting go and the man he said he'd been before the demons of his ordeal had taken hold. He was unburdened by them now, and he was giving *me* that small glimpse of him. No one else, just me. That man had been there all along, it'd just taken this moment for him to see it too.

Heather's stepped out from behind me and bumped into me in her haste to raise her weapon. The gun jerked in her hand in my peripheral vision and his smile turned to a grimace.

"No!" I screamed.

A shot rang out, and her gun jerked again. Mick dropped to his knees.

Two shots went off in rapid succession. Heather doubled over, then folded. Her body hit the floor beside me as I cringed from the sounds.

Alex lowered his weapon and looked at me, but my eyes were already swinging back to Mick. He was on his side, blood soaking his shirt.

Flying across the room, I stumbled and fell to my knees beside him.

"God, Mick, no!" I screamed as I pushed him to his back.

My gut clenched when I saw the blood spreading over his shirt near his ribs. My hand immediately went to the area and covered it. Desperate to stop the life from leaving his body, I pressed down and heard him moan.

Glancing up at his face I let out a high-pitched sob. There was a long gash across his face that was pouring blood down his cheek.

"Alisa," Alex said beside me.

Focusing on his voice, I looked up as he knelt on the floor with me.

"Not him, Alex. Please not him. Please, I can't do this."

"It's okay, we're going to get him some help. Crazy bastard just stepped right in front of her. What the fuck was he thinking?"

Alex peeled his jacket off and took his phone out. He pressed the material against Mick's face to stem some of the blood flow as he dialed.

"Yeah," he said after a moment. "I need an ambulance and the police at *Erebus Club*. There's been a shooting. Two dead downstairs and one bleeding. Fuck, just get here, and someone call Chief Galloway, his son is the one that's been shot."

He listened for a moment then tossed the phone aside.

"They're coming?" I asked between sobs.

"Yeah, they're coming. It's okay. God, I'm sorry, Alisa. This is my fault. I should have seen it a long time ago. She could have killed you. I've been so damn blind."

I shook my head. "You couldn't have known."

"I should have. Fuck. That woman only wanted money," he growled. "All this for money."

I looked over my shoulder where Heather lay on the floor. "Is she dead?"

"Yeah," he said. "And I'm not checking on her to see if she isn't."

A sob left my body followed by another one until I was shaking with them. The blood that drenched Mick's shirt and my hands was still flowing, but not as fast.

"Alex."

"He'll make it. As much as I wanted to kill him a few times, I've gotten used to him. I'm going to beat the hell out of him when he gets better for knocking you up."

A half laugh, half sob slipped out of me. "I'll help."

Mick's eyes opened for a moment then he groaned again. "Alisa."

"They're on their way, Mick, just hold on. I need you, please don't leave me alone. I love you, just hang on."

His eyes roamed my face for a moment then he let out a groan. "Love you."

"I know," I whispered.

"Cameras. Recorded it."

Alex's head swiveled around the room then he nodded. "Got it. Where's the recording?"

Mick's eyes closed, but his hand reached out to touch my arm.

Alex leaned over him and asked again, "Where's the recording, Mick? Stay with us."

"Mason," he whispered.

Alex and I looked at each other then back down at him. He groaned again, but his hand was still on my arm. I brought it to my lips and kissed his fingertips.

Sirens could be heard in the distance, steadily getting closer. It sounded like half the city was coming to the club.

Alex reached for his phone and dialed a number.

"Mason, it's your brother. Shit went bad at the club."

He listened for a minute. "He's still breathing, ambulance is coming. He said something about the cameras. Look Heather said a bunch of shit..."

He nodded like he was listening.

"Yeah, Heather. I can't explain right now. But if you want those recordings to end up in the right hands before Kingston's finest get here then we need to know where the recordings are. Otherwise all we've got is a bunch of dead bodies, one of which is my ex-girlfriend who's been fucking my old man. She said some shit that'll help bring him down."

I squeezed Mick's hand, watching his face as he grimaced. The pain was probably excruciating at this point, and I didn't know if he had any internal injuries from the bullet that hit his side. My hand slid around his waist to his back but the only thing I felt was the sticky blood pooling in his shirt and on the floor.

Alex continued to talk as he got up from the floor and went to the desk. He rifled around in the drawers, searching for something.

I swung my gaze back to Mick and leaned over him. "They're coming. You'll be okay."

"Baby," he whispered before he grimaced again.

"That's right, we're going to have a baby. If you sleep, dream about me, Mick. Just me and the baby. I love you."

Alex rushed out of the room and I heard voices yelling downstairs.

"Here!" I screamed. "We're here!"

There were multiple sounds of footsteps coming up the stairs as I kept my eyes on Mick. He'd taken a bullet for me, killed for me, loved me and scared me. There was so much to this man laying on the floor in front of me.

My life couldn't possibly be the same without him as much as it was also completely different with him. I needed him. Everything about him. I didn't care about the reputation he and his brother had. Didn't care about whatever they were doing. I just knew that my heart hurt thinking about a life that didn't include the beautiful, complicated man in front of me.

A hand nudged me to the side, tearing my eyes away from Mick. Two men bent over him and immediately started examining him, speaking rapidly.

I started crying again as they worked on him. When a hand slid around my waist, I turned to see an older man that looked a bit like the Galloway brothers. Not so much in the eyes, but the set of his jaw and lips were nearly the same. His eyes were focused on Mick, an expression of pained concern flashed across his face.

He backed up and took me with him as another emergency worker approached us. She checked out my hands, wiping most of the blood away even after I told her I was fine.

"We'll go to the hospital," he said, distracted by the men that were lifting Mick. "Jesus, what happened here?"

Alex approached us and held out his hand. "Chief, glad you got my message. We need to talk."

The older man blinked then turned toward Alex. He nodded then mumbled, "Not here. I'll take you both in my car."

He whistled loudly, and several uniformed officers turned toward him as he barked orders. He sounded exactly like his sons when they got in heated debates.

Alex held his hand out and I hugged him as the medical team passed us in a rush through the door.

"Can we trust him?" I whispered to Alex.

"Yeah," he replied. "But we have to be careful. Let's go with him and see what he has to say."

Nodding, I followed Alex and the older Galloway through the door and down the stairs. There were more officers in the room and I realized I hadn't checked on Holly with everything that happened.

"Where's Holly? Is she okay?"

Alex clenched his jaw for a moment as we stepped outside. There was a light rain that was coming down, with dark clouds in the sky. The ambulance sirens started wailing as they pulled away from the curb. Two police cars raced ahead of it.

"Yeah, she's okay. Paul was sitting with her in my car."

He scanned the street for a moment then frowned.

Paul was speaking to an officer by one of their vehicles, but I didn't see Holly anywhere.

Alex grabbed an officer as we passed him on the sidewalk. "Have you seen the girl that was with that man earlier?"

The man looked over at Paul. "Yeah, they took her to the hospital to get checked out. Said she was in shock I think."

Alex sucked in an audible breath, but only nodded.

We followed Mick's dad down the sidewalk to a non-descript sedan while Alex pulled his phone out of his pocket. He dialed a number and stepped to the side as I slid into the back seat of the vehicle.

The older man got into the driver's side and glanced at me through the rearview mirror.

"I'm Sean."

"Alisa," I replied.

"Yeah, I know. Looked in on you at the hospital. Meant to talk to you after what happened at the apartment, but the detectives wrapped everything up. Talked to the boys instead."

I nodded, anxious to go to the hospital.

"Just wanted you to know that Mick's a good man. He'll make it. That boy has more drive and fight than anyone. Wish I had a hundred of him in the department."

"You should tell him that," I replied softly as I looked through the window at Alex, who had just gotten off the phone.

"I would if he'd listen," he said gruffly. "So maybe you can tell him for me. Yeah?"

Looking down at my hands, I wasn't sure what to make of that message, or whether I'd be able to tell Mick. He probably wouldn't listen to me either, given his relationship with his father.

Alex slid into the car and glanced at me then turned back to Sean.

"Just talked with Mason, he's at the hospital already."

Sean put the car in gear and let the siren run before we rolled down the street.

"What do you have, Alex?" he asked.

"A recording. Our father was involved."

Sean whistled. "Fuck. Had a feeling you were going to say that. Didn't want to hear it, but I knew you were going to say it. This a conversation we can have right now?"

Alex glanced at me again and I gave him a small smile.

"I think we should. Alisa already knows most of it."

"Okay, shoot."

Alex proceeded to relay the events of the last few weeks as Sean drove us through the wet and rainy streets. Sean blanched at the information about Heather and our father, but didn't look surprised.

"I get it, Alex. I do. I work with the man all the time and believe me, I know he's as dirty as they come. It's always been lack of evidence. He has everyone running scared every time they even think about disagreeing with him. Frankly, even if Heather did say something in that room, it's her word against his, your word against his and no one wins."

"According to Heather, he killed George for wanting to run for mayor."

Sean shook his head. "You know this, Alex. Evidence is golden. We can't prove anything which means we have zero reason to investigate him."

"He beat my sister. Took a belt to her for years. If she testifies, then what?"

Sean took a sharp right toward the multi-story building we were headed to.

"If she testifies then she's brought into court and crucified by one of his lawyers. Again, her word against his and if they get their hands on one shred of the truth about Mick or even you, they'll raise hell until your life is ripped apart. I may be the Chief, but that department isn't mine and never was. It's run by the Kings. I get my orders and we do what we need to, but I know who's pulling my strings."

Alex looked through the window as Sean circled around the parking lot for a space.

"So, even with the recording, we can't use it?"

Sean pulled into a spot, parked then looked at my brother. "You can use it. But you're going to have to get your hands dirty to do it. You guys have been up to quite a bit lately, so I know you'll figure out how to use it and when. Politics, Alex. Use your head. You grew up with them and you know how to play this game. Think about it. And we never had this conversation."

The three of us headed into the hospital and were directed to a waiting area on the third floor. Mick had gone into surgery immediately upon arrival. The nurses wouldn't tell us anything as we waited. Only that we'd probably have a long wait.

After a couple of hours, a few officers joined Sean and spoke to him quietly out of earshot. Alex paced for a few minutes, then headed toward the nurse's station where he started asking them about Holly. When he found out where she was, we headed to see her on a different floor.

Alex was the first to enter her room as I hung back and peeked around the edge of the door. Unlike my idiot brother, I didn't want to disturb her if she was in the middle of something. He didn't seem to care as he ambled over to her bed and touched her arm for a brief second.

She woke up startled, jerking her arm away as she stared up at my brother.

"Hey, Holly," I said from the edge of the room.

Her eyes slid to mine, and she gave me a small smile. "Hey you."

"I'm so sorry..."

She shook her head. "I'm okay, really. I'm just tired."

Her eyes darted to Alex for a moment as she chewed at her lip.

"Is your family coming up here?" he asked.

"Uhm, no. I'm just in here getting some fluids until they get my paperwork done. What happened?"

Alex opened his mouth and I touched his arm to stop him. "Alex, can you see if her paperwork is going to take long? Maybe she can come upstairs with us."

He nodded and left after glancing at her again.

"Holly, what happened?"

She held up her hand. "Stop. I'm okay. Everybody thinks I need some sort of hand holding here. Nothing happened, despite what it looked like."

I looked at her in confusion. "What do you mean? What did what look like?"

"I've got a small gash on my head from one of those guys when he pushed me to the floor. He...he tried to do something, but Paul came in and I think I passed out. Your brother thinks something bad happened, but Paul got to me first. He needs to calm down."

I smirked. "He's just a good guy."

She shrugged. "Whatever. Make him stop."

Laughing for a moment, it took my mind off Mick. Then the smile faded from my face as I thought of him upstairs in surgery.

Alex came back in and gave Holly the information on her release which would take another hour. When he offered to stay with her, she gave me a look.

Extracting him from the room was impossible, so I left them both and made my way back to the waiting room.

Mason met me halfway to my chair when I returned. Giving me a huge hug, he squeezed me tightly then stood back with a smile. Jack was next, who hugged me a little less tightly and smiled at me a little less widely, but I could tell he was glad to see me, nonetheless.

Paul was sitting in the corner reading a magazine and immediately gravitated toward us.

"The doctor came out a little while ago. He's going to be okay. Uglier, but okay. Might be a nasty scar."

A long breath that I didn't even know I was holding, escaped me. My knees went weak and Mason gently guide me into a chair.

"Hey, we can go in and see him in a little bit. Don't get upset, he'll be okay. Well, as okay as Mick gets, which we both know is fucked up crazy most—"

"Shut up, Mason," I said with a small laugh.

My thoughts turned to Mick and his recovery. It was going to be a long road for both of us the next few months, but in the end, I knew that we'd come out okay. No matter what, we were forever bound to each other.

CHAPTER TWENTY-THREE

Mick

"I don't need a wheelchair, Alisa. This is ridiculous," I said as I watched her retreating back. She disappeared into the bedroom and I sighed.

"She's just worried, you've been in the hospital for a week," Paul said as he wheeled me through the living room.

"It was a fractured rib. They removed the bullet, put me on some meds and I'm good. Painful and still fucking painful, but it doesn't require me to be wheeled around. I'm fine."

"You're the boss, but if it were me, I'd let the woman have what she wants for a little while."

I sighed and flinched from the pressure on my right side. It was sore and uncomfortable to say the least, but didn't prevent me from walking. The wheelchair she'd gotten me was overkill and would immediately be burned or thrown off the roof as soon as I could muster lifting it. But Paul had a point. She was sweet, and it was just her way, even if it was a little overboard.

"Alright, I'll give her a day, after that, lose this thing, Paul, or you're fired."

"You got it," he said with a deep laugh as he walked away.

The worst part about being in the damn thing was I was tired of being in bed or sitting. I felt like I'd done enough of that in the hospital and didn't want to do it anymore. My legs needed to stretch before I forgot how to use them.

I pushed on the sides to try and roll toward the bedroom and immediately regretted it. The pinch in my side reminded me that I was still recovering.

Sighing, I stood up and pushed the chair toward the bedroom then sat back down in it when I heard her walking around behind the door.

"Alisa?"

"Give me a sec. Do you need help?" she replied.

Rolling my eyes, I scooted the chair forward with my feet and nudged the door out of the way.

Scanning the room, I didn't see her. There were a few items of clothing on the edge of the made bed. She hadn't been sleeping here in a week, so things looked exactly like they had been when we'd left the house a week prior.

Shuffling forward, I grabbed the clothes and threw them in the hamper.

"What are you doing in here?" she asked behind me.

"Helping with the clothes," I muttered. "You know I can handle clothes and walking at this point."

"You were supposed to stay out there."

"Why?" I said as I glanced over my shoulder at her. I blinked, riveted on what she was wearing. "What are you doing?"

She shrugged then smirked as I turned the chair around to face her. She had on a white lingerie set with a short little skirt that had a medical symbol on it. The garters and stockings alone were enough to pique my interest, but the lacy top that clung to her body looked like it was about to spill over, freeing the prefect globes underneath.

My dick, that was nearly always semi-hard around her, started to take notice.

"Alisa?" I asked as my eyes feasted on her.

"I thought maybe I could be your naughty nurse today," she pouted.

My mouth opened, but I couldn't manage to form a single coherent sentence, so I nodded. My side was sore, my cheek still had stitches from the missed bullet that Heather nearly put in my head, but none of the aches and pains mattered now as I watched her.

She gave me a small smile while she played with a tiny satin ribbon that was on the front of her panties.

"You're so beautiful," I managed to say.

"So are you," she said as she walked closer to me in her own seductive way. It wasn't practiced, couldn't be described as alluring, but the way her hips swayed naturally had been a turn on for me for a long time. And fuck, her ass in that outfit probably looked even sweeter.

"Be a good girl and turn around."

She complied, and I groaned. Pushing myself up from the chair, I slid behind her and wrapped my hand around her waist.

Kissing the side of her neck softly, I heard her sigh. I'd never get enough of her scent and taste.

"Mick," she whispered. "You're supposed to be sitting down. I don't want you to hurt yourself."

"Fuck that," I said as I slid my hand into the edge of her panties. "I'm not going to sit over there where I can't touch you. Do you know how bad I want to bend you over right now?"

"That's not the point, Mick," she said, with a whimper as my other hand cupped one of her breasts and squeezed. "I was going to—"

"Who has control, baby?" I said as I nipped at her ear.

She giggled. "You do."

A loud banging from the other room arrested my hand from sliding over her clit. Growling, I kissed at her neck as my hips pressed into the soft mounds of her ass.

"Who is that?"

"Ignore it," I mumbled as my mouth found her ear.

The loud banging continued.

Sighing, I retreated with a kiss on her shoulder. "For fuck's sake. I swear to God, I'm going to shoot someone. Get on the bed, I want to taste you when I get back. And you better not be too attached to those panties. They're coming off."

Stalking through the house, I winced once and let out a quick breath. She might have to ride me for the afternoon, after I killed whoever was at the door.

I adjusted myself and flung the door open.

"This better be a fucking emergency," I barked.

Three sets of eyes met mine. Alex, Mason and Jack stared back at me. Only Mason smirked. Fucker could probably tell why I was pissed. He had a nose for my moods.

"We stopped by to talk," Alex said as he went past me into the living room. "We have some things to go over that you missed while you were in the hospital. Where's Alisa?"

"Taking a nap," I snapped.

Mason chuckled. "Right. Well, I'm sure she won't miss your ugly mug for a while."

Shaking my head, I stalked into the kitchen, my mind on her, as usual, rather than the three assholes invading my house. I wasn't completely unaware of how I looked at the moment with the bruises, but Alisa hadn't seemed to mind it at all given her little surprise in the bedroom.

"Fuck off, Mason," I mumbled as I grabbed a water out of the refrigerator. "What do you guys need? Make it quick."

Mason followed me out of the circular kitchen to the living room where Jack and Alex sat on the sofa. Alex looked distracted and Jack looked as non-emotional as ever.

Alex held up a thumb-drive and set it on the coffee table. I recognized it from the club and assumed it was the recording of what happened in the office a week ago.

"And?" I said frowning at Alex.

"I reviewed it. It has everything on there that we need, the problem is it would be circumstantial according to your dad and based on some research I did this week. I hate to say it, but it's useless. The only thing that it would do is stir the hornet's nest, and prove that Heather was a crazed lunatic. Paul isn't facing any charges based on Holly's statement to the police. They both claimed it was self-defense and your dad shut it down pretty quickly."

"My dad..." I mumbled. "Well, that's another one we owe him."

Mason crossed his arms over his chest and looked annoyed. "You've got to get over it, Mick. He'd do anything for us if that isn't proof enough. He's not the same man, just like you aren't the same man. People change."

"Okay," I said in a resigned tone as I shot Mason an annoyed look. "So, other than it being useless, which I don't think it is, what are you suggesting?"

"Your dad said something about using it at the right time against him. But not through court or police interaction I'm assuming."

"The right time," I said to myself, thinking about what he might have meant. "Hmm, I'll think about it. I'm sure we can figure that one out without running to his office to ask. Probably did it on purpose. Cryptic bastard."

Mason let out a sigh beside me. "Okay, so forget about dad for a second. What about Denny and the rest of those assholes? Sorry, Alex but your family sucks."

Alex shrugged. "The problem is, they're all in very public high-profile positions. But that doesn't mean we can't make life difficult for them. Again, I'll restate that gathering information and making it public to the press would be bad enough."

"Doesn't seem like enough," Jack said. "The shit I saw some days, the way they treat people."

"Were there any associates in your department, Jack?" I asked.

"They were there, but it was also the deals they made. We were told to look the other way if any of our investigations turned up something that might be questionable for that family."

I shook my head. "Of course. I say we hit them where we can. This isn't going to end tomorrow. It's not even close to being done. Denny learned a lesson if nothing else, but I doubt that'll stop him. We'll figure out what to do."

"Ben and Eli," Mason said.

"What about them?"

"Paul has been working with them. Says they're good. They've got connections with the gang that operates in the area. He said that they don't have any love for the Kings. They've seen some of their henchmen bullying the families in the area. They know the Kings are trying to squeeze these families for personal gain."

"But why, is the question."

"Ben said something interesting the other day. They get the feeling that if the King family keeps the population on this side of the city poor, and unable to fight them as a whole, then they've effectively tamped down half the city. They've made them afraid to speak out or report what they're doing so they'll continue to have power."

Alex chimed in. "Basically, divide the city in other words. Make it so hard, as they struggle to make ends meet, that they don't care what happens in the long term. Divide and conquer."

Mason nodded. "Maybe they can ask their brother…"

Holding up a hand to interrupt. "As much as I'd love to see Denny's house torn to shreds, we have an obligation to both Alex and Alisa to tread carefully. Their mother is still there for the time being. I'm not saying they can't cause a few problems, but I have no idea what their brother would do because I don't know him well. We've had a couple of conversations, as odd as that was, but not enough to get a feel for him."

"I'm sure they'd be willing."

Weighing that option, I glanced at Alex. "That's your call. If you want to move against your dad one of these days, then maybe you can work a deal with the gang. Or we can on your behalf."

Alex nodded, looking distracted for a moment. "We'll see. I think I'd like a turn at him again before that. The problem with not acting, now that we know what he's done, courtesy of Heather, is that he may continue to try and kill Alisa just out of spite."

I glanced at the closed bedroom door thinking of the beautiful woman beyond. "That's unacceptable. We'll make it clear enough that if he lays one finger on her again, he'll get one last visit. Where is he?"

"Barbados. However, he's telling people he's in Iowa for health reasons or some garbage. I didn't pay much attention to it."

"Start paying attention, Alex. You know the ins and outs of how your family operates. You're the only one they don't really question right now."

"I don't know about that. My father…"

"Won't say a damn thing, just like you said. It's all in how he wants to be perceived. If he'd said anything to anyone, you'd be facing that loan issue with Warren. Speaking of which, how's Heather's father?"

"He was terse but polite."

"Likely due to your family's influence. Play it. It's a roll. We know how you honestly feel and that's not going to change. We need you, but you have to be careful."

He looked annoyed for a moment. "I can take care of myself. Just take care of Alisa."

I rolled my eyes. I had to admire his love for his sister, but he seriously pissed me off when he got in protective mode with her.

"Speaking of…I need all of you to leave so I can go check on her. She's been stressed and she's carrying my kid. Get out."

Mason smirked before he ambled toward the door as Jack followed. Alex approached me with an expression that was thoughtful.

"Are you putting another bodyguard on her?" he asked. "I don't trust Denny."

"We'll both have one now, but I'll be adding to that at some point. If she goes out without me, she'll have two. Alex, you might want to think about hiring your own. I know he won't say anything publicly about what happened, but it doesn't mean he won't come after you privately just to settle the score."

"He's more likely to hit me financially just to bend to his whims. We'll see. Jack comes in often enough."

"Jack seems like a good man, but there's going to be a day when he's not there. You need to cover your ass and the people around you. It's going to get a lot uglier before it gets better and I don't want to see Alisa in pain, if something happens to you."

Alex chuckled. "I'll think about it. We've already started a war here, Mick. To call it anything else would be pure stupidity. I'm fully aware that I'm in the middle of it too."

I shook my head slowly. "No, you're not."

"What do you mean?" he responded with a frown.

"Other than your father, no one knows that you're really involved."

"The club," he responded. "Half the police force saw me there. They know I killed Heather."

"Doesn't matter, you were there for Alisa. You heard the official statement. Brother shows up after call from sister, or whatever shit my father said. They don't really know. I'm not saying they won't figure it out eventually, but right now you have one golden opportunity to play their game at their level. Take it, mingle, dig. Go make some friends in their realm that'll work with us. The one thing we lack is the same kind of limitless funding."

"I can tell you how to get that, but you're not going to like it."

I sighed deeply. "I don't see myself crossing certain lines here yet. I may never. Are we talking drugs, prostitution?"

"It might get to that. That local gang you have running around isn't the only muscle in town."

"How do you know that?"

He tipped his head to the side and smirked. "Defense attorney. I've seen them all."

Laughing, I led him out of the apartment, nodding at Paul, who was in the hallway talking with Mason. When they loaded on the elevator and the doors closed, I turned to Paul.

"No more visitors or people die."

"Got it, boss," he replied.

"Tell Eli, we need him at the loft on full rotation for both of us, starting today. Ben is still on Mason."

He nodded before I shut the door and leaned against it. We were fighting a war with the Kings. Alex couldn't have put it any better. My eyes drifted to the living room then the bedroom beyond.

I'd fight any war for her, because of her, with her. But I was beginning to think that I was also fighting for a lot of other people too. We all were. Somehow all of this had gone from pure protectiveness, to revenge, and now holding our own against a foe who was far more experienced in how this game worked.

We'd done things for the right reasons. We'd just gone about it in such a way that none of us could ever go back.

And now we were...

A thought formed in my head as I glanced at the couch we'd just been sitting on. Whether we wanted to admit it or not we were criminals. An organized group of criminals. Which meant we were much like the Kings.

The bitterness of that conclusion stuck in my mouth for a moment. I wondered if the other men around me, the ones I would trust with my life, had formed the same conclusion yet.

Pushing myself off the wall, I walked toward the bedroom in the mood to be surrounded by her scent.

She was on her side, curled halfway into a ball, stockings still on, but panties missing. I grinned as I undressed, then crawled in beside her. Facing her, I listened to the faint sounds of her sleeping as I ran a hand over her bare hip. Sliding down softly, my fingers lingered over her stomach.

My baby. My woman.

When I finally closed my eyes, I dreamt of them.

EPILOGUE

Mick
Four months later...

I watched the amber liquid in my glass as I listened to Ben and Eli talk about their brother. He was now dead, killed by an unknown assailant in an alley.

They sat across from me, fidgeting in their seats the way they normally did when they both came to see me. They weren't much younger than I was, but for some reason they acted like they were intimidated. I could name a few reasons why they should be, but it seemed out of place considering their family was associated with a gang.

For months they'd been telling me about the escalation of some violence in the area, worried that something critical might happen. The bank had foreclosed on several houses in the neighborhood putting families out of places to live and causing a small migration of people to flee to different areas. If I read the situation right, which I'd like to think that I was, the King family was moving people out in order to broker a deal for what they were terming a "revitalization" of the older part of Kingston.

On the surface, it looked like a step to bring new businesses to the area, but underneath it all, it was just a ploy to displace who they considered unsavory and move them to areas where they deemed fit.

The plans they set in motion, started shortly after Denny King had gotten back from an extended leave due to health issues. I read it clear enough. He was pissed, and he was calling in his family to put pressure on the businesses and people who now looked up to us in the area.

A better play on his part would have been to ingratiate the people who lived and worked in this part of the city. They might have idolized his family as visionaries. Put more clinics and shelters in, created more jobs. Instead they were doing exactly what they always did. Being pretentious fucks, who cared very little about people with minimal means at their disposal.

So, we did what we could to counteract it. Helped local businesses with small loans from time to time that they paid us back for. Offered free advertising on occasion at the club and helped with the very same things that the Kings refused to do, which was support a struggling community being crippled by their long reach.

In the last month alone, Ben and Eli's brother had caught several people in the middle of crimes against the locals. Through pressure under interrogation, they'd admitted eagerly that they'd been hired by one King family member or another to commit crimes. Arson, assault, theft, mayhem and murder. The list of crimes in the neighborhood had doubled for a while.

Until we started sending Denny a finger or two.

The old building that Alex bought out from his partners in his firm, worked well for a number of reasons. It was a legitimate business during the day, in which Jack and Mason could work out of without question. Alex had decided not to put his name on the door, and from what I understood, had buried his ownership of the building somehow.

They'd all gone with something rather simple on the door. The Mack Agency was officially open for business, of which there was very little, but it served as a good front for Mason and Jack, and had provided a private environment in the basement for nice long chats with our criminal friends.

My eyes drifted up to Mason who was leaning up against the far wall with his arms over his chest. He was listening to the brothers as they explained what happened.

"He was just caught out in the open. I don't know why he didn't have anyone with him. He's not stupid," Eli said.

Ben sat with a blank stare for a moment then gave me a quick glance. "The gang is in disarray. They're fighting over who succeeds. It's not as easy as you think."

"And do they want one of you to do it? You were his brothers. Your brother is dead. Family succession?"

Ben and Eli glanced at each other and fidgeted again.

When I looked back at Mason, he shrugged.

The pair in front of me was nervous for some reason. Eli rarely popped his knuckles unless he had something on his mind, and Ben tended to pull on his left ear when he was thinking about something more than women and alcohol. Something I had to repeatedly remind him not to do, as it messed with his earpiece and could emit high-pitched feedback in the rest of our bodyguard's earpieces. I needed to ask Reid if there was a different solution, but I hated talking to the man.

"Guys, I understand if that's how it has to go. I don't want to lose either one of you. You're family to us as far as I'm concerned, but it's the way it is. It makes sense for one or both of you to take over the gang."

"That's not it," Ben, the older of the two, replied. "It's not us that they want."

Frowning, I tilted my head and waited.

"They want you and Mason."

My eyebrows arched. "We're not gang members, though. We've never crossed paths with them other than a few conversations with your brother, and a few of his friends about the people who live around here."

"Doesn't matter," Eli responded. "They respect both of you. They think you might legitimize the group, make it more organized."

I blew a long breath out and sat back in my chair. "This is something coming from the whole group or just some?"

"It was voted on," Ben responded. "There was a big meeting and we were invited. It kind of surprised us, since we've been kept out of the loop for a while now. But nearly the entire group was there."

"Minus how many?"

He shrugged. "Maybe ten who were working."

"I still don't understand the connection."

Ben was pensive for a moment. "It's like this, they know you. They also know what you and Mason are trying to do. They see it, we see it. You're trying to help this community. We have families here too and we see what's happening more than most. They don't have a leader right now and they don't want to break up and war with each other in the end because that's not going to help. Most of us grew up in the streets and we know what can happen. And while you two are fighting a war for us, we don't want to fight each other."

The implications of this kind of mentality wasn't lost on me. The gang members had been operating in the area, according to Jack, for a few years. They'd grown in reputation, but were still considered a smaller group in terms of the amount of members. His estimate was about sixty or so, give or take. His assessment of them was somewhat positive, given his background in dealing with organized criminals when he was working on the force, but he still considered them lethal.

"I'll think about it," I responded. "Tell them out of respect for your brother, I'm taking time to consider the gracious offer and I'll have an answer to them by the end of the week. In the meantime, they can consider Ben my personal liaison. I need to discuss this with Mason. Ben, take the night off, we'll talk soon."

The brothers stood and nodded their thanks as they left the room, closing the door behind them.

"What the fuck?" Mason asked as he took a seat in front of the desk.

"I have no idea."

"Let Ben handle it and keep him on the payroll."

"What?"

He shrugged. "He becomes the leader through you. You pay him, but don't have to deal with the day to day shit. If you want something done, he makes sure it happens, but your hands are clean in the end."

"So, we're taking over a gang?"

He chuckled. "We're adding a few more people to our list of friends."

"Did that just come out of your fucking mouth? It actually sounded intelligent."

"Jackass. I'm not as stupid as I look."

I swallowed my drink and gave him a doubtful look. "You deal with Ben. You're closer to him. And for fuck's sake, tell them that we run a semi-clean business and all that crap. You're going to have to deal with the majority of all this one of these days. After we bring down the King family I want to spend my time watching my kids grow up."

"Right," he said with a non-committal tone. "It'll never be over, Mick."

A knock at the door, was the only warning before Alisa walked in. She was carrying a shopping bag with her.

"Later," Mason said as he got up. Before he left he planted a chaste kiss on top of Alisa's head even though he knew it infuriated me every time he did it. God only knew where his mouth had been.

"So, I have some clothes," she said as she laid the bag on the desk in front of me.

"Hmm," I said as she rattled off her shopping adventure. I was more interested in the dress she was wearing and what was under it. Her belly was starting to become more pronounced as she carried the baby, but something about her being pregnant made my already uncontrollable libido around her go haywire. It was like the more I saw her grow, the more I wanted to put five more in her immediately.

Grabbing her hips, I lifted her onto my desk and ran my hands along her thighs.

"Are you even listening?" she asked when my hand slid under the hem of her skirt.

"Mmhmm. Every word."

"So, you're okay with triplets?"

I blinked for a moment, my hand freezing in mid-exploration.

"The wha—?"

She smiled sweetly down at me. "Didn't think so. No, it's still one baby. But you should pay more attention and keep your mind out of my panties for once. The doctor called, and I bought some clothes. Would you like to see?"

She was going to pay for that one later when I finally got her in bed. Triplets. Fuck me. Small heart attack avoided.

"Sure," I said as I ran a finger along the inside of her thigh.

She brought the bag around and dumped the contents in my lap. Once again, my attempts at seducing her on the desk were thwarted by having to catch half the clothing.

"Blue?" I asked as I lifted a tiny outfit.

She smirked at me. "Told you the doctor called. I went in this afternoon and we looked."

"You didn't tell me. I should have been there."

Her hands slid around my face as she smiled. "And ruin my surprise? No. The doctor hates you anyway. So, this just made it easier."

Frowning at her for only a second, I glanced down at her belly. "My boy."

"Yeah," she said, tears filling her eyes. "Your boy."

Standing, I grabbed her around the waist and leaned into her. When her hips met mine, I slanted my mouth over hers and gave her a deep kiss.

"You're my life, Alisa," I whispered against her lips after a moment, savoring the taste of her.

"And you're mine," she said. "Always."

I glanced at the couch over her shoulder and smirked. My day had been long and interesting, to say the least, but it was about to get so much better with her in my arms.

The End

COMING SOON!

ALEX: KINGSTON CORRUPTION BOOK TWO

Alex
Three years earlier...

"Congratulations on the case, Alex," the blonde next to me said. I couldn't remember her name, but I smiled at her anyway.

"Thanks, it was pretty tough," I responded then tipped my glass of brandy back. It was smooth as it went down, and I had no doubt that my father had spent quite a bit of money on it.

The blonde bumped into me as she made her way past me. She gave me a clever smile meant to entice my interest, but it did little for me. She was just another amongst our circle that knew who I was and wanted something.

I felt a rough slap on my back and flinched.

"Son," my father's deep voice said. I glanced at him as he watched the blonde walk away. Her thin waist led south to her best feature. Clad in a silk open back dress, as she swung her hips, the material glided over her taut ass.

My father's eyebrows shot up in a lecherous way as he turned back to me. He'd been admiring the view.

"You could do worse son. That's Howard Morton's daughter, Shannon. You know he's loaded and she wouldn't be hard on the eyes if you dated."

I chuckled. "Dad, I'm not really looking. I don't have a lot of time on my hands. We just opened the office and I have a million things I need to do."

"It's never too early to start looking. Hell, marry one, bed her and forget her. Simple as that."

Clearing my throat, I scanned the room, trying not to comment on my father's opinion of how a marriage should function. It wasn't a secret that he'd married for money. They all did. It was a King family trait and tradition.

The disturbing part was that there were plenty of women in the upper echelon of Kingston, that for some reason didn't mind being seen as a means to an end. My family saw them as assets and they saw us as ostentatiously rich, born with a last name that signified our place in the city's long history.

I spotted two of the lawyers in the firm across my father's enormous living room and raised my glass to them in greeting. They did the same, then went back to their conversation. There were so many people mingling and talking that it was a waste to have music playing lightly in the background but occasionally I'd hear it filter through the chatter.

A woman approached us carrying a tray of champagne. As my father grabbed a glass, I set my tumbler on the tray and took notice of her. She was brunette with soft features and lips that any number of women in the room would have paid a fortune to replicate. She didn't look at us, never once glanced up, simply looked at us mid chest and no further like many of the servers at these parties did.

When she left, my eyes followed her, wondering if she'd been born with money whether she would have been married to one of the rich assholes my father called friends. The likely answer was yes. She was no less pretty than the people she served tonight.

"Eye on the prize, Alex," my father said beside me.

"What?" I responded, dragging my eyes away from the pretty brunette.

He laughed and took a drink and he nodded toward the woman. "If you want to make her a pet project, do it. But we're here tonight celebrating your first case and a win for you. Forget the staff and mingle."

I rolled my eyes and shrugged. "She's pretty, that's all."

My father eyed her and pursed his lips. "If you say so."

"And it wasn't really a win."

"Now, Alex, we said we weren't going to talk about it."

"I didn't win that trial fairly."

His jaw twitched for a moment before he gave a tight smile to one of his attorneys. After a moment and another drink, he leaned toward me and gave me a serious glare.

"We're not talking about this again. You won't bring it up, you won't think about it. You won the case and that's all anyone cares about. Winning, son. You defended a man that committed a crime, proved his innocence in a court of law and it's done."

I shook my head feeling as strangely as I'd felt right after the verdict was read in court. Not guilty. The man I'd defended was now free. The problem was, I'd had very little to do with it, and I knew he was guilty.

He gave me a small grin. "Come to the office in a few minutes. We'll have a talk. Meanwhile, enjoy your night. This is all for you and everyone here wants to see you succeed. Lose the attitude and have another drink."

I tipped my head at him, acknowledging that I'd heard him. One thing about him that I'd learned a long time ago was that arguing with him was pointless. He'd been an attorney for most of my life before he'd become Kingston's District Attorney. He knew how to press the right buttons to get me worked up, which he did frequently. But as my father I owed him my career and college education.

Ambling toward the open bar in the corner of the room, I passed several people that knew me, some family, and some people they knew. Lavish parties were normal in this house, and although the faces sometimes changed, the connections didn't. The Mayor and half the city council was here, attorneys and business associates. Everyone was decked out in suits and expensive clothing.

All to celebrate a win that wasn't really mine. But it helped the firm, launched my career and made me one of the most sought after defense attorneys now that a month had passed since the verdict. Hell, the judge who ruled on it was probably here too.

I wasn't going to lie to myself and say that I didn't enjoy the reputation I'd suddenly built. It felt good to be known for something other than my last name. But the way I'd won didn't sit well some days.

Shannon circled the room like a shark smelling fresh prey and cornered me for a few minutes, chatting about the latest news and my success. She was good, I'd give her that. She stuck to topics that might interest me rather than ones that likely interested her. She'd been groomed to be the perfect woman on the arm of a rich man.

After a few minutes, I made my excuses to leave, extracting myself from any further matchmaking ideas she might have and went to my father's office.

Shutting the door behind me with a soft click, I glanced at my father sitting behind his desk writing something, while the brunette I'd seen earlier sat on the couch. She leaned back with a glazed look on her face and gave me a lazy smile.

Dad glanced up at me and waived me forward. "Come in, I have a gift."

As I approached, he signed what looked like a check and handed it to me.

"What's this?" I asked as the brunette behind me giggled.

He smirked and glanced toward the woman. "It's a check. A present for a job well done. For my son, not the defense attorney that Kingston now respects. Take it. And then take her."

I didn't reach for the paper in his hand but looked over my shoulder instead. The woman was standing and unbuttoning her shirt as her slacks slid down her thighs.

I blinked when I turned back to the man behind the desk. "What's this about?"

He waved the check at me with annoyed look. I took it from him as he stood up. He reached in a drawer to his right then motioned for the woman behind me to come join us.

When she did, he produced a small baggie of white powder that he laid out in a line on the desk. The woman laughed for a moment as she sidled up to me.

"Enjoy, Alex," my father said with an almost proud look in his eyes. "If you haven't figured it out yet, anyone can be bought. You want her, you can have her. You want to win, you can and you did. All it took was money. Everything you ever wanted is yours. Lose the tie, put a little of that up your nose like you did in college, and I'll clean it all up later."

With that, he came around the desk, and passed by both of us without saying anything more. The door shut as he exited, and I watched the woman in front of me snort a line of cocaine. She smiled and giggled once then she got on her knees in front of me.

Looking at the check in my hand I noted it was written for the exact amount that I owed on my house. Something that would benefit me a great deal as I started my practice and paying off some of the loan on the office building that two other attorneys and I had just started working out of.

I looked up at the ceiling and leaned back against the desk as the woman in front of me unzipped my pants and tugged at them. I jerked and slid my hand into her hair when her eager wet mouth finally found me.

Being a King was good sometimes, but I felt like my accomplishments had been bought and paid for. The part that angered me and settled like a festering pit of hell in my stomach, was how utterly tempting it was to let them. Especially in moments like this.

THANK YOU!

Dear fabulous reader,

Thank you for reading my book! If you enjoyed this book, would you be kind enough to leave a review and give your personal feedback? It would be greatly appreciated!

ABOUT THE AUTHOR

Jennifer Vester is a romance author whose ambition is to entertain readers with quirky, off-beat female characters and the men that love them. Her work is infused with humor and suspense, while exploring relationships from the female perspective. Characters are often facing difficulties in life and love.

For more information, please visit:
Join my Reader's Group on Facebook! @VestersVixens
Follow on Facebook and sign up for my Newsletter: @AuthorJenniferVester
Author Website: www.JenniferVester.com

Printed in Great Britain
by Amazon